MAN IN THE MIST

Lavender shivered as she stood in the cabin doorway trying to focus on the stranger approaching through the mist. It was a man, broad and tall. She cocked her gun and waited.

It was Cole Younger.

"Cole!" she cried, rushing into his open arms.

"Lavender," he murmured, burying his face in her hair. "I should get back on my horse and ride out of your life, but I can't. Neither of us knows what the future holds, but at least we have tonight."

Lavender pulled the sheet up to her chin, shaking with anticipation as Cole joined her in bed. "Let me look at your beauty," he whispered, and he pulled the sheet from her body. Then he wooed her with love, invited her suppleness with his hands. And Lavender could feel Cole's response as she pressed her body to his. At that moment, the words Cole spoke earlier entered Lavender's thoughts: *At least we have tonight*. And Lavender clung to him in desperation. If tonight was all they had, she would make it one he wouldn't forget. . . .

BESTSELLING ROMANCES BY JANELLE TAYLOR

SAVAGE ECSTASY (824, $3.50)

It was like lightning striking, the first time the Indian brave Gray Eagle looked into the eyes of the beautiful young settler Alisha. And from the moment he saw her, he knew that he must possess her—and make her his slave!

DEFIANT ECSTASY (931, $3.50)

When Gray Eagle returned to Fort Pierre's gates with his hundred warriors behind him, Alisha's heart skipped a beat: would Gray Eagle destroy her—or make his destiny her own?

FORBIDDEN ECSTASY (1014, $3.50)

Gray Eagle had promised Alisha his heart forever—nothing could keep him from her. But when Alisha woke to find her red-skinned lover gone, she felt abandoned and alone. Lost between two worlds, desperate and fearful of betrayal, Alisha hungered for the return of her FORBIDDEN ECSTASY.

LEATHER AND LACE

#1

LAVENDER BLOSSOM
BY DOROTHY DIXON

ZEBRA BOOKS
KENSINGTON PUBLISHING CORP.

ZEBRA BOOKS

are published by

KENSINGTON PUBLISHING CORP.
475 Park Avenue South
New York, N.Y. 10016

Printed in the United States of America

To
My Dad
Adlai Stevenson Dixon

Chapter 1

Deep in the heart of the Ozark hills, along the soft, lush, emerald green banks of the Marais des Cygnes River, a new day was slashing the horizon. Not much more than a promise now, faintly pink-edged like a baby's fingers, groping . . . stretching.

Stars were fading but the night-hush still held the forested land in its grip.

This hush lay like an aura of cottonwood mist blanketing the low ground and veiling the log cabin, a stone's throw from the water, not too close, of course, because spring floods can be treacherous.

The log cabin built by John Younger for his bride, Lavender, was a stout house made with thick, strong, double walls of oak logs with a ponderous door. It was built to withstand the elements and even Indian attacks, if necessary.

However, John Younger had no fear of Indians. In fact, he feared no one, man or beast, except Quantrill. He would admit this fact and feel no shame in doing so. He feared Quantrill as did everyone else who knew the guerrilla leader.

Most of all he feared Quantrill's hair-trigger temper. It was said he inherited his uncontrollable temper from his mother and he often bragged about that.

Charley Quantrill was an ex-schoolteacher and was extraordinarily handsome with the face of a cherub and the soul of a demon.

John admired Quantrill and believed his embellished tale of how he and a brother had set out for the gold fields of California. He told how one night, while camped on the Cottonwood River they were attacked by a band of Jayhawkers, abolitionist guerrilla soldiers of Missouri and Kansas. His brother was killed and he was left for dead. In the days following, buzzards tried to tear his brother's rotting body to shreds while he fought them off. Then miraculously, a Shawnee Indian appeared, buried his brother and with herbs nursed Quantrill back to life.

Charley Quantrill hated the Jayhawkers with an almost insane fury and vowed to avenge his brother's death. His followers, and there were hundreds of them, followed him zealously as he burned and plundered and murdered. They followed him with a fervent feeling of justification, remembering always, with Quantrill's constant prodding, what those Jayhawking bastards did to his kin.

John had not been with Quantrill when he sacked and burned Lawrence, Kansas on August 13, 1863 killing one-hundred and forty men, women and children, burning one-hundred and eighty-five buildings and plundering and looting.

John was only twelve years of age at the time of the sacking and was not yet a rider under the black flag of Quantrill. He was sorry that he had missed out on this event but had listened to Frank James and his brothers, Cole and Jim Younger, so often that he had come to feel that he was actually present.

John Younger was compactly built, not too tall, with brown hair, the soft color of the wing of a thrush. There was a curl in his forelock. Lavender, his bride of six months, called this curl a good luck charm and liked to twine it around her finger. His eyes were blue, thickly, darkly lashed and his face had a faint apricot flush.

The mist veiled the two occupants in the bed too with a kind of pearl glow which lay heavily on the Flower Garden quilt that Lavender's mother had tucked so lovingly into the back of the covered wagon that brought the newlyweds to the home that John had built in the Ozark Hills.

Part of Mama's heart, Lavender knew, had been put in the tiny, neat stitches. And she always felt secure somehow with the quilt over her. It was almost like Mama was with her.

She lay now, her long slender fingers on the quilt and her beautiful face close to John's. Her skin was very fair, her face round like a doll's face, and her hair so gold that John said the sun had somehow gotten tangled up in it.

Once she whispered in sleep, softly, "John" and the man stirred. But she settled down and there was deep silence in the bare bedroom which lay at the far end of the single-roomed cabin. There was a stone fireplace of rich, pink-rounded stones of the Ozark hills, gleaming like jewels in the morning glow.

Later she awoke and stared at her sleeping husband, remembering the first time she saw him. It had been at a church box social. She had wrapped her box so carefully. Mint, her sister, had tied a red bow on her box but Lavender had put a bouquet of daisies on hers over a cluster of oak leaves.

9

She stood back now to admire her masterpiece. "It's beautiful," she declared.

"I can't imagine a man wanting to buy a box with daisies on it," Mint scoffed.

"I like things different," Lavender said.

"Yes, you're just like Mama. Mama always likes things different, such as naming you, Lavender, and me, Mint and our brother, Jacob, after her favorite character in the Bible."

"Well, we'll see whose box gets the most bids," Lavender said.

"My red bow will make everyone sit up and take notice," Mint predicted. "I hope Charles Engleman bids on my box."

"And I hope a stranger bids on mine. Someone on a white horse like a knight in the stories."

Mint laughed. "A knight who comes riding out of the West! Lavender, you are a dreamer. No one is going to come riding out of the West."

"I can hope, can't I?" Lavender asked wistfully.

It was a beautiful day for a box social. The boxes were lined up on a table in the churchyard beneath the trees near the white church. Lavender, looking at the colorful display of boxes, was sure hers was the prettiest.

The bidding started.

Mint's box was sold to Charles Engleman as she had hoped. When the Reverend Hopkins held up Lavender's box she heard the usual voices enthusiastically bidding and she sighed. She hadn't fried chicken and tucked in a napkin just to eat with Duke or Clem or Fraser or George.

"Twenty-five cents."

"Thirty-five cents."

10

"Fifty cents."

"Oh, let someone else bid," she prayed silently.

And then a strange deep voice rang out, "One-dollar."

She turned around to look at the bidder and she saw a stranger, a very handsome stranger. Clem bid again and a deep silence enveloped the gathering. No one ever bid more than a dollar for a box! The stranger's voice rang out again, "One-dollar and a half."

Clem was angry now. His voice was edged with steel as he yelled, "One-dollar and sixty cents."

She clamped her lips shut. She was afraid she was going to shout for Clem to hush.

"Three-dollars," the stranger said firmly.

They sat across from each other in the churchyard and Lavender smiled at the man as she opened her box.

"Three dollars is a lot of money," she observed, putting aside the daisies.

"There's more where that three dollars came from."

"Really!"

He laughed. "I'd have bid ten dollars just to meet you. I saw you coming into the churchyard and I stopped for a better look. Seeing it was a box social, I came in."

She fluttered her long dark lashes and grinned at him, asking, "Do you have a white horse?"

He nodded and Lavender giggled to herself. She was right and Mint was wrong. A knight on a white horse did come riding by! She gave him the napkin and said, "I hope you won't be disappointed in the food in my box."

"Don't ask me how I like the food until I've tasted your fried chicken."

11

"How do you know there's fried chicken?" she demanded.

"All country girls have fried chicken in their boxes," he said.

She pouted, "Don't call me a country girl."

"You don't look like a country girl and you don't act like a country girl. Country girls tie their boxes with ribbon but you, my lovely Lavender, have class. No ribbon for you. You have the taste of a queen."

"Thank you."

They ate in silence for awhile, then she asked, "You know my name but I don't know yours. Shall I call you Sir Knight on a white horse?"

He laughed showing even white teeth. "It's Brandy."

"That's an odd name but I like it."

Later she asked, "Brandy, are you going to be around here long or are you just passing through?"

"I'll be here long enough to get really acquainted with you."

"My father doesn't allow me to see strangers," she said demurely.

"I won't be a stranger after today." And he winked at her.

"Oh." And she thought, what a charmer he is and how handsome with that shock of curly hair and smooth peachy skin!

He had charmed her father, Matt Mueller, too, who surprisingly enough agreed to let Lavender ride with the stranger the next day. Brandy represented himself to be a cattle buyer and Matt was impressed.

They had ridden into the hills, their horses galloping through the fresh spring air. Life was suddenly too wonderful to Lavender. This all seemed like a dream.

She thought the sky had never been bluer, the songs of the meadowlarks never sweeter and the wild roses never more fragrant.

They rode every day for a week and she counted the hours wasted when she was not with him.

Mint, looking at Lavender's sparkling eyes one evening as they prepared for bed, said, "Lavender, you don't know a thing about Brandy. Even his name doesn't sound real. He comes riding in here on a white horse and you think he's the knight on a white horse you've been waiting for. Don't fall in love with him. Somehow . . . somehow I don't trust him."

Lavender bristled. "You're jealous," she accused.

"No, I'm not jealous. It's just, I don't want to see you get hurt."

Lavender smiled sweetly and got into bed to dream sweet dreams of Brandy.

It happened the next day. Lavender's eyes were like blue stars. A flush of happiness enveloped her. Her voice trilled like a bell. It was as if the whole world was radiant and glowing with ecstasy. They had ridden to the edge of the forest and had tied their horses to a tree and stood now close together.

"Lavender," he whispered. "You are a golden girl. Your beautiful face is like the face of a doll. You walk so proud. Your eyes are the color of the wild larkspurs."

She looked at him with wide open slightly-puzzled eyes. "Brandy, my sister, Mint, thinks I don't know enough about you."

"One thing you know is that I love you."

Lavender could not answer. Her heart beat slowly . . . slowly and thickly with an exquisite throbbing. He pulled her roughly to him now and she felt his hardness.

Tighter, tighter, she felt her body blend into his.

"Brandy," she whispered. "What are you doing to me?"

"Loving you," he said huskily.

"Oh, Brandy," she murmured and began to cry, putting her arms tight around his neck.

All around them the sweet spring fragrance enveloped them; the birds sweetly chorused nearby over and around them.

She was in heaven, she thought. This must be like heaven. She could never remember being so happy. She clung to him and his lips touched her hair and his teeth nipped at her ears and neck.

He was untying their horses and leading them into the woods. She followed. He retied the horses and they went farther into the forest. Here the sunlight shone lacily down through the oak trees into a secluded enclosure. The world was transformed into a magic place of shadows and white glow.

Violets bloomed profusely everywhere. Their fragrance enveloped them with beauty.

"My darling," he said softly and she slipped her fingers, smooth and warm and young, into his and his lips were upon hers. Her eyes were closed, her beautiful young body supple and soft in his arms.

"You do love me?" he asked very low.

"I do love you," she breathed.

"Nothing else matters, does it?"

"No, nothing else matters."

He drew her down gently to the moss-covered ground. Nearby a brook rippled. She was suddenly aware of its muted murmurings as he undressed her tenderly. She felt like a helpless doll allowing him to fondle and caress her as he removed her clothing.

It seemed to take a long time but suddenly, time did not matter. They alone existed in a Paradise laden with fragrance and birdsong.

He got hung up on her breasts.

"They are like firm young peaches," he whispered. "So sweet."

He nuzzled and nibbled while she whimpered, consumed with an ecstasy she had never before experienced.

"Brandy," she cried. "Stop, please please stop. I've never been with a man."

He murmured, "A virgin is like unripened fruit."

She began to sob as he caressed her inner thighs. She was still protesting but her protests grew fainter now. And then he was on her, holding her, nibbling at her young breasts. She was trembling and sobbing as he entered.

She caught her breath sharply and moaned with pain. She was weeping with the agony of ecstasy and a strange pain she had never before known. In some dark corner of her mind she feared he would tear her asunder.

Then there was a final deep thrust and she was being borne on wings of a glorious radiance that enveloped her with stardust.

Up . . . up . . . up . . . She wanted always to feel like this.

When it was over, he cuddled her saying softly, "My little virgin."

She marvelled that he seemed so delighted that she was a virgin.

"I'll have to tell Charley about this," he exulted.

"Tell Charley about what?" she asked, shocked.

"About your being a virgin," he answered.

"Brandy, you can't do that! You mustn't do that!"

"I won't if you don't want me to," he said reluctantly. "It's just that Charley sets such a store on virgins."

"Is Charley your brother or a friend?"

"A friend," he said bluntly.

"I can't believe you would actually tell anyone about us. I . . ." she paused, fumbling for words.

He began to pull up his pants. "I'm bloody," he said beaming. "You sure enough was a virgin."

"I hurt," she said simply.

"That's 'cause it's the first time. It won't hurt so much the next time."

He went then to dip his handkerchief in the nearby water and came back to wash the blood tenderly from her inner thighs. Again and again, he made the trip to the water, stroking, loving her.

"Don't touch me down there anymore, Brandy," she begged. "I'm so weak and I'm beginning to feel strange again."

"Strange?" he questioned, laughing. "That's because you want it again."

He flung himself down beside her and entered her again. It was even better this time and she looked at him with the sunlight filtering through the trees and marveled at the beauty of his brown hair and sun kissed skin.

She came back to the present now with a start and looking at the sleeping John; she remembered the shock she had received when he told her that his name wasn't Brandy Wells. It was John Younger and the Charley he had referred to was Charley Quantrill.

"You rode under the black flag of Quantrill!" she cried.

"Proudly," he said.

She had assumed they would be married immediately, and was surprised at his reluctance to name a wedding date.

"I don't think I'm ready to get married and settle down," he said awkwardly. "I'm too young to get married."

"My pa was only eighteen when he got married," she said, feeling a fingertip of ice on her heart. "You said you were going on twenty."

She began to cry.

"Don't cry," he said. "We'll get married. I guess I can get used to double-harnessing. Ma ain't goin' to like it and neither is Charley Quantrill. He don't like his men gettin' married."

They decided it would be best not to tell Lavender's folks that Brandy Wells was really John Younger. At least not now. Later, perhaps, they could be told. They would be married now and go away. He had a cabin in the Ozark Hills. Really just a rough hideaway but he could make it liveable. They could stay at the Crossroads Inn while he rejuvenated and rebuilt the cabin.

After a simple ceremony attended by all their neighbors and a wedding feast at the Muellers, Mint and Lavender clung to each other.

"You'll write?" Mint questioned.

"Yes," Lavender promised. "And as soon as we're settled, you must come for a visit."

Mama had tucked the quilt in their wagon and they

17

had gone away together.

Was she happy? she asked herself now. She supposed she was.

She did not quite understand her young husband and his moods. She knew he was restless and not quite satisfied in his role of a farmer.

She recalled now her first meeting with Ma Younger. One Sunday morning he informed her they were going to visit Ma. She remembered now how, during that ride, she had looked at John in the shade of the buggy top and thought how lucky she was to be married to someone who had given up the life of an outlaw to settle down to being a farmer. He must love her.

She had not expected to meet anyone like Ma Younger. Never in her wildest dreams had she thought John would have such a woman as Ma for a mother. Ma, who came out of the big house when they drove up, and peered suspiciously. Lavender had only a moment to gasp, "You didn't write to your mother and tell her that we're married?" She knew without asking that he hadn't.

"Hell, no," he said. "You don't tell Ma nothin'."

Ma came up to the buggy and stared.

"This is Lavender," the man said. "And, Lavender, this is my Ma."

"Too puny," Ma rasped, looking at Lavender.

John jumped from the buggy and helped Lavender down and they stood facing Ma. Lavender smiled and went to stand close to the woman. And then she froze because Ma was looking her over from head to foot as though she were a horse John had brought home for inspection.

"Can't bear you a passel of sons!" the stooped, dirty woman barked.

"We don't need a passel of sons," John had answered, laughing.

They were joined now by two young men and John introduced them as his brothers, Jim and Bob. They sidestepped Ma and Lavender had the impression that they were more or less afraid of her. But why should twenty-two year old James and seventeen year old Bob be afraid of Ma? John had told her their ages and had bragged that they too were followers of Quantrill.

Bob answered, "Ma gave us orders at Christmas to come home and clean up some chores this month."

This tickled John and he laughed heartily, "That Quantrill is about the toughest meanest man there is and tiny Ma says she wants Jim and Bob home at a certain time and he lets them go!"

"Why aren't you with Quantrill?" Ma asked John.

"I was doin' some special business for him up near Westport and I met this angel and we got married."

This announcement was greeted by dead silence. Then Ma spoke. "You know," she said harshly, "that Charley Quantrill don't want his men havin' a wife."

"I'm leavin' Quantrill. I aim to settle down."

Lavender tore her thoughts away from the babble of outrage that had erupted from Ma at John's words. It was better not to think about the scene that followed.

Lavender, on the way home that Sunday, asked John why his two brothers were afraid of Ma.

John had laughed. "Yep, I guess they are afraid of Ma. She's got a temper like Charley Quantrill and it's better not to make either one of them mad."

"She's mad at us," Lavender put in.

"That she is," he conceded, "but did you notice I didn't back down to her? I stand up to Ma."

John told her that Ma had not always been like she was now. She had once been a real lady. She had once worn white gloves and taffeta dresses all covered with lace. That was before the Colonel, John's father, had been financially ruined by ruthless Kansas Jayhawkers and later brutally robbed and murdered by a Union officer.

"They turned us out in the bitter cold," John reminisced angrily. "Ma was sick with pneumonia and coughin' her lungs out. Bob, too. Wouldn't surprise me none if they both died with consumption some day."

Lavender said nothing but she wondered how a woman who had once been a great lady could turn into a slattern.

She went back to sleep now and when she awakened later she thought of how much she resented Ma. John always defended Ma, saying she was old and sick. Just yesterday, she had sent the Dalton boy to tell John to fetch Cole to her as she was ailing.

Cole was Ma's favorite. He was John's hero too. John never tired of talking about Cole. Cole was seven years older than John. No one could shoot straighter or ride a horse better than Cole, according to John.

Lavender sighed now and snuggled closer to John. He pulled up his long nightshirt which Lavender had sewn for him. He liked to sleep naked and wore the nightshirt only to please her.

He pulled it over his head now. "That's better," he said. "Now yours." And he pulled her long heavy gown off.

"This is much better," he said.

They lay there a moment, bare body to bare body.

"I have to leave you," he said presently.

20

"Don't go, John, don't go," she begged. "Besides you have so much to do on the cabin yet before it's all finished."

"You wanted to move in before it was finished," he reminded her.

"I was tired staying at the Crossroads."

"Then don't complain about it now," he said brusquely. "Besides, you know I have to go fetch Cole."

"Just because Ma says so."

He did not answer but twined his legs around her and began to stroke her gently. She often thought that John was moody and often hard to understand but in bed he was a master. She wondered where he had learned to love or maybe it was born in him.

But then again, perhaps he had learned his secret of making her quiver with yearning for him from some of Quantrill's women. These women, who were camp followers, rode with Quantrill's band and slept with the men at night. When John first told her about these women, she thought he was making it up. But he convinced her there really was a Kate Clarke who was Quantrill's woman. And there were many camp followers.

She often wondered if John welcomed Ma's instructions to fetch Cole as this gave him the opportunity to slip away from their cabin and plunge deep into the forest to find Quantrill's camp.

When they were first married, Lavender had enjoyed hearing John tell of the women who were camp followers.

"Any man can have any woman he wants," he had explained simply enough. "That is anyone but Kate and she belongs to Quantrill. Once," and John had laughed

21

at the memory, "a new woman came to camp. Her name was Queenie and Quantrill took a likin' to her. Quantrill went and took this woman, Queenie. All hell broke loose!"

But now she had no desire to hear of the women and their antics. When John would start to tell stories of their toughness or sexiness, Lavender would put her hands over her ears. "Don't tell me about them. I don't want to hear about them. I just want to forget that you ever rode with Quantrill's band and made love with women like that."

"Women like what?" he demanded.

"Cheap women. Women who live like animals."

"You used to like to hear about the women," he reminded her.

"I don't any more," she answered. No need to tell him she was sick with jealousy at the thought of him with another woman.

She often wondered how often John had made love with these women. A man got very lonely, she imagined, out under the cold, glittering stars, especially when he heard lovemaking in the camp and wanted to share the pleasure too.

Now John would ride away from her to summon Cole and she would be left alone again. She hated to be left alone. The nearest neighbor was miles away. There was always the possibility too, that John would not return. He might decide to rejoin Quantrill and Cole to ride madly over the Missouri hills in search of danger and excitement.

In all these months of being married to John Younger, Lavender never felt quite sure of him. Not only was he uncommunicative but often cold and aloof.

At those times, she would try to be very sweet and loving but he would ignore her and it was then this inner fear would surface in her that someday the old lust for adventure would lure him away from her.

Chapter 2

Lavender, in spite of the loneliness when John was away, loved the Ozark Hills. The beautiful, wild free land! The quietness, the peace that was like a benediction. She loved the towering trees, the hills, the valleys and always, always the birds. So many, many birds. Bluejays, and redbirds and robins and over all the beauty, the sweet trill of the larks.

But she did not like the crows. She could not stand the crows. And they were everywhere. They were, she thought, like death, black and evil.

John laughed at her and told her she must have Indian blood in her veins. The Indians, he said, had a superstition that the crows were evil.

"They frighten me," she said. "I don't like them."

This had amused the man for her to be afraid of a bird when she was afraid of nothing else. Lightning could streak the sky with silver, the rain could come down in torrents, the thunder could roar, nothing bothered her. Not even snakes, scorpions or wolves. Only the crows. Especially one crow in particular.

This morning after John had kissed her and ridden off, promising to return as quickly as possible, she busied herself tidying the cabin. She had cleared the breakfast table when she heard the crow screaming outside her window. She went outside and cried, "Go away" but it was as if the black, glossy-winged creature wanted to torment her.

All day the crow swept low over the roof, balancing himself on the oak tree nearby and cawing. It made her nervous as the long day dragged to a close.

She milked the cow and forced herself to eat some bread and sorghum and drink some coffee, and then go wearily to bed.

She lay there, thinking of John and when did she ever stop thinking of him? Where was he on this early fall night? Dashing through some goldenrod clad field or trotting down a bluebell-lined road with the band under the black flag of Quantrill? Or perhaps he was sitting around a campfire with his brothers, Cole, Jim and Bob and the James brothers. He liked Frank James and hated Frank's brother, Jesse. He had told her that often enough.

Or were the cold stars looking down on him as he was pursued by Army officers? He had no business even being with a band of bloody cutthroats. He should stay at home where he belonged.

She thought of Quantrill! She had met Quantrill only once and that was three months ago. She would never forget that meeting. She would never forget those gray eyes staring at her, eyes as flat and cold as an Indian arrowhead.

Quantrill, followed by a band of about fifty or sixty men, had swept into their yard one evening at twilight. And John had changed instantly. From sitting beside her and looking out into the twilight at peace and it had seemed to Lavender they had never been so happy, he had jumped to his feet in a very fever of excitement and delight. In an awed voice he had cried, "It's Quantrill! Here at my place!"

He was beside himself with joy at seeing his old comrades. Quantrill swaggered forward and she saw a man with bushy, reddish hair, very fair skin and the coldest, most beautiful eyes she had ever seen.

John introduced her proudly and Quantrill stared at her and swept his hat off majestically and bowed low. Lavender tried to remember some of the things John had told her about this man. She knew that sometimes he went by the name of Charley Quantrill and sometimes he was known as William and that before the outbreak of hostilities along the Kansas and Missouri borders, he worked as a horse thief in Kansas under the alias of Charley Hart.

Quantrill's eyes were of a light gray, so light they bordered on white especially when he was angry.

He claimed he had received permission from Jefferson Davis in Richmond in 1861 to operate along the border. That seemed not to matter now as he operated wherever he wished.

Quantrill continued to stare at Lavender, and when he spoke Lavender was startled by the soft tone of his voice. Almost with a kind of reverence in it. "Your woman is beautiful," he said to John. His voice was well-modulated. But then, he was well-educated. She remembered John telling her Quantrill had been a schoolteacher. A schoolteacher turned guerrilla.

He smiled at her while John beamed, pleased.

"She smells good too," he said approvingly. "My woman smells like a barnyard."

"Your woman is tough," a rough voice cut in and Lavender looked away from Quantrill to see several

26

women coming forward. The woman, who had spoken, came close and stared at her.

Lavender knew instantly that this must be Kate Clarke, Quantrill's woman, about whom she had heard. Kate had beady eyes peering from an incredibly dirty face. Her straight brown hair was held back by a single leather thong.

She glared at Lavender. "I'll bet this one," she jerked her head toward Lavender, "couldn't skin a rabbit."

John spoke up, "She doesn't need to skin a rabbit. I do the dirty work for her."

Quantrill laughed. Lavender thought he looked better when he laughed. But then she looked at his eyes and noticed that his eyes did not laugh. His lips laughed only and they were parted over perfect white teeth.

Lavender remembered now how John had told her, in one of those first hushed and beautiful nights when they had been so close, that Quantrill was the biggest liar on earth. He was really a Northerner, a native of Ohio, who had taught school in Kansas before the war.

John said Quantrill lied when he said he had come to Kansas from Maryland before the war to join a brother on a trip to California. John said Quantrill could tell a lie with such sincerity one believed whatever he said.

"How can you believe anything he says when you know he's a liar?" Lavender asked.

"Because he's such a clever liar," John said grinning. "When he tells that story about the Shawnee Indian saving his life he's so convincing I believe him and I know it's a lie from start to finish. It's a story everyone seemed to accept as fact. After recovery from his wounds, Quantrill claimed he had joined Montgomery's Jayhawkers, under an assumed name, to seek revenge."

John told her too, that most of Quantrill's guerrillas were farm boys with the exception of one of his lieutenants, George Todd, who was a bridge mason. They had come from some of the best rural families of western Missouri, the majority of them driven to insurrection by the treatment their relatives had received from the Kansas Union troops who occupied the area.

He told her too that there was only one question asked anyone who wished to join Quantrill's band and that was, "Will you follow orders, be true to your comrades, and kill those who serve and support the Union?"

She lay now in her lonely bed and reached out to touch the Smith & Wesson Schofield revolver John had given her for protection and which she kept under her pillow. It gave her a sense of security but she wished John was here. She wanted him. Wanted to feel his body close to hers, wanted to feel him loving her, wanting her passionately.

Then she heard the sound of horses' hooves. John! John was coming and sooner than she had expected. John was coming home and she was out of bed and running to the door. She flung it open and saw there were four horses and four figures astride the horses. Peering into the darkness she saw that one of the figures was John and he was calling, "Lavender."

She hurriedly lit a lamp and waited for the four to come into the cabin. As she waited, she thought that they would want coffee, of course. She built up the embers in the fireplace. The black iron kettle was always full of water.

And then suddenly John was in the kitchen and introducing her to Cole, his brother. Lavender looked up into her brother-in-law's face for the first time and suddenly, she knew why John idolized him and why Ma Younger thought Cole could do no wrong. She could almost hear Ma Younger saying, "Cole is worth more than all my other boys put together. He can ride farther and faster and shoot straighter than any of my boys."

She had sometimes gotten tired of hearing John praise Cole. But she had always been anxious to meet him. He had not been with Quantrill's band the evening they had raced into their yard.

At that time, Quantrill had explained to John, "Cole was detained. Had to detour to the south."

This explanation was greeted with snickers by some of the band.

"I know Cole," John laughed. "All the women love Cole."

And even as the men watered their horses and later galloped off into the dusky twilight, they were still talking of Cole. Now looking at him, she knew why. Just looking at him she knew. There was something about him, something magnetic that drew people to him. He grinned down at her with the face of an angel. His hair was pure gold and his eyes the gray of a dove's wing. The air about him seemed charged with a kind of vibrancy.

"Lavender," he said and the words were a caress. He took her hand in his and held it. "I've been anxious to meet John's wife."

A woman edged close to him now and Lavender came back to the present with a start.

"I'm Melon," she said smiling, "and this," she nodded to the woman standing nearby, "is Ruby."

Lavender instantly took their coats. Then filling the big coffee-pot with hot water, poured in coffee grounds and set cups on the table.

They were presently seated around the kitchen table while Lavender poured the hot black liquid into the cups. Cole produced a bottle of whisky and generously laced his and John's cup. Ruby held out her cup.

"Mine, too," she said.

Now Lavender could study her guests at leisure. Ruby was Indian dark with jet-black hair and dark brows and a square firm jaw. Melon was delicate as a flowerlet with pale skin and soft features and light brown hair. Ruby kept staring first at Cole and then at John but she said nothing as she sipped her coffee.

"Found them easy," John told Lavender between gulps of coffee.

"Where?" she asked.

"Down by the Springs," John answered. "Had a right nice camp. Plenty of water and fish for the takin'."

"Don't mention fish to me," Ruby said, wrinkling her pert nose.

"There's nothing as good as fresh fish fried over open fire," Cole said.

"I'll take roasted rabbit any time," Melon put in.

"More coffee?" Lavender asked.

"Yes," Cole said looking straight into her eyes.

"You're sure pretty," Melon said to Lavender when she returned with the coffeepot. "I was mighty anxious to see the woman who could make John give up ridin' with Quantrill."

"And give up all the women," Ruby put in with a smirk.

"What women?" Lavender asked. But she knew, she knew.

"The women that sleep with the men," Ruby said knowingly. "Don't say you don't know. There's never

30

enough women to go around, so we always take turns. You move from one to another."

Lavender flushed.

"There's nothin' more excitin' than wonderin' who you'll have next."

"Shut up, Ruby," Melon said.

"Why should I shut up? You know it's fun. None of us wanted to get Tom Williams. He was too rough on a woman. Then there was Bill Andrews. He . . ."

Melon interrupted Ruby, "Shut up. Can't you see Lavender doesn't want to hear this?"

"You got a mighty nice place here, John," Cole said. "Sure would like a place like this myself someday."

Lavender, silently sipping her coffee, tried to visualize Cole sleeping with a different woman each night. And sleeping with this Ruby person? She forced her mind away from the thought. And she wondered again as she had wondered a thousand times before how many women John had slept with. And had it been more thrilling underneath the star-studded nights on the ground with these camp-following women than with her in a soft bed?

"We'll just bed down here before the fireplace if it's all right with you, Lavender," Cole was saying presently.

"Of course," she said.

And later, all through the long night, she watched the red glow of the fire and the three figures before the fire, huddled together. It had started to rain and the wind whistled around the cabin and the rain beat on the roof. Plink . . . plink . . . plink . . .

Lavender, nestled beneath the quilts, felt John's body warm beside her. He was a light sleeper, probably

31

because of his years of following the trail. The slightest noise would cause him to be instantly alert. But tonight, he slept the sleep of the dead. But not she. She could not sleep. She could not even shut her eyes knowing that Cole and Melon and Ruby were slumbering before the fireplace.

She thought of the two women. Ruby with her dark wings of eyebrows jutting upward above dark eyes and Melon with her little-girl manner of looking at Cole and John. The glow from the fire made a golden halo in front of the fireplace and the glow danced on the three figures. She watched as Ruby snuggled close to the sleeping Cole.

What if . . . what if . . . the shameless Ruby began to make love to Cole before her watching eyes? And Cole? What would Cole do? Cole with the face of an angel and the golden hair and lean body. Cole. She had to stop thinking about him. Angrily, she turned on her side. She had to go to sleep.

Chapter 3

The visitors stayed, and as the days went by Lavender found that she loved Melon. Melon was helpful and always willing to share in any task.

Ruby, however, was surly and lazy. She seemed to come alive only when Cole or John was near. Otherwise she spent most of her time sitting before the fire.

"Why don't you get up off that lazy behind of yours and help?" Melon blazed one day.

"I'm no servant," Ruby retorted.

"You think you're too damn good to help."

"Leave me alone. I'm not going to do anything I don't want to."

"She's the laziest no good gal this side of Westport," Melon told Lavender later. "She's just like her sister, Kate Clarke."

Lavender was stunned. "Ruby is Kate Clarke's sister?"

"Didn't you know? I thought John had told you," Melon answered and her hands flew up to her mouth as they did when she was nervous. "I guess I thought everyone knew Ruby is Kate's sister."

Lavender stared at Melon. No, John had not told her that this snip of a girl, Ruby, was Kate's sister. Well, she hadn't liked Kate and she didn't like Ruby either. She resented the way Ruby smiled at John. In fact, flirted with him. She had a way of sidling up to him and lowering her lashes and talking with him.

"That Ruby is a bad one," Melon went on and her voice cracked with hate. "Puts on like butter wouldn't melt in her mouth and inside, she's rotten to the core. I've seen her stir up the whole camp. She had man against man. Quantrill told Cole to get rid of her. Kate put on an awful act of crying and taking on but Quantrill wouldn't give in. I think Kate was just actin' up. She don't like Ruby 'cause Ruby was always tryin' to take her place with Quantrill. When John came to fetch Cole, Quantrill told him to take Ruby along. We're going to ditch her in Westport."

"She wants John," Lavender said.

"And she wants Cole and every other man she sees. Sure, she'd settle for John. I tell you she's oversexed and she's a she-devil."

Lavender wished the visitors would leave. Life had been, at least, peaceful before they arrived. Now she was on edge because of Ruby and always, painfully aware of Cole's presence.

"I thought your Ma wanted Cole to come home," she said to John.

"Hell, Cole don't care what Ma wants. Cole does what he wants to and right now, he wants to stay here. He thinks you're beautiful."

The late fall days went by and the visitors made no move to go. John urged them to stay. He was delighted to have Cole help around the farm and each day they would disappear into the forest. Lavender could hear their axes ringing. They were laying up firewood for the long, cold winter.

It was gratifying to Lavender to think that Cole thought her beautiful. She often looked up suddenly to find him looking at her, staring at her in admiration and this gave her a pleasant little glow.

She could not understand John. Since Cole's arrival he spent every moment with him. He had never been very talkative with her but with Cole he talked incessantly. It was as though he gave all his energy to Cole and had none left over for her. The nights were the hardest to bear. The only time she had ever really felt close to John was when they were in bed. But now it was as if he was frozen by the sight of the three figures before the fireplace. She wanted him to love her. She wanted him to pull her close and take her gown off and make love.

He would whisper, "Goodnight," and turn his back on her. And she would lie, tense and angry, feeling frustration sear her. Pushing hard up to him, he would edge closer to the other side of the bed ignoring her. And there was nothing for her to do but go to sleep!

She was aware that Cole and Melon often disappeared into the woods. She could well imagine what took place at such meetings. Once she heard Ruby begging him to take her. "You always take Melon," she pouted. "It's my turn."

Lavender, at the kitchen table, was peeling potatoes for supper and turned to look at the two standing by the door. She saw the dimples dancing in Ruby's cheeks as she looked up provocatively at the man.

Overhead the sky was overcast and dark. It was going to rain. Lavender had not seen the crow all day and for that she was glad.

"We're going to have a storm," the man said shortly,

looking outside at the banked dark clouds. In the distance, the cicadas hummed and groaned ominously.

"That's when it's best. Remember, Cole, remember how good it was that night on the banks of the Blue River? Remember?"

They stepped outside the door but Lavender could hear what they were saying.

"Yeah," Cole said. "I remember. I remember I was sleeping. I was tired. Had been riding all day. You came to me naked and your body bloomed like lily-sheen in the moonlight."

"I remember," she said.

He smiled now, remembering. He had looked at her with her dark hair shining in the moonlight and the light of passion glowing in her dark eyes and he had taken her with wild abandon. After all, she was pretty and very willing. He had known, and known instantly, that she was not a virgin.

He had questioned her about this later. He was curious how one so young had lost her virginity. Ruby had been frank about that. "It was one of the Blantons. Dan Blanton. He laid for me in the woods and took me. It hurt awful and I cried. And yet . . . yet it was good. And after that I had to have it all the time. Dan got shot up and that was the end of him."

Cole had been curious. "How many others have you had?"

"I don't know. I lost count after meeting up with Quantrill's Raiders."

"Meeting up?"

"You know what I mean. I stole a horse and ran away from home and went lookin' for my sister Kate. Found her too."

"You'll end up like Kate," he predicted.

"And what's the matter with Kate?" she asked bristling defiantly.

"She's hard as an oak. Walks like a man and talks like a man."

"But she ain't a man in bed. Quantrill says she's the best lay he ever had. Long as she pleases him, guess that's all that really matters."

"She'll get old and slow and he'll kick her out."

Ruby had scoffed at this observation.

"A man," Cole said, "likes a woman to be soft and womanly."

"Like me, Cole, like me."

"Hell, no," he answered sharply. "You're as tough as rawhide."

Lavender, still watching Ruby trying to entice Cole, saw a flash of blinding light zigzag across the darkening sky. Ruby grabbed at the man. He shook her off. "Looks like a bad storm coming up," he called in to Lavender. "I'll put the chickens in the shed."

"I wonder if Cole will ever settle down and get married," Lavender said to Melon.

"Cole ain't the marryin' kind," Melon answered.

"I know you love him," Lavender said. "It would be wonderful if you two could get married."

"Cole ain't the marryin' kind," Melon answered again. "Sure I love him. I've loved him since the first time I laid eyes on him."

The two women were making vinegar. Ruby, sitting in the sun nearby, watched. Melon was picking the stems and leaves from the clover blossoms while Lavender measured out two quarts of sugar and one quart of molasses.

"Ruby," Lavender said. "would you please bring me the kettle of hot water from the fireplace?"

"Get it yourself. I ain't your servant."

Wham!

Lavender heard the slap before she turned around and she knew it was Cole delivering the punishment to Ruby.

"When Lavender says for you to do something, you do it," he commanded, "or you'll get a taste of leather."

Ruby hurried to bring the iron kettle full of water. There was a red mark on her cheek and she glared at Lavender. She brought the kettle to where Lavender was working and deliberately slopped the boiling water on Lavender's foot. Lavender cried out with pain and Melon cursed Ruby under her breath.

Cole, who had turned away and was going back to join John in the lean-to that served as a barn, was instantly at Lavender's side.

"Are you all right?" he asked gently.

He took hold of Ruby and dragging her roughly by her arm took her to the other side of the cabin. As he walked, shoving the reluctant and frightened girl, he was taking off his belt.

"You've been asking for this for a long time," he said, "and now you're going to get it."

"I won't do it anymore," Ruby whimpered. "I won't do it anymore."

"Lift your skirts," he commanded.

Lavender and Melon looked at each other and Melon giggled. "She's finally going to get what's coming to her," Melon exulted. "Wish I could see it." Presently they heard the swish, swish of Cole's belt and Ruby's screams of pain.

Lavender was amazed at Melon's knowledge. It seemed she knew everything, knew how to make starch and perfume and even face powder.

"But I had to learn all those things," Melon said. "We were very poor. My pa was a dreamer. He thought he would strike it rich by going out West. We never even had a wagon. We walked."

"Walked?"

"Walked mile after mile after mile. That sun was abeatin' down and my lips got cracked and dry. My poor Ma finally couldn't go anymore. She just laid down and died. We buried her out on the prairie and we started walkin' some more."

"Poor Melon."

"We finally made it to the gold diggings. Pa went off and left me with a family by the name of Higgins. Pa went off to dig gold and I never saw him again. Mr. Higgins was a mean, stingy man. Ma Higgins did the best she could. She was always having a baby and most of 'em died when they was birthed. I earned my keep. Had to work hard but I learned how to cook and how to get by on nothin'."

"I wish I was as smart as you about keeping house," Lavender said.

"I'll show you what I know. It looks like Cole ain't about to move on right away. How about johnny cake? Can you make that?"

"No."

"That's one recipe I ain't about to forget," Melon said. "One day, 'bout noon it was, a band of Indians knocked on the front door. Mrs. Higgins was scairt and so was I. But she didn't blink an eyelash. She rustled up a batch of johnny cakes. Here's the recipe. It's a poem so it's easy to remember.

> Two cups Indian, one cup wheat
> One cup good eggs that you can eat,
> One-half cup molasses too.
> One big spoon sugar added thereto,
> Salt and soda, each a small spoon.
> Mix it up quickly and bake it soon.

"And did the Indians like it?"

"That old Chief touched Ma Higgins on the shoulder when they left and mumbled 'good cook.' But the best is the recipe for roast goose," Melon continued. "Maybe we can roast a goose before we leave, that is if Cole or John can get one. You kill a fat goose and dress it. Wash it in hot soapy water and rinse in cold water. Dry and hang it up in the woodshed overnight. Next morning early, mash a kettle of potatoes with cream and butter and chopped onion and lots of salt and pepper. Stuff the potatoes into the goose and sew it shut. Rub the skin with salt and pepper and sage and put in not too hot an oven. Dip the grease up every hour or so and save for cold on the lungs and for shoes."

Lavender laughed at this last.

Melon went on, "Then there's corncob sirup. Boil one dozen clean corncobs, red ones are best, from one to two hours in enough water to leave one pint of liquid when done. Then strain and add two pounds brown sugar. Boil as long as you wish as some like a thick sirup and others like a thin sirup."

"How can you remember all those recipes?" Lavender asked.

"I had to remember or else," Melon answered. "Ma

Higgins was right nice but that Pa Higgins he was mean. He was a great one for hittin'. He was always slappin' me in the face. That is until I got to be about fifteen or so. Then he saw I had a right good shape and he began to want to feel. By that time Ma Higgins was plumb wore out havin' babies and being sick and workin' so hard. Pa Higgins used to lay for me and I took off one day. Hitched a ride to Denver and got a job as a dance hall girl."

"A dance hall girl!" Lavender echoed, remembering the many times she and Mint had giggled over a picture of a dance hall girl. They had whispered together too, marvelling at the exposed breasts and feathers dancing in curls and even been a bit envious.

"It wasn't so bad," Melon went on. "I liked it. No more slavin' for the Higgins. No more trying to keep out of Pa Higgins way. And it was fun wearin' pretty dresses and having men like me."

"Having men like you?"

"Sure we had to cotton up to the men. Well, there I was alivin' it up. Then one day Cole Younger came in and I took one look and knew he was my man. All the other men just became nothin'. I knew I'd follow him to the ends of the world."

"And you followed with him to Quantrill?"

"Yes and I had to be with other men there but it's worth it just to be near Cole." Yes, Lavender thought, she could understand how Cole would make a woman feel like that.

"Now," Melon presently said briskly, "how about you and me makin' some wild grape dumplings for supper?"

"Does Cole like wild grape dumplings?"

"Sure does."

"And you aim to please Cole?"

"In every way I can," Melon said. "Oh, Lavender, I love that man. I would die for him."

Lavender wondered how it would feel to love a man so much that you would lay down your life for him. She thought she loved John but now seeing Melon's love for Cole, she sometimes wondered. But then John was so different from Cole. Cole, laughing lovable Cole!

As if reading her thoughts, Melon said. "You must never compare John to Cole. There's only one Cole in the whole wide world. I know John seems cold and distant compared to Cole but that's just his way. After all, they've lived through bloodshed and persecution."

"I know," Lavender said. "That's why I try to understand John when he gets moody and restless. He told me he had to kill a man when he was only barely fifteen years old."

"Cole told me about that. Seems John, just a mere boy, was arguing with a bully."

"It was a man named Gillcreas. He was a mean man. Everyone was afraid of him but not John. John stood up to him and Gillcreas went to get a heavy sling shot. John had a revolver. Gillcreas was going to kill John but John got him first."

"John is bound to carry the memory with him,"

"A coroner's jury acquitted John because it was self-defense."

"Things like that can freeze a man's soul," Melon said softly.

"It made John tough and sometimes unfeeling," Lavender sighed. "Then there was that time when a band of Vigilantes came to the Youngers' home and were mad because Cole wasn't there and they took John to the barn and hanged him. Each time he was near dead, they brought him back by throwing water on him and then they'd jerk the rope around his neck again. John wouldn't tell them one word about his brothers, Cole and Jim. They left him for dead."

"That's why we women got to be lovin' to our men to make up for all they been through," Melon said as she went to fetch the wild grapes Cole had gathered that morning.

"Let's take the stems off," she said, "and cover them with water and boil about fifteen minutes. Then we'll strain them and add one cup of sugar and some water and bring 'em to a boil."

Lavender followed Melon's instructions and sieved together two cups flour, one-half cup sugar, some baking powder and salt. Then cut in four tablespoons of shortening and mixed with three-fourths cup sweet milk to make a soft dough. Lavender watched as Melon dropped the dough from a teaspoon, one at a time. The chunks of dough, about the size of a small egg, bobbed about in the boiling juice.

"You're a good cook," Lavender complimented.

"Yeah," Melon laughed. "I'd make Cole a mighty fine wife."

"I wish you could marry him," Lavender said wistfully. "You love him so much."

"I wish he'd ask me."

"He ain't goin' to ask you," Ruby cut in. She had come silently into the kitchen and stood now, with hands on her hips, grinning at them.

"You don't know nothin' about it," Melon cried.

"You think you're so smart," Ruby sneered. "Don't you know Cole ain't the marryin' kind? One of these days, I'll bet Cole is just goin' to ride off and leave you."

"We're both goin' to ride off and leave *you*," Melon said. "And it won't be long. We're takin' you to Westport and leavin' you."

"And what would I be doin' in Westport, smartie?"

"Your sister, Kate, said you got an aunt there."

"Hah!" Ruby yelled. "If anybody thinks I'm gonna live with old Aunt Minnie, they're crazy!"

"One thing sure, you ain't gonna go with Cole and me."

"We'll see about that."

"We're goin' to ditch you," Melon said definitely. "That's for sure."

That night when Lavender and John were in bed, she whispered to him, "Do you think Cole will really take Ruby to Westport and leave her?"

"Sure. Them's Quantrill's orders."

"She'll put up a fight," Lavender predicted.

"Yeah, she's a wildcat but Cole can handle her," the man said. "Quantrill said to get rid of her and Cole will get rid of her."

"If Quantrill said to get rid of her by killing her, would Cole kill her?" Lavender asked.

"Hell, yes. When you ride with Quantrill, you do what Quantrill says."

For a moment, Lavender was stunned. "You mean he would kill her if Charley Quantrill said to kill her?"

"Hell, yes."

Presently she tapped him on the shoulder. "When," she whispered, "are they leaving?"

"Don't know. They ain't in a hurry. Cole's helping put in firewood for the winter. They might as well stay a spell."

44

"I love Melon," Lavender murmured.

John did not answer and Lavender lay awake for a long while thinking. She would miss Melon when she left. She would not miss Ruby. And Cole? Yes, she would miss Cole very much.

The days went by and the leaves hung gold and red and brown. "It's 'Dog Days,'" Cole said and the others agreed.

They knew all about 'Dog Days.' 'Dog Days,' the season when snakes bite without warning because they're shedding their skins and are too blind to tell friend from foe. The season when fierce red wasps build their paper nests and now and then swarm out in droves.

Grass crackled underfoot and forest foliage hung listless through the long hot afternoons. Jimson weed opened its purplish trumpet-flowers at dusk to the big sphinx moths. Tall horseweed and ambrosia trifida grew everywhere. And at night, the air overhead was filled with hundreds of nighthawks or bull-bats. And always, lonely whippoorwills mourned.

"We should be moving on," Cole said. "The snow will soon fly."

"Stay with us," John urged. "We've got plenty to eat. There's no need for you to push on. It'll soon be freezin' weather. You know Charley Quantrill will be holin' up somewhere for the winter."

"You're persuadin' me," Cole laughed.

At Thanksgiving, Melon and Lavender roasted a wild turkey. They made lemon crackers from dried pink-flowered sheep sorrel and had acorn bread. Cole and John said it was the best meal they ever had.

In December, Cole declared it would not be Christmas without a Christmas tree and invited Lavender to go with him out into the hills to find the right tree.

"I want to go," Ruby cried eagerly.

"No, Lavender will know the kind of tree that will be just right," Cole said firmly.

He was waiting for her now outside the door. The winter day was cold and sunless. No breath of wintry air stirred in the bare world surrounding the cabin. The trees were silent dark sentinels. Lavender had hung several dish towels on the line earlier in the day and they hung frozen in grotesque shapes. The sky was low and menacing with snow.

Lavender joined Cole now and as they walked, a hundred cowbirds rose suddenly making a lacy black and gray patchwork pattern in the sky. She pulled a heavy scarf closer around her shoulders and adjusted the heavy black woolen bonnet over her golden curls. Dimpling up at him, her eyes were very blue and sparkling.

"You need a heavy coat," he said.

"I'm warm enough," she answered.

"The ground is slippery in places, Lavender," he cautioned. "Watch your step."

"I will. I will, dear."

The word had slipped out. She stopped short and looked up at him. The sharp wind whirled about them making the golden tendrils dance on her forehead. He stopped walking and looked at her. "Lavender, Lavender," he whispered. "You are so beautiful."

Then quite simply, he put his arms around her and kissed her tenderly on the mouth.

46

"Don't," she gasped.

He held her tightly. "I have to kiss you," he said gently and Lavender's breath was gone again.

"I love you," the man said, his cheek hard against her cheek. "I love you."

She clung to him then but did not answer. She continued to smile mysteriously into his eyes. He kissed her again, this time full on her beautiful mouth.

"Oh, Cole," Lavender murmured. - The serene cadence of her voice made the two words somehow thrilling.

There was a madness hammering in her blood, a madness that made her want to hold onto Cole forever. She suddenly knew how Melon felt. Radiant with happiness, she laughed joyously as her fingers found his. They stepped apart to look at each other. For a quick moment her thoughts flashed to John and were back again, sobered. Cole kissed her again. "I love you," he said huskily.

Abruptly she turned away. "Cole," she said, "we had better find that Christmas tree."

They walked silently then for perhaps a half mile until she found a tree that was shaped beautifully and was not too large. Silently, he chopped the tree she had selected and in silence they started to walk back to the cabin. The wind had strengthened and overhead a ragged edge of clouds, hard driven by the wind, marched toward the northeast. Lavender, walking by Cole with her hand on his arm for support, was thinking of the precious moment when he had kissed her and thinking about it, felt her heart soften with happiness.

"But what sort of woman are you?" she asked herself sternly. "What sort of a woman to want this man to kiss you and never let you go?"

And what sort of man is he to say he loves me when I am married to his brother? she thought. And there was no answer.

Christmas was a happy time. There was plenty of wild game for the taking. There were potatoes and beets and apples that had been carefully buried for the winter's use. And always, there was Melon to sing for them in the long winter evenings.

"Your voice is so beautiful," Lavender told her guest more than once.

"I guess I can always get a job singing in a saloon," Melon laughed.

She sang,

> *"O'er the valleys the snow wreaths*
> *are drifting,*
> *Hanging their garlands on laurel*
> *and pine.*
> *Blanketing the fields with an exquisite*
> *beauty.*
> *Feathering the lacy sprays of the vine,*
> *Cushioning like down on the bosom of*
> *the river."*

The two men and Lavender applauded vigorously while Ruby glared.

"My ma used to sing a song called, 'The Despised Singer,' " Cole said. "Do you know that song?"

Melon bowed and began to sing in her rich voice,

> *"There stood in olden ages,*

> *A castle high and grand;*
> *Wide gleamed its shining turrets,*
> *E'en to the ocean strand;*
> *And round it fragrant gardens*
> *A wreath of beauty made;*
> *There sprang the freshest flowers,*
> *In rainbow tints arrayed."*

"Speakin' of Ma," John said. "Guess she'll be plenty mad 'cause you didn't show up when she wanted you to."

Cole laughed.

"You were always Ma's favorite," John said bitterly. Cole laughed again. "No, it's just that I never took no sass off of Ma.

John looked dubious but said nothing.

Melon swung into,

> *"Oh, the rolling prairie,*
> *Broad and wild and free,*
> *Oh, the rolling prairie,*
> *Is the home for me."*

When John spoke again, it was to say belligerently to Cole, "I always stood up to Ma. You know I always stood up to Ma."

"Of course you did," Cole said soothingly. "It takes a lot of guts to stand up to Ma but you had the guts to do it."

On Christmas Eve, they hung up their stockings. Cole insisted on this. John and Lavender and Melon joined in the fun. Ruby scoffed. Looking out at the star-spangled night, Lavender thought she had never been so happy.

"I see a star," she said in awe.

Cole came to the door to see the star blinking and shining with unusual brightness. "That," he said, "is the North Star."

Later, they found a present in each of their stockings. Lavender and Melon had made cookies shaped like a fat Santa Claus and had two in each stocking. Cole had carved something for each of them. Figures, tiny and perfect and beautiful. Lavender held hers close. "It's beautiful," she cried admiring the tiny statue of a woman, which looked strangely like herself. "I'll keep it always."

She smiled at him and knew she would treasure his gift forever, just as she treasured the memory of that day in the forest when he held her close.

Their Christmas tree stood in all its popcorn-wreathed glory in a corner of the room and made the room come alive with pine fragrance. Melon, looking at it, said wistfully, "I always wanted a Christmas tree and never had one before. Pa Higgins said it was a lot of foolishness."

"Anything that makes people happy," Cole said and looked at Lavender, "is good."

And Lavender, looking at Cole smiled and felt the magic again. Life, suddenly, was too wonderful.

Chapter 4

All day the snow fell with a soft feathery softness that reminded Lavender of a picture postcard, all glittery and shining. Cole went out to bring in an armload of firewood and Lavender went with him to help. Cole protested, saying the weather was too rough. Lavender should stay in the cabin where it was warm.

"I love the snow," she cried, dancing beside him and raising her beautiful face for the snowflakes to kiss. When they reached the stacked logs, Cole gently pushed her in back of the logs away from the view of anyone looking from the cabin and pulled her close to him. In such a moment, life was too gloriously full for Lavender. To see Cole smiling down at her, with the hint of a smile brightening his eyes and touching the corners of his mouth, was pure joy.

"Lavender," he whispered. "I love you."

She put her face close against his face. Then their lips were together and he held her tightly.

"Do you love me?" he asked.

"I don't know," she said very low while all the sweet colors of April glowed in her face. She could find nothing more to say, her throat thickened, her heart hammered.

"I love you," he repeated. "I marvel that the others do

51

not notice. I feel like a blushing schoolboy when I get near you."

"I know," she whispered.

"You don't have to say it, but I know you love me too."

For answer, she kissed him.

When they returned to the cabin, his arms were loaded with wood while she carried only a few sticks. "You have plenty," he said firmly, and she loved him for his thoughtfulness. John would have carelessly loaded her arms full of the logs.

"You look like a snow man," Ruby giggled, hurrying to Cole and brushing the flakes from his lashes and cheeks. Melon took his coat and glared at Ruby who was dancing around him as he deposited the thick pieces of wood into the bin.

John came in now from milking the lone cow. The bucket of milk he carried wore a covering of snow.

"You should have covered it, John," Lavender said, taking the pail from him. "But no matter. Will Bess be warm enough?"

"She's fine. Snug and warm as can be. Chickens are all nested too."

After supper, they gathered around the fireplace. Lavender's hands, never idle, were busy with needle and thread. John had smoothed and rounded a piece of wood which Lavender used to darn socks and she sat now darning. Melon and Ruby had pushed their chairs close to the fire and now John came and Cole.

Cole stopped in back of Lavender's chair and put his hand gently on her back. She felt on fire from his touch. But she sat unmoving, her hands busy with needle and thread. Tears dazzled in her eyes and in the mellow glow of firelight, her hair turned to pure gold and her eyes to deep purple. He drew his chair close to hers.

Presently, Cole began to talk and Lavender became lost in the beauty of his voice. She had always felt ashamed somehow of John's connection with Quantrill's Raiders but now with Cole talking of Quantrill, she found herself fascinated.

"The first time I met Quantrill I was a mere lad. Rex, my dog, and I cut through a cornfield, south of Harrisonville after delivering the mail. We ran into a hangin'. First hangin' I ever saw. I'll never forget it. The fellow was danglin' on the end of a rope. He had red hair and his face was kind of blue. It was a bitter cold day and I stood there shiverin'."

Cole told how hidden in the bushes, he watched in sick wonder. Then Rex had whimpered and the leader of the men doing the hanging demanded that whoever was there, show himself. "I ran," Cole went on. "Then a bullet whizzed by my head and I stopped dead in my tracks."

"Weren't you scared?" Melon asked.

"I was scared stiff," Cole laughed, remembering. "But I didn't let them know. They dragged me to the leader who said, 'Whoa, boy.'"

Cole continued, "That man had the coldest eyes I ever saw. He jerked his head toward the man dangling from the tree limb and asked me if I had seen the hangin'."

Silence. Silence. Lavender broke the silence. "What happened?" she breathed. Cole went on, "I said I had seen the hangin' and the man asked me what I thought of it. He asked if the hangin' had made me sick?"

"What did you say?" Ruby asked.

"I lied. I said it didn't make me sick and the man smiled in a pleased sort of way. 'Good boy!' he said and asked me if I knew who he was."

"Did you have any idea it could be Quantrill?" This from Lavender.

"I was too scared to think. I just wanted to get away from there. Then the leader told me proudly that he was Charley Quantrill. Believe me, I had heard of Quantrill."

John spoke now, "I'll never forget how you came tearing into the house that night. 'I saw Quantrill' you kept saying over and over. 'His men hung a man. I saw the man dangling on a rope.' "

"I remember," Cole said.

"You kept bragging about meeting Quantrill. You thought he was a great man."

"I did and I always have and I always will."

"Me, too," John agreed. "When he looks at you with those gray-white eyes you know you'd follow him anywhere."

"That's true," Cole said.

"Remember," John went on, "how excited Pa got? He and Ma said we were not to mention the hanging. Things were pretty bad then and Pa was afraid the Federal Troops would accuse you of having a hand in the affair."

"Yes, I remember," Cole said. "That was 1861. It was just after southern guns had fired on the *Star Of The Steamer*."

"Tell us more," Lavender begged.

"Remember Captain Walley?" John asked Cole now.

"That bastard!" Cole exploded. "Forgive me, ladies, but I get mad just hearing his name."

"I was hoping," John said, "that you'd shoot him."

"He always ran like the coward he was."

"He was just plain no good," John went on. "He hated you, Cole, because Sis wouldn't have anything to do with him. He blamed you for that. He had a right nice wife, if I remember rightly, but that didn't stop him from running after the girls."

"That's right," Cole reminisced. "Remember at that dance at Colonel Mockbees in Harrisonville when that imp of a sister of ours declared loudly so everyone could hear, 'I don't care to dance with you, Captain Walley.'"

John laughed, "I can see her yet. Her red curls dancing on her neck and that green skirt billowing around."

"Her spirit almost got me killed!" Cole said ruefully.

"What happened then?" Lavender asked.

"There wasn't anything left to do," Cole went on, "but join up with Quantrill. Walley was hot on my trail spreading the rumor I was a rebel."

"Did Quantrill remember you when he saw you again?" This from Melon.

"He did. He remembered the lad who saw the hanging. He remembered taking a shot at me too."

"And missed on purpose," John added.

"You're right. He's a dead shot."

"He's almost as good as you, Cole, and that's sayin' something!"

Cole beamed, pleased. Lavender looked at him and smiled. All the while they sat around the fire, he had not given her a glance or said a word to her. Yet she knew in her heart that he was thinking of that moment that morning when he had held her close.

John spoke now, "Cole, remember the time we were

trapped in the old Flannery house in Jackson County? Captain Peabody of the Federal Militia with more than a hundred soldiers and Jayhawkers surrounded us?"

"Sure do."

"Quantrill yelled out the window that he needed a few minutes. The request was granted and while the Feds celebrated outside, we plotted inside. Quantrill placed each of us in advantageous positions and boldly flung open the door, shouting, 'Quantrill's men never surrender.'"

"I remember," John said drily.

"Before those Feds could recover from their surprise many of them were dead from our gunfire. When they fired the house, we put pillows and rags on the windowsills with a hat on each. Then charged out of the house while the Feds were reloading."

"I remember," John said again.

Cole talked on and on of Quantrill and the adventures they had shared. He finished with, "Don't you miss those old days, John?"

"Yes."

Ruby smirked and winked. "Bet he misses those nights," she said, "when he could lay a different woman every night."

Cole and Melon glared at Ruby who laughed maliciously, "Hell, Lavender ain't so dumb. She knows what went on."

Cole frowned and was silent for awhile. When he spoke again it was to ask John, "Do you remember young Blythe?"

"Yeah, I remember," John answered. "I remember, he was twelve years old. Thirty of them Feds rode into Blue Cut after killing the boy. They was all laughin' and singin'. We mowed them down! Twenty-eight of them went down under our fire!"

"We did a good job," Cole said.

"You're still doing a good job," John complimented.

"But the war is long over. We should be settling down."

"They won't let you," John said.

"You did it, John. I'd like to change places with you." And he looked at Lavender and she smiled at him. Her heart was singing with wild excitement and delight.

Chapter 5

The long winter days went by. The land was held in an icy grip. Cole and John and Ruby played endless games of poker and Melon and Lavender did the household chores. Cole sometimes talked of going westward. He called the West "The Land Of Milk and Honey." He talked of Indian war whoops and the crack of Winchesters. He spoke of the wild and flamboyant lure of gold fields.

He reminded his listeners that during the Civil War, the trans-Mississippi Great Plains was opened up by the Union government to free homesteading. An Act of Congress gave one-hundred sixty acres of land to anyone willing to work it.

"Well, I ain't willin' to work it," John said.

Melon began to sing,

> *To the West, to the West,*
> * to the land of the free,*
> *Where mighty Missouri rolls*
> * down to the sea.*
> *Where a man is a man*
> * if he's willing to toil.*
> *And the humblest may gather*
> * the fruits of the soil.*

Where the young may exult and
  the aged may rest.
Away, far away,
  to the land of the west.

"A man could make a new start there," Cole said.

"Oh, hell," John snorted. "A Younger is a Younger and there's no chance of making a new start anywhere. They'll never let us live in peace."

"You're livin' in peace here," Cole reminded him.

"I don't call this livin'," John scoffed. "This ain't nothin' but a little dirt farm and I ain't nothin' but a dirt farmer."

"Well, I'm just a-dreamin' about goin' west," Cole said. "With Ma ailin' with consumption and goin' to her Maker before long, I can't leave."

"You wouldn't want to leave Charley Quantrill would you?" John asked. "Especially now that he's ailin'?"

Cole did not answer.

As signs of spring eventually began to appear and the creek overflowed with melting snow, Cole announced they would be leaving soon.

"It's time to move on," he said.

And Lavender felt time stand still. She could not let him go. She could not stand living in this Godforsaken place with the silent and morose John.

The first flush of green was showing. It had been a day rich with sunshine and fragrance and birdsong. Now at twilight, Lavender and Cole stood together in the path at the end of the lane. Far off a night-bird wailed plaintively but the quiet hush of coming night lay like a benediction over the earth. "I wish things had

59

been different," Cole said. "I wish we . . ."

Lavender interrupted him, "It's too late to think such thoughts."

"I want you, my darling," he said very low. "I see you at night, so beautiful, so wonderful, in that bed with John and I cannot bear it."

"And I see you there in front of the fireplace with Melon and Ruby and I cannot bear it," she whispered.

"I know, my darling, I know. That's why it is time to leave. It's torture, pure torture, to see your beauty, your sweetness and not have you."

"I'll miss you, Cole," she said wistfully.

For answer he held her close and kissed her hair, her eyelids, her lips.

Later, as they walked back to the cabin, she asked, "What are you going to do with Ruby?"

He grinned. "I'm going to dump that wildcat at her relative's home, just as I promised."

"Ruby loves you," Lavender said.

"She's an oversexed, ignorant woman who will never amount to anything. I didn't want to bring her with me but Quantrill wouldn't have her in camp anymore."

"If he loved Kate it looks as though he would have let her sister stay in camp."

He answered gently, "Lavender, my darling, you are a sweetheart and a beauty but very naive. Men like Quantrill don't love. They can't let themselves love. Something dries up in them. Maybe the juices of compassion. They just take and take. They never give. He'll use Kate until she's worn out and then discard her."

"I'm glad you're not like Quantrill."

"I used to worry that I would get like him. Hard and tough and mean, but Lavender, I figured out how

60

Quant and I differ. He never laughs. Sometimes he seems to laugh but he really isn't laughing. That mind of his never stops figuring what to do next."

"I know what you mean, Cole," she said. "When he and his Raiders came to the cabin, he laughed with his mouth but his eyes did not laugh."

"I get along with him because I know how to handle him. You were clever to notice his eyes, Lavender. There are many men dead because they didn't read the storm warnings in those steely eyes of his."

They were almost back at the cabin when she spoke again of Kate. "Kate seemed to love Quantrill so much the evening they stopped here," she said.

"She worships him. He is her god."

"What happens to women like Kate when the men they love get rid of them?"

"They drift to another camp and usually end up as camp cooks. Women like Kate are born losers. Women like that can't expect much."

She asked curiously, "What do you mean by women like that?"

"Cheap women."

She wanted to ask him if he had made love to many of the women in camp but she stifled the impulse. He stopped walking now. It was their last chance to be unseen by the occupants of the cabin. The fragrance of violets enveloped them and stars shone in the darkening sky.

"I'll remember this moment all my life," she whispered as he crushed her to him. "Oh, Cole, I love you."

For answer, he rained tender kisses on her face. She felt his passion as he held her close. He was visibly shaken when he finally released her.

"We had better go back," he said huskily. Just before they reached the cabin, she asked, "Where are you going after you deliver Ruby?"

"To visit Ma and then rejoin Quantrill," he said simply. "Quant's a sick man, Lavender. I can't desert him."

"Cole, don't you think you'll ever want to settle down? Won't you ever tire of riding with Quantrill?" she asked.

"Lavender, I dream of settling down. I dream of you and me riding off to the West together. I've always had a dream of striking gold. I've seen those wagons with signs, 'Pike's Peak or bust' and I've wanted to trail after them."

"You'll make your dream come true, Cole, I know you will."

"Do you know in Central City, Colorado there's silver flecks in the mirrors of the Teller House? The parlors are elegant. Furnished with walnut and damask, and carpets of the finest Brussels. There's a big square grand piano in the lobby."

"Have you ever been there, Cole?"

"No, but I got first-hand information from one of the Raiders," Cole explained. "He told me about the miners in their heavy boots and swinging their lunch-pails singing in melodious harmony as they came from the mines. They're Cornishmen and are called 'Cousin Jacks.' "

"I wish I could hear them sing."

"He told me he owned a partnership in a diggin' called Butterscotch Gulch. He knows all about minin' that hole in the ground. He talks of pumps and the shriek of steam hoists and the narrow-gauge railway hauling in machinery for mine shafts and for the stamping mills. Tom Born, that's his name, always talks of going back. Wants me to go with him."

"Oh, Cole," Lavender murmured. "It sounds so exciting."

"It would be more exciting if I could go with you beside me."

"Oh, Cole," she whispered, looking up at him with the light of sunrise in her eyes.

"Let us hold fast to that dream," he said.

"It would only be a dream, Cole," she said, sighing. "Cole, I should tell you not to dream. I should tell you to be practical, to marry Melon and go west with her."

"My darling," he said very low. "You should know better without saying that. You know Melon and I will never marry. Melon is a fine woman. I would never say a word against her. But, Lavender, there are women that men do not marry. When a man marries, he wants a woman like you, fine and clean and pure."

"Oh, Cole," she said and her voice held all the joy of springtime.

That night Cole announced they would leave the day after tomorrow and asked Lavender if she would mind baking a few extra biscuits to be eaten on the trail. Ruby was jubilant to be on their way. She still did not believe that Cole meant to drop her off in Westport. She believed she would rejoin Quantrill's band. Melon said simply, "I'll miss you, Lavender."

Two days later, they were ready to leave. Ruby was radiant. Cole was very quiet, as was Melon. As Lavender wrapped biscuits and salt pork and cake for the travelers, she was conscious, through the confusion of her senses, of a feverish incessant prayer, "Oh, God

63

help me! Let me not miss him too much!"

She could not think of the days ahead without Cole. His quiet smile, his gray eyes, his laughter. How could she go through the days without him!

They had only a stolen moment together. "Goodbye, my darling," he said softly. "You've changed things. That's all right. Nothing will ever be quite the same again. And yet, I'm so glad just to have known you, to have loved you. Goodbye, my dearest, and let's never forget our dream."

For the briefest moment she was in his arms. She felt his cheek hard against her own.

"Take care of yourself for me," she whispered.

Her heart was dead within her. In a few moments he would be gone and she would probably never see him again. Ah, but she would see him again! He might come riding back any day. He and Quantrill and the others could come sweeping into the yard.

Or she could follow him and her heart veered upward on a surge of joy. She could follow him. She could become as Kate Clarke. She could sleep beside him beneath a canopy of stars. She could wait on him, love him and be always with him. But then . . . then she would be like Melon and Kate and Ruby and he had said, "Lavender, you know there are some women that men do not marry. When a man marries, he wants a woman like you, fine and clean and pure."

Well, there was no use to dream such dreams or even think such thoughts. Besides, there was John. She watched them presently ride off. Melon's kiss was warm on her cheek. Ruby's casual and hurried "Bye" rang in her ears and Cole's quiet smile and the look in his eyes lingered in her heart. Cole did not look back, nor did

Ruby but Melon turned and smiled and waved until they were out of sight.

Lavender went into the cabin and knew she would eat and sleep and talk pleasantly to John. He must never know that because a square, gray-eyed man with an unforgettable smile and a way of holding his head had come into her life, she would never be the same again.

Yes, she must be pleasant to John. John, who somehow in these winter months had become almost a stranger to her. She was sure he had taken Ruby to the woods on more than one occasion but somehow she did not care. The old jealousy she had once felt was gone.

The days went by and her confusion and unhappiness subsided somewhat. She kept busy. She transplanted seedling trees near the cabin. She dug up violet plants and planted rows of them close to the house. She brought flame azaleas from the woods and Dutchmen's-breeches and wild lily-of-the-valley and gold thread and remembered to gather the marsh marigold and nightshade and the wild rose for color.

And she made perfume, remembering Melon's directions, carefully spreading fresh, unsalted butter on two plates of the same size. Then she filled one plate with the wild rose petals and the other with violet blooms and turned the twin plate over it, letting it stand for twenty-four hours. Then she scraped the butter from the plates and put in some alcohol and bottled it, corking it tightly.

She sensed that John was as restless as she. When he came in from planting he would stare morosely into space. Finally, he blurted out angrily, "I can't stand this. I miss Cole. I wish I was with him."

"You miss the excitement."

"Yes, yes," he cried, pounding his fists together. "I miss the campfires and the wondering what's going to happen next. I miss Cole and I miss that devil, Charley Quantrill."

"You didn't miss them so much before Cole and Melon and Ruby came," she said.

"No, seeing Cole brought it all back. The excitement and all and how good food is cooked over a campfire and how we rode, a hundred strong. I miss the danger. I felt like I was alive. Now I feel dead."

"You miss Ruby," she accused.

His face brightened into a smile. "That tramp!"

"You miss sleeping out under the stars with a woman in your arms?"

"Hell, no," he said lamely and she did not believe him. And she did not care how many Rubys he slept with.

"If you want to, we can sleep out under the stars," she presently suggested.

"You ain't as willin'," he sneered, "as Ruby."

He turned away then and Lavender thought as she had thought a thousand times since Cole and Melon and Ruby had ridden away that they had taken something with them of life and laughter and love.

She missed Cole with an ache that consumed her. She wondered if he missed her too, if he sometimes thought of her and thought of their dream. Her days were filled with a vague discontent. She could not quite put her finger on it. But plunging her fingers into the soft creamy dough that would be bread, or churning the heavy cream, she felt miserable.

She missed seeing Cole smile at her across the breakfast table, missed seeing him grinning down at her

66

in admiration, missed the glint of the sun on his light hair. And there was no moment that she did not think of him.

And always she thought of those moments when he had taken her in his arms and held her close. Especially that first time he had taken her when they went in search of a Christmas tree. Even yet, she could close her eyes and see the cold blue sky above them and smell the fragrance of the pines and feel the kiss of snow feathers on her face.

She could hear the crunch of the newly-fallen snow beneath her shoes. She remembered the tenderness of his touch, and the expression on his face, his way of closing his gray eyes half way. She was on fire with wanting to see him again.

She thought of Ruby. Had Cole actually taken her to Westport and left her there? Ruby, with the wildness in her, that same wildness and toughness that drove her sister, Kate, to live the life of a man. It must take a lot of courage, Lavender thought now, to brave danger and hardships to be with your man, sleeping at night on the hard cold earth and climbing hills and fording rivers.

She wondered if she, Lavender, would have the stamina and energy and love for John to follow him through the forest. No, she had to admit honestly to herself, she would not follow John through such hardships.

And then came the kindred thought. Would she be willing to follow Cole? And she knew she would. She would follow him through the sleet of winter, the fragrance of spring and glory of summer, the radiance of fall. Yes, she would share hunger, suffering, sorrow and danger with him. Just the thought of sleeping in his arms at night filled her with ecstasy.

It was the summer of 1870. Although the War was now over five years, she often saw tattered and torn uniforms of both Union and Confederate veterans in her occasional visits to the Crossroads General Store. She felt sorry for these men. They seemed to have no purpose but to drift.

In June, the Dalton boy came tearing into their yard. Lavender knew him only as the Dalton boy. She had never heard his first name. She thought of him as Ma Younger's messenger. He was yelling for John before he jumped off his horse. "John, your Ma's ailin' bad. Doc Ranger says you should fetch Cole and come."

"Do you want me to come, John?" she asked, wanting to go. She would get to see Cole again. She could hear his voice again. Perhaps they could have a moment together!

"No need for you to go," John rasped. "No need to go. If Ma's ailin' that bad, I'll have to fetch Cole and Jim and Bob and get there fast."

"I can ride fast like the wind," she cried eagerly.

"You didn't have no use for Ma anyway," he said spitefully.

"Don't say that, John. I only saw Ma once. How could I not have any use for her?" she demanded.

"Hell, I could tell."

When presently he and the Dalton boy rode away in search of Cole, she stifled an impulse to go to Ma's. It would be a long hard ride alone but she could manage. But no, John might make a terrible scene. She thought of Ma Younger and how awful she had looked the first time she saw her. Ma Younger with her dirty gray hair, her wizened hands, her bony neck.

John had blamed Ma's consumptive condition on the self-appointed Vigilantes who forced her to march through the cold and snow of a winter night. Poor Ma, who had known so much sorrow. Ma, who had once been a fine lady in white gloves. Lavender hoped John's sister, Henrietta, would see that Ma was buried in white gloves. Men would never think of things like that.

Three weeks later, John returned. He was alone. He said little but that Ma had died. She had clung to life until her boys came home.

"She wasn't about to die without seein' Cole one more time. She didn't care if Jim or Bob or me were there. Only Cole."

"She loved you, John," Lavender said.

"Ma didn't care about anyone or anything but Cole," John said darkly.

Lavender presently asked if Cole had taken Ruby to Westport.

"He got rid of that wildcat just like Quant told him to."

"I guess she didn't want to stay there," Lavender put in.

"Hell, no. Cole said she screamed like a banshee. Cole just rode off. He was glad to get rid of that whore."

"Do you call all camp followers whores?" she asked.

"What else are they? Ladies of the night?"

He grinned and reached out to her. She was startled by this action. He seemed almost a stranger, she thought looking at him. Like someone she had known long ago. And then suddenly, unaccountably, he seemed to revert to the John she had known in their courtship. She did try to meet him halfway. It seemed now he could not get enough of her body. To the reluctant Lavender it seemed he was always wanting to fondle and caress her.

When she went to bed at night, he was always there first, waiting, grinning up at her.

"You didn't want me when Cole and Melon and Ruby were here," she told him one night.

"Couldn't," he answered. "Too many people listenin' and watchin'."

"Ruby didn't mind hugging Cole and kissing him at night," she pointed out.

"Yeah, but they didn't do nothin'."

"They didn't have to. Sometimes he took Melon to the woods. You can imagine why!"

John laughed.

Presently he said, "You're a good woman, Lavender. I couldn't jump on you in front of them sleeping by the fire. I just sort of froze up."

"What do you mean froze up?" she shot back quick as a wink. "Did you freeze up when you were with one of your whores?"

"That was different."

"Why was it different."

"Everybody was doin' it."

There seemed nothing to say to that and so she was silent. She felt his body warm against hers and knew that lovemaking without love is not enjoyable. She gave John her body but not her heart. Had she ever really loved him? She tried to remember how she had felt before Cole had entered her life.

Mama had always told her and Mint that it was a woman's duty to endure what Mama called a man's foolishness. Lavender had liked the foolishness when she and John were first married but now she was only patiently enduring. She thought now of those nights when she had pressed close to John when Cole and Melon and Ruby had first arrived. Her frustrated body had needed satisfaction and John had denied her. She didn't need or want him now.

Long after John would fall peacefully asleep, Lavender would remain awake, staring into the darkness, remembering, always remembering Cole. Remembering Cole and their dream. She would review in her mind's eye each precious moment they had shared. His tenderness, his smile, his kisses and the quiet glances he had given her when they were with the others. And always, her thoughts would linger on that evening when they stood together in the violet-fragranced lane in darkening twilight and he had crushed her to him and she had felt his mounting passion.

The next day she looked at herself somberly in the speckled mirror that John had brought to her so proudly after their marriage. She had often wondered where he had gotten the mirror and wondered whose face its shining black-ridged surface had mirrored. But she had dared not ask.

The reflection that stared back at her today was that of a very beautiful woman, the gold hair, the smooth white skin and the eyes, so thickly darkly lashed.

She stared into the mirror and asked herself, "What kind of a woman are you? What kind of a woman to be married to a man and dream of his brother? How can you lie in bed night after night and pretend love when all the while you are aching for your husband to stop touching you so you can dream dreams about someone else?" And there was no answer.

71

Fall came and the leaves hung red and gold. The crow that had tormented her for so long disappeared and she wondered about him, as one would wonder about an evil friend.

One fall evening after supper John suggested they walk. Lavender was tired. She had made soap that day and her hands felt red and blistered. As she had stirred the hot grease she had remembered the last time she had made soap. It had been a cold winter day and Melon had helped her. The ground had worn a frosty coat and the tree leaves hung dry and most branches were bare and the air had a wintry snap to it. The sky, gray as an arrowhead, loomed overhead.

Melon and she had worked hard and the air was rancid with the smell of hot grease and lye. They had come into the house with their hands raw and red and cold for the wind had whipped relentlessly through the yard. Ruby had been sitting before the fireplace. She hardly ever bothered to talk to Lavender or Melon. It was only to the men that she smiled and appeared interested in their conversation.

When they came back into the kitchen she was gone. Neither of the two women thought much of her absence. She had an odd habit of disappearing, of wandering into the woods in search of Cole and John. It was much later when she came back into the house. Lavender glanced at her and Melon whispered that Ruby looked like a cat that had swallowed a fat mouse.

"You've been up to no good," Melon told Ruby.

"Mind your own business," Ruby rasped.

John came in presently. His face was flushed and Lavender knew, without asking, that he and Ruby had been together. And strangely, she felt no jealousy, she felt nothing.

She was remembering the incident now as they strolled slowly down the lane. Lavender stooped to pick a flower saying, "Look, John, it's Queen Anne's lace. Isn't it beautiful?"

"That's bird's-nest," John said definitely.

"We always called it Queen Anne's Lace," Lavender said.

"It's bird's-nest," John said almost angrily. "See—this one is dried up."

Lavender saw how the dry flowers had curled to form a deep bird's nest.

"You're right," Lavender conceded wearily. John must always be right.

She blinked back sudden tears and began to gather the black-eyed Susans that lined the path. Mama called these yellow-petaled flowers, yellow daisies. The leaves were rough and hairy and now beginning to turn brown. She wished John wouldn't be so domineering. It made her feel young and childish when he maintained he was always right. John, who had walked ahead of her, turned back now with a handful of long green stems with great leaves that joined around the stem and formed cups. "Indian cup," he said and Lavender saw the leaf cups actually held water.

Cicadas hummed melodiously when they walked back to the cabin. Lavender felt tired and glad to go early to bed.

In the coming days, she found she was always weary and this weariness made her irritable and queasy to her stomach. John, too, was on edge, and she found him staring often into space and dreaming. She knew he was thinking of Quantrill. And of Cole and the excitement they were living.

Well, she thought defensively, if that was what John wanted, he had no right to ask her to marry him. Oh, if only she could go back in time. If only she had met Cole Younger instead of John! If only it had been Cole who had come riding by on a white horse that day of the box social. If only she was Mrs. Cole Younger instead of Mrs. John Younger, how proud she would be!

She did not know just when it was that she realized she was to be a mother. But gradually, she knew she should not feel so ill or so tired. She tried not to think about it but the thought persisted that she might be "in the family way" as Mama would say. Oh, she wanted her mother. She wanted someone to be kind and loving to her.

And she was certain, she was afraid to tell John. He had become so strange of late, so distant that, at times, she was almost afraid of him. After their marriage when they had first come to the cabin, he had farmed their small piece of cleared land happily, if not too industriously. Now he complained constantly. At night, he would pull her to him and take her almost cruelly and afterwards, fling her away from him as if he hated her and hated himself.

Well, she would have to tell him. There was no need to put off the telling any longer. She could almost sense his distress and disgust.

On a wild wet rainy night, she told him quite simply, "John, we're going to have a baby. I have to tell you. We have to plan. Maybe Mrs. Bradley from the Corners would come here when my time comes or I could go home to Mama before it's near the time."

He stared at her for a long moment, saying nothing. She could hear her heart thumping . . . thumping . . .

74

thumping. "John," she said, "did you hear me?"

He glared at her.

"We're going to have a baby," she repeated the words slowly in the deadly silence. She saw the familiar red flush stain his cheeks. His lips curled back and she knew he was very angry. She threw back her shoulders defiantly. She was with child and he might as well acknowledge that fact. There was no going back.

"You might as well be glad about it," she said flatly. He continued to stare at her with fists clenched, saying nothing.

"It will be a boy," she said definitely. "It will be a boy and he can help you farm and hunt."

"Farm and hunt!" He spat the words.

She fled from his anger and went to bed where she cried herself to sleep. Even the dream she shared with Cole was small comfort tonight.

When she awakened the following morning, she knew instantly that something was different. Something was all wrong. She looked at the pillow beside her own and it was smooth. She had been so tired she had slept the sleep of the dead. He had not awakened her by his rough demanding touch because he had not come to bed.

She felt the strange silence as she went to the stove and built up the fire so she could have hot coffee. She wondered if perhaps one of the horses or maybe the cow had been taken sick and John had spent the night in the lean-to that served as a barn. Or perhaps someone from the Corners had needed help and had come for him. But no, he would have told her. Surely he would have told her.

She made herself eat breakfast, a slice of salt pork and fried eggs and bread. She would have to decide what to do if John had actually gone off and left her. But surely, he wouldn't just go off and leave her!

Perhaps he had gone to the Corners for supplies. They were short of a number of things. She fed the chickens and the cow and the horses. She kept busy and when supper-time came she fried potatoes and a slice of ham and put biscuits in the oven.

She told herself over and over that maybe the Dalton boy or maybe even Bob Younger or Jim Younger had come by. Perhaps one of their relatives was ill and John hadn't wanted to worry her and had gone quietly away. But no, she would have heard horses' hooves sweep into the yard. Besides John's horse had been led out of its stall. She could tell from the prints. It had been very carefully led. John had stolen away like a thief in the night.

Day followed night and night followed day but John did not return. Sometimes she thought she should go home to Mama. Then again, she knew she must wait to see if John would return. When he had been gone a month she felt in her heart that he would not return. And she knew she did not really care if he came back or not.

It had been raining all day. She had completed the evening chores and came into the cabin drenched. She shed her wet garments and put on her gown. No one would be liable to come this evening, not when the roads were mire and the rain kept coming down in buckets.

She was lonely. She thought now of how restless John

had become especially since his mother's death. She remembered how irritable he was and found it easy to believe that he had returned to his old life of riding with Quantrill.

The thought of being tied down with a baby, as well as a wife, had been too much for him. He had just ridden away from the responsibilities.

She looked out the window. It was twilight now. Rain pelted on her violets and other flowers she had so lovingly planted. She made herself eat a cold biscuit and sorghum and drink some milk. Sitting at the table, she thought she heard the sound of horses' hooves. John! John was coming back!

But maybe it wasn't John. Maybe it was someone else. She got the gun from its place over the fireplace and waited. The horseman was in the yard. She saw him jump from his horse and walk toward the cabin door where she waited with gun raised ready to shoot.

Chapter 6

The rain splashed against Lavender as she stood in the doorway waiting. She could see that the man approaching was not John. The visitor was much taller. She waited. The gun was cocked. She was ready.

Perhaps, she thought, it was someone bringing her word of John. Perhaps he was hurt or dead! Or perhaps he was sending word that he did not intend to return. The only noise was the sloshing sound of the man's footsteps against the heavy beat of the rain.

She saw the rain dripping from his wide-brimmed hat and as he came closer, she recognized him.

Cole! It was Cole!

"Cole!" she cried and she was in his arms. All her worry about John's leaving disappeared. Nothing mattered. Nothing would ever matter again. She would always have this moment to remember.

They went into the kitchen and he took off his dripping coat and hat. He was looking at her anxiously, "Lavender, are you all right?"

She could not answer. She could only look at him. Cole! Cole Younger here!

"I needed you and you came," she breathed.

She presently brought him hot coffee and salt pork and biscuits and they sat at the table with the lamp between them. In the lamp's glow, he could only stare at her.

"Lavender," he said. "You are so beautiful. I think of you day and night. When I got back with Quantrill all I could think of was you. I thought of how beautiful you are, the way your golden hair curls around your beautiful face and how blue your eyes are and your skin and . . ." his voice broke and when he spoke again it was to say mildly, "It was hell."

"I know," she murmured softly. "I know."

"John came into camp. When I saw him I thought something must be wrong with you. He said simply he needed time away from the farm," Cole said. "He's a fool. I don't see how he could spend one night away from you." She did not answer.

"He is just a lad," Cole said.

"You don't have to defend him," she said softly and smiled at him. "I know all about John."

"Let's forget about John," he said gently. "Quantrill sent John on an errand up to Illinois country. Quant's smart. He wanted to make John feel important and Quantrill guessed how I feel about you. When John rode northward, I came south."

"Partly to see if I was all right?" she queried.

"More than that, my darling. To feast my eyes on your sweetness, your loveliness again."

"Oh, Cole." And she thought to herself, what a darling you are Cole Younger! And what a weakling my husband is! No wonder John had told Cole she was all right. He just didn't want to talk about the farm or the baby or the unexciting life he led.

She decided now she wouldn't mention the baby. She didn't want his pity. It was better that he did not know she was with child.

"I told you months ago that I loved you," he reminded her. Tears filled her eyes and ran down her smooth peachy young cheeks. "Oh, Cole, I love you too."

"I never knew I could love a woman as I love you, Lavender," he said softly, sincerely. "The minute I saw you the very first time, it was as though the world and time stood still. I never knew a woman could mean everything to me."

She smiled lovingly, aching for him to take her in his arms.

"I tell myself you are my brother's wife. I tell myself this love I have for you is all wrong. But it doesn't matter what I tell myself. It doesn't matter. All I know is that I am on fire with wanting you."

The rain continued to beat against the cabin. The branches of the giant oaks, heavy-laden from the rain, pressed on the roof and beat with a heavy ominous sound but inside the cabin it was warm and cozy. She presently brushed her hair and got in bed. She felt no shame as she waited for him. She loved him with all her heart and soul and this night belonged to them alone.

As she pulled the sheet up to her chin, she waited trembling with anticipation. Two tallow dips were burning.

Cole came toward the bed and seemed to fill the room with his presence. He loomed in front of her. The gleaming glow of the dips turned his hair to pure gold.

He sat on the bed and spoke softly, taking her hands in his, "Lavender, I should get on my horse and ride out of your life but I can't. Whatever the future holds, we do not know. But tonight is ours."

"Ours," she echoed.

"When you live as I do, you have to snatch what happiness you can. There may never be a tomorrow. There is only this moment."

She nodded. She understood. He drew off his boots with the bootjack that stood always at the fireplace. Then unbuttoning his shirt, he stood and let his pants slide to the floor. In bed, he took her tenderly in his arms and she relaxed against him. For a long moment he said nothing, then whispered, "Lavender, my beautiful, beautiful Lavender."

She lay hypnotized by his nearness, smelling the good healthy scent of him. He pulled her gown upward from her willing body, over her head.

"Let me look at your beauty," he whispered as he pulled back the sheet from her body. He drank in her loveliness for a long moment then he breathed in awe, "Lavender, your breasts are the breasts of a goddess."

He was tender and so gentle, not at all like John. Cole wooed her with love and she relaxed and became as clay in his hands.

She coiled her arms around his naked waist and ran her fingers up and down his back feeling the strong rippling muscles, the firm skin. She felt his response as she pressed her body to his and felt his hardness. He was whispering sweet words to her and she felt that she had never been alive before this moment.

Unconsciously her hips began to undulate. He was whispering, "I love you, love you, love you." Her body took up the sweet rhythm to his words. His eager hands captured her breasts and kissed them, tasting them, nibbling them. Then he was on her, taking her, loving her, penetrating her with love.

She moaned, she moved beneath him and they breathed together in mounting and complete ecstasy. Then he rolled over on his back, still breathing hard and she touched him tenderly and he looked deep into her eyes. Her eyes glinted purple in the golden glow from the tallow dips. Her trembling lips smiled at him and there was a glitter of a tear.

"It was so wonderful," she exulted and kissed his cheek. Her face was radiant in the dim light. He stroked the curls back from her face and held her close. She felt desire rising in her again and she pressed close to him.

They loved again and this time it was even better. The waves of ecstasy enveloped them in great pulsating waves. Afterwards she told him, "I never knew it could be so wonderful."

"Our love has made it so."

She clung to him and his lips tenderly touched her hair as he eased himself off her and lay beside her holding her close.

And so they slept for a while and then he awakened her with kisses and they loved again and she felt herself lifted to heights of glory she had never in her wildest dreams imagined.

"Cole, how can I let you go?" she asked later.

He did not answer for a moment and then he spoke solemnly, "We must always treasure the memory of this night. God alone knows what the future holds."

Toward morning he awakened her and they talked.

"Dearest," he said. "I know your life with John isn't easy. It's like John is two people."

"Yes, sometimes he is agreeable and other times he is cold and silent. I can't reach him when he gets frozen like he does."

"John's been through a lot," Cole said. "He's been through hell."

"I'll bet you've had bad experiences too," she said. "I know you told of some of them last winter and I'm sure there were many, many more."

"Yes, but Lavender, John is seven years younger than me. And he's different. He has always had a chip on his shoulder. You know he was only fifteen years old when he became involved with a man named Gillcreas. Gillcreas said something bad about me and Quantrill and one thing led to another. John was a good shot and when Gillcreas shot at him, he shot back. The old man missed but John's aim was true. John was let off scot free but it left its mark. Then Ma, at the close of the War, went back to the farm in Jackson County. The Youngers were poor, Lavender. Our money had been scattered during the War and we had only the land."

He was silent, remembering as she snuggled close to him. "Jim and John and me intended to work the land," he went on. "It was good rich land. We could have made a go of it. We could have rebuilt the family fortune and lived respectable, lawful lives."

Lavender listened, her eyes never leaving his face.

"Neugent's Militia persecuted us. They hated the Youngers. We had to fight to survive. I finally left home thinking the Neugent so-called Vigilantes would stop persecuting my mother and brothers."

"Oh, Cole," she murmured sympathetically, kissing him.

"You know how my father was ambushed and killed. Jayhawkers shot him down in cold blood," he said bitterly, "and they took Ma from a sick-bed and made her set fire to her own house. Half-dead from consumption, my poor Ma was forced to trudge miles in the darkness and bitter cold to find shelter."

"Oh, Cole, I never knew."

"Didn't John tell you?"

"He never talked much about it, only now and then he would start to tell about something that happened, and then he would get very angry and wouldn't say anything else," she answered. "He did tell me about your Pa being shot down."

"John's all frozen up on the inside. He should talk to you about these things. It's bad to keep your thoughts bottled up."

They were silent then until presently he sighed and said, "Lavender, when Melon and Ruby and I were here last winter I used to look at you in the bed with John and I would be so jealous of him. I wanted you. I wanted to hold you, to cover you with kisses and John would lie next to you like a stick."

"I know."

"You mustn't blame him too much. The War and its aftermath has scarred us. How can we settle down to farming when we have lived as we have? We aren't normal. We've been hunted, tracked down and forced to endure untold hardships. I remember how you looked when Ruby told of the men taking the women, but Lavender, we had to take what pleasuring was offered when we could. We never knew if there would be another opportunity."

The mention of Ruby made Lavender giggle, "Poor Ruby," she said. "She loved you."

He smiled. "Believe me, I was glad to get rid of that wildcat."

"I loved Melon," Lavender said.

"She talks often of you."

"She's had a hard life. She deserves better."

"She's happy. There's not much future for a woman like Melon. No folks. No one to care. She, like the Raiders, has to take her happiness where she can."

She snuggled closer to him, saying, "Oh, Cole, you make it all seem so clear. A woman needs a man to talk to her."

"John never had much to say when he was a mere lad and as he got older and endured so many hardships he said less. He was just a boy, Lavender, when he rode off to join Quantrill. Now there is no peace for the men who galloped under the black flag of Quantrill."

"It's not fair," she said.

"No," he echoed. "It's not fair. Outlawry and strife born of the Civil War have joined forces. Hate still flames in our hearts because we remember the bloody time of burning homes and massacre. The bodies of the slaughtered have fertilized our land."

"Maybe that is why John is so restless and so dissatisfied," she said wistfully.

"No doubt," he agreed. "But, Lavender, how can you expect him to hoe a furrow and shuck corn after the excitement of tearing open a town with blazing guns and shattering glass? And what is milking a cow to the blood-tingling minutes when your horse leaps forward and you are one of a hundred screaming demons of destruction?"

She sighed. "That's why I will never regret this short time we have together. It will be a beautiful memory for me to treasure forever."

She began to cry, clinging to him.

"Don't cry, darling," he comforted her. She wanted

to tell him she was going to have a baby and that she was worried that John was not going to come back and she was afraid to be alone. But no, this was not the time. She would not spoil this happy time.

Later she watched him ride away and her heart was dead within her. She had clung to him and his lips had touched her hair and her lips.

"Always remember that I love you, my darling," he had whispered in parting. "Only God knows the future, sweetheart. Perhaps someday we will be together."

Chapter 7

"Always remember that I love you, my darling," Cole had told her and she clung to his words like a talisman in the coming weeks. He had whispered too, "Only God knows the future, sweetheart. Perhaps someday we will be together."

She lived day to day always wondering if John would return. She reasoned to herself that if he had no intention of returning, Cole would know and would come for her.

Week followed week and winter was not far off. Mr. Granneman from the Corners rode out to see if all was well with the Wells. Lavender had forgotten that John had adopted the name of Brandy Wells in this, his new home and for a moment she was ready to correct Earl Granneman.

"The missus was mighty worried cause she ain't seen you or Brandy," he explained.

Lavender thanked him for his kindness and assured him all was well with them. Brandy, she explained, had been called away on family business. No, she did not know when he would return.

"Guess you're gettin' short on supplies?" he asked. "I'll be glad to send my son, Otto, out with what you need."

Lavender felt the tears well up in her eyes. She had felt so abandoned. No one cared, she thought. No one cared that she was left alone in this cabin.

"Thank you, Mr. Granneman," she said gratefully. "I wonder if Otto would harvest my wheat for half of it. With my half I can lay in plenty of supplies for this winter."

"It's a deal," the old man said. "It's a deal if you promise to let the missus and me know if you need anything before Brandy comes back."

She promised.

"I see you have plenty of firewood," he said. "I'll have Otto check from time to time to see that there's plenty. But I expect Brandy will be home before long."

"Yes," she said, wondering if the old man really believed her.

The wheat was harvested; late, but harvested. Lavender breathed a sigh of relief when Otto and the wheat disappeared in the distance and the sound of the creaking wagon faded away. She had plenty of supplies to last through the winter months. And in the early spring she would ride on Sugar, her horse, to Mama's and have her baby. She prayed for an early spring. She would be awkward and big by then. She supposed Mama would be horrified to see her come home by horseback. She planned during the coming weeks. She would dispose of the chickens by eating them. That would stretch her food supply. She would drop Bess off at the Grannemans on her way.

Winter set in with a raging blizzard. She fought her way to the barn to feed Bess and milk her and feed Sugar and feed the chickens. She thought of last winter and those unforgettable evenings around the fireplace.

88

She thought of Melon, sweet and lovable, and of fiery over-sexed Ruby and silent moody John and she thought of the handsome Cole. Cole, her lover. She thought of their stolen kisses and she thought of the memorable night with him, of their passion. And as day followed day, she could not understand why he did not come to see how she was.

Christmas came and went and her body thickened.

She was thankful that after that first big blizzard the weather mellowed. There was much rain and the dampness penetrated the cabin making everything feel clammy in spite of a roaring fire in the fireplace and the black iron stove.

January passed and February came with a few feathery snowflakes but barely enough to whiten the ground. March and her violets were green and full of blossoms. She knew she could wait no longer. She looked at the green shoots of the other flowers she had so lovingly planted and wondered if she would ever see them again.

It was late spring of 1871. Lavender was back home. And yet she felt a stranger in familiar surroundings. The house was the same, a big old white house set back from the road and surrounded by oaks. The Wakarusa River in the distance looked the same and Pa's land looked as it always had in the spring.

The rich soil, broken with ox-drawn plows, lay upturned in thick folds as black as a crow's wing. On the fringes of the plowed land, bluestem grass held fast to the heavy soil as though determined to resist the encroaching civilization's efforts to tear it asunder. Wild hyacinths and blazing stars bloomed in profusion as larks trailed melody over the village nearby.

Lavender saw that the soft rays of the sun still touched on every color in the rainbow from the sky that looked as though someone had dipped a brush into azure water color and drawn it across the horizon to the flame-breasted robins hopping daintily over the rich earth. The pink wild roses were blooming and to the west, two miles hence, the Oregon Trail was vivid with spider lilies.

Lavender tried to analyze her feelings about returning home. Everything seemed so different. Even Mama and Pa seemed different. They had been surprised at her return. And shocked by her appearance so swollen with child. They demanded to know Brandy's whereabouts. And under their incessant questioning she broke down and admitted that his name wasn't Brandy Wells at all. It was John Younger.

This knowledge had left them speechless with horror and indignation. Their daughter married to a Younger! Staunch supporters of the Union, they considered the Youngers and the James on the same level as the Devil.

"He'll get what's comin' to him if he comes around here," Pa vowed. "He's a killer. Just as it says in the Good Book about the blood runnin' up to the horses' haunches; that's the way the blood ran in Lawrence, Kansas. They burned the town. They killed women and children."

"Pa," Lavender defended John quickly. "Pa, John was but a boy when Lawrence was sacked. He had no part in that." She did not say how often she had heard John express regrets that he had been too young to partake of the gory happenings at Lawrenceville, also called Lawrence.

90

"He's got the killer blood in him," Pa cried. "And your baby will have the killer blood in it."

"Hush, Pa," Mama begged.

Lavender wished now she had stayed in her cabin. She missed Jacob and Mint too. When the three of them had been growing up in this house, there had been fun and laughter. Now there was the gloom of death here.

Mama and Pa were bitter. Bitter because they felt Jacob had deserted them. He had gone blithely off to the gold fields in search of gold. Pa felt he should have stayed on the farm and helped him.

"Just when he was old enough to be of real help he gets on that damned train and goes west," Pa complained. "Ever since he heard about the Central and Union Pacific lines joinin' up at that Promontory Point in Utah in 1869 he talked of nothin' else. Vowed he'd ride that train."

They were bitter about Mint too. Mint, who just two weeks ago had eloped with a stranger named Will Ruggles.

"Just rode off into the night. Never said 'Goodbye' or 'Go to hell' or nothing."

Lavender missed Mint and had looked forward to seeing her. They had written a few times after Lavender's marriage. Lavender had found it hard to put on paper the details of her new life. She could not tell of John's cold strange behavior or of Cole or Ruby or Melon. She did tell her of the cabin in the woods and how she hated the crows. She told of planting the violets and the scrub trees close to the cabin.

Mint, in turn, had written. Evidently Charles Engleman had faded out of the picture soon after Lavender's marriage. She had mentioned other would-be suitors, boys with whom they had grown up but of this Will Ruggles, she had said nothing. Perhaps she had not known of this Will when she had written the last letter last winter. Mail was slow and one had to go to the Corners to pick it up.

It must be terrible, Lavender thought often in these long days of waiting, to get old like Mama and Pa and have your children desert you.

And always, she remembered Pa's words about her baby having killer blood. This is ridiculous, she told herself over and over. A baby is so soft, so sweet, so loveable. A baby doesn't have killer blood! But still, Pa's words lingered.

It was on a wild wet day that she knew the time was near. Mama had summoned two neighboring farm women to assist in the birth. It had been raining all day and Lavender felt chilled and frightened. The usual hush and air of anticipation customary where a birth is imminent fogged heavily over the bedroom.

She looked out at the rain sloshing against the windowpanes and at the gray gloomy day as she lay on the bed where she and Mint had giggled in the old days. Where had the years gone? If only time could be rolled back and she and Mint could laugh and plan and dream again? But life went on and with it came sorrow and disillusionment and unhappiness. But then there were the happy times, those times of joy and ecstasy she had shared with Cole. Cole. Cole. Cole, where are you? Where are you when I need you?

She lay like a waxen doll on the bed. Her golden hair had been brushed back from her hot forehead but tendrils of curls framed her round face. Her cheeks were flushed and her lashes lay like dark butterfly wings against her soft young cheeks.

She braced herself against the pain that swept her body like a knife. She would think of something else. She would think about Cole. But then Cole apparently hadn't cared enough about her to come back to her. When he found that John had deserted her he should have come back to the cabin and taken care of her. But no, she mustn't think such thoughts. Something had happened or Cole would have returned. She had to cling to Cole and their dream. Without Cole she had nothing.

Mama and Pa were disappointed in her. They had been so shocked and heartsick when she revealed that she was married to a Younger. And Pa had talked about Lawrenceville. Thoughts of Lawrenceville came swooping down on her now. She tried to shut them out but could not. She could almost hear John talking about Lawrenceville. Even though he had not been there he had heard all about it many times from Quantrill, who delighted in the memory. John had been only twelve years old but through the years, the telling and retelling of the story made it seem vividly real to him.

In those first days of their marriage, he had talked of Lawrenceville. Perhaps he thought it made him seem a man of the world, a man who had taken part in the writing of history. She did not know. She knew only that in those first days of marriage she had delighted to listen to him.

And she *had* listened to the eager wild John Younger. She had neither approved nor condemned. The past, she told herself, did not matter. Only the future mattered and it lay ahead, glowing and shining. Lawrenceville! John had made the telling so real she had felt herself a part of the planning for the sacking and burning. Plans had been made in the Pardee home in Johnson County, Missouri. On a hot summer night, the Pardee parlor had been crowded with men. Quantrill strode into the middle of the room. He carried a heavy Navy Dragoon pistol with which he rapped on the table to command attention.

"Men," he hissed. "This is August the nineteenth and we must make our decision on something big at hand."

Although small and feminine looking, every man in the room looked at him with admiration and respect. Dick Yaeger suggested, "Lawrence is close. Let's raise some hell over there."

This had pleased Quantrill and his eyes danced. Lawrence, considered to be the most beautiful town in Kansas, had long been marked for destruction by Quantrill. Sometime before, Kansas outlaws had laid waste to a little town in Missouri named Osceola. Quantrill had been run out of Lawrence as a thief just prior to the Civil War so he was aching for revenge.

Quantrill complimented Dick now, "Good for you, Dick," he said. "Fletch Taylor here has been to Lawrenceville and done some spying."

"Yeah," Fletch boasted. "I've been there. I lived at the Eldridge house and even talked to that bastard, General Lane." They all hated General Lane and there were cries now of "Let's get rid of him."

Fletch grinned and hurried on, "I wanted to kill that damned Yankee right then and there."

They then discussed the pros and cons of raiding Lawrence. Finally Quantrill shouted for quiet. "Men," he said, "We've heard Fletch's report. It won't be an easy task but victory will be ours. Shall we take

Lawrence or shall we not?"

"We shall," the men shouted in unison.

"Let's burn it to the ground as Lane did Osceola," Quantrill said.

So on the morning of August 20th 1863, the Raiders marched from Lone Jack, Missouri, toward the Kansas border. Three-hundred men in all. One-hundred and fifty men were Quantrill's followers, the other one-hundred and fifty men were supplied by General Sterling Price and they were under the authority of Colonel Holt, a regular Confederate officer. No one ever knew if General Price actually knew of Quantrill's murderous intent. At eleven o'clock that night, they passed Gardner, Kansas, which sits on the old Santa Fe Trail. There, for the fun of it, they burned several homes and killed a few men. Even then, no one sent word to alert Lawrenceville sleeping placidly under the autumn stars.

Almost one-hundred and fifty were murdered because the people of Lawrence were complacent and didn't believe that anything could happen to their town. The town had been warned repeatedly that Quantrill intended to destroy it. But the guards had become careless. And finally there were no guards at all. The beautiful town was completely asleep to its terrible danger.

Lavender's mind veered away now from the horror. John had said Cole and Frank James had been in the group but she was sure that Cole would not shoot anyone in cold blood. She did not know about Frank James.

She opened her eyes now. "Mama," she whispered. "Mama."

Mama came to her bedside. Her quick nervous brown hands patted Lavender reassuringly.

"Mama is here," she said softly.

Lavender looked up at her. This was the old Mama, the Mama who had tucked her in bed at night, not the disapproving Mama who was disappointed in her because she had fallen in love with a stranger on a white horse and married him and the stranger had turned out to be John Younger.

"Mama, I hurt," she whispered.

The two other women in the room came close to Lavender. Sympathetic pity was on their faces.

"Poor girl," the one whispered to the other. "She needs that no good husband."

"Hush," Ma commanded.

"It's the truth," the woman flared. "A woman needs a good husban' standin' by at birthin' time. A beautiful sweet girl like Lavender don't deserve goin' through this alone. When she married that stranger, Brandy Wells, I thought no good would come of it."

"It's a shame, that it is," the other woman put in now. "I'll never forget the day this poor girl came draggin' up the road in front of my house. Plumb worn out and loaded down with a few belongings. Yes, plumb tuckered out after that long trip alone from down in those Ozark hills. Says her husband had to go away on family business. Ha!"

Mama took the two women gently by the arms and led them to the kitchen, suggesting a hot cup of coffee. Lavender lay thinking. She was dazed with pain, but she thought of John. How shocked these women would be if they knew she was Mrs. John Younger instead of Mrs. Brandy Wells! Being Mrs. Brandy Wells was bad enough in their eyes but they would be like Pa and Mama when it came to seeing her as Mrs. John Younger. Well, she thought sadly now, John Younger didn't want her and he didn't want the baby either. He wanted his old carefree life.

She cried out now in sudden pain as a sharp labor pain surged through her. Her cry brought the three women from the kitchen.

"Be brave," Mama said.

Lavender moaned.

"Just bear down. It won't be long."

Twilight came and the rain continued to beat against the windowpane. After a while a kind of dreaminess began to steal over Lavender. Time slipped away and it was a crisp winter day and the scent of pine filled the air. The snow flakes had tinseled her hair as Cole smiled at her with the hint of a smile brightening his gray eyes.

"I love you," he had said. "I love you."

And he had taken her in his arms. She had put her face against his and felt a wild joy take possession of her. All the sweet colors of April had glowed in her face and her throat had thickened and her heart had hammered. She remembered it all, every precious moment.

"Cole," she murmured. "Cole."

"She's cold," one of the women, Mrs. Ellis, said. "I'll fetch a blanket."

Lavender thought of that night when they had stood together in the gathering twilight at the end of the lane. A nightbird had wailed plaintively but the quietness of the evening had lain like a benediction over them. And he had told her that when a man married, he wanted a woman like her. Happy memories. Happy thoughts. With the pain racking her body, it was heavenly to think

97

of those happy moments with Cole.

She thought now of their last stolen moment together. "Goodbye, my darling," he had said softly. "You've changed things. That's all right. Nothing will ever be quite the same again. And yet, I'm so glad just to have known you, to have loved you. Goodbye, my dearest, and let's never forget our dream."

For the briefest moment she had been in his arms. She had felt his cheek hard against her own. And then there had been that time when he had come to her and they had loved through the night. What a time of ecstasy that was!

She relived that time now, remembering how it felt to feel his body warm against hers. A heavy drowsiness mercifully took possession of her, dragging at her mind and body. She surrendered to this fog of unreality until she was roused again to waves of racking pain. She heard the women in the room talking and felt Mama's hands gripping hers and then Mrs. Burns, the other woman in the group, gave a glad cry, "It's burst. It's a comin'."

In her stupor, she heard Mrs. Ellis say, "The Bible says, 'Unto the woman He said, I will greatly multiply thy sorrow and thy conception: in sorrow thou shalt bring forth children.' "

Lavender writhed in agony and then it was over. I'm a mother, she thought in wonder.

Mama had her baby and she was smacking it, but it made no sound. Lavender tensed, listening. She felt the silence. So thick she could taste it. A great fright seized her. Something must be wrong with her baby. Babies always cried when they were borned. Babies cried and cried. She raised herself up and called sharply, "Mama."

Someone else had the baby now and Mama came close to the bed. Lavender saw there were tears in her eyes and she looked pale and worn.

"Lavender," she said softly. "It was a little girl."

"Was," Lavender whispered.

"Was," Mama repeated. "Your baby was born dead. She just didn't breathe."

"Oh, Mama, Mama," Lavender wept.

"God knows best," Mrs. Ellis said and Lavender stared at the windowpane at which the wind and rain was lashing. Presently Mama brought her baby in. It looked like a tiny doll. It was dressed in a baby dress.

"One of your baby dresses," Mama explained. "One I had saved."

Lavender looked at the tiny face and saw it looked like a white rose. "Her name," she whispered, "is Rose."

Chapter 8

Mint's letter came on a day when Lavender was helping Mama make candles. She had regained her strength, the birth of the stillborn baby Rose seemed like a dream to her now. There was nothing to do but live one day at a time.

Today she and Mama had been threading wicks into candle molds, poking the long wick-string through all of six molds, carefully looping the tops over a stick to keep them from slipping. Then the molds must be plunged into hot water to loosen the hard grease. She liked working the shining cream-colored candles out of their containers.

Pa had gone down to the general store to get the mail and had come back waving a letter from Mint. He was excited. This was the first word they had gotten from her in the months she had been gone.

"You read better'n me," Pa said handing the letter to Lavender.

She opened the envelope and found it was really just a note stating Mint was well and happy. Will had a farm near the Big Blue River. She was glad of this, she wrote, because she missed seeing the Wakarusa. And she missed Mama and Pa and wondered if they had heard from Lavender.

"She sounds happy," Lavender said slowly as she folded the letter and gave it to Pa.

"That Big Blue ain't nothin' like the Wakarusa," Pa said definitely. "I know all about that Big Blue. I crossed it in 1844. Seemed nothin' bad 'cause I was young and strong but it can be ragin' with whirlpools. I remember we camped at the Alcove Spring campground. There were mosquitoes as big as polecats. I remember we went west from St. Joseph and crossed at Marysville."

"Mint must live near Marysville," Lavender said glancing at the postmark as Pa clutched the letter.

"I tell you that water was so purty. About fifty yards wide. It was purty when we saw it one evenin' and it looked like it would be right easy to cross. But a storm came up and we had to camp an extra day or two. When we tried to cross, it was near death for us. Our horse leaders got tangled up. I had to plunge in to get them straightened out. I remember when we came up the bank there were three graves nearby. Things like that you don't forget."

Pa liked to talk about the old days when he had emigrated west. He had gone as far west as the Platte River. Lavender had been raised on stories of his trip. She could shut her eyes now and remember the joy she had felt when she was a little girl and he told of his adventures. Especially when he went to the Platte in a covered wagon. She relived his experiences, thrilling to the beauty of twilight on the prairie. She saw the rays of the late afternoon sun casting gold-strewn shadows across the low rolling hills.

She heard the bees making last buzzing journeys into blossoms and saw honey locusts lift arms of benediction to the red and yellow and violet-colored sky. The wild morning glories had long since closed their white cups and the evening star gleamed white in the darkening sky.

She could imagine she was in a covered wagon with a young and eager Pa as it jostled along the worn ruts of the Trail. Westport Landing, with all its hustle and bustle of departing wagon trains and its crowds of cowboys and leather-faced Indians was behind them. The turnoff was before them. The wagons trailed along, one behind the other. Canvas tops billowed in the prairie breeze and wooden buckets hanging on the sides of the wagon beds made a gay, almost musical sound as they rattled together.

When the signal was given to stop for the night, the wagons ricocheted off into odd tangents forming a circle. The horses were unharnessed quickly by the men and the women crawled stiffly down from the wagon seats. They stretched their arms and legs and walked around a few minutes, loosening up limbs that had become stiff during the long jostling ride. Then it was time to cook supper. Boys and girls hurried to gather wood for the fire, shouting back and forth. To hear them calling, "Hello," to one another, one would think they hadn't seen each other for a week. And yet they had been together off and on all day picking mayflower buds and dogtooth violets as they ran alongside the wagons. Some had even found rare anemones and Dutchman's breeches, and all had joined in playing games of tag.

There had been a little girl named Emma Susan and she had taken a liking to Pa and Pa took her under his wing. Pa liked to talk about Emma Susan and Lavender had begged for stories about the little girl. She even tried to be like Emma Susan since Pa always talked as though she was someone special. When Pa told about the day he had warned Emma Susan about tagging along too far behind the wagon train to gather flowers, Lavender pretended she was Emma Susan and Pa was warning her.

"I know you like to gather flowers, Emma Susan," he said. "But remember to stay close to the wagons. This is beautiful country but there is much that is strange and wild."

"I'll remember," she had promised.

Emma Susan had tried to keep her promise but the beauty of the red blossoms she had seen by the side of the road just before they stopped for the night drew her like a magnet. She had never seen such blossoms before. They looked like strawberries growing on stems. She decided to gather some quickly and hurry back.

Lavender spent many an hour play-acting that she was Emma Susan. She saw herself straining to see in the dusk that the flowers were farther from the road than she had thought. And the circle of wagons seemed a long way off. For a quick moment she considered turning around and going back to the wagons without the flowers. But lured by their beauty, she hurried on. The stems were thicker and tougher than she had expected and she had to tug and pull to break them.

Then before her frightened eyes, a figure stepped from behind a tree. It was an Indian. His eyes were like big black beads and he had black hair dangling down to his shoulders. As Emma Susan stood petrified with fear, he spoke in low guttural tones as two other ruddy figures slid silently from the shadows. Emma Susan was sure they were going to scalp her. She had heard fearsome stories about little girls being scalped.

Then she heard horses' hooves. Clippety-clop. Clippety-clop. Pa had come to rescue her. In Lavender's imagination she could feel Pa's strong arms holding her close as they rode to join the wagon train. But that wasn't the end of the story and many a night Lavender shivered in her bed reliving Emma Susan's adventures. There were those in the wagon train who were very angry at Emma Susan for wandering off. Especially angry when they heard how the Indians had confronted her.

One woman became hysterical, crying that they would all be murdered in their beds by the Indians. Another predicted darkly that the Indians would follow them all the way westward. As they ate supper, gathered close to the campfire, they were quiet and talkative by turns. There was evidence of uneasiness though it was submerged in the usual banter and plans for the next day.

"Just a few days farther west," Old John, the wagon master said, "and we come to the turn off. It'll be like a buffalo trail. Be mighty rough goin' but I 'spect you'll like what's at the end of that old buffalo trail."

They had heard this story before but they listened expectantly for his booming voice to roar, "The Land of Milk and Honey." His listeners smiled. This was what they liked to hear. Their tanned faces and wind-reddened eyes were aglow with the dream.

The women looked at their work-worn hands and dreamed of a day when life would be easier. The men dreamed of acres of their own. They were anxious to build an empire out in this wild rough country. Even though they talked of the land that would be theirs, they fell silent now and then. They were all wondering if the Indians would molest them. Now that darkness had fallen, they became more tense and worried.

In the distance, a long fringe of trees was silhouetted darkly against the night. Pa had wished there was a high hill nearby. But there was nothing but low, rolling hills . . . nothing that offered any natural protection.

Silence had fallen over the camp as the supper cleanup was completed and preparations made for the night. A coyote howled nearby and even the tall grass seemed to shiver. There was a feeling of fear, like the cold dampness that comes after a fall rain. They lingered by the fire. They felt safer huddled around the bright flames.

Pa had seen the shadowy figure first. A shadowy figure stealing like a panther toward the wagons. Then that figure was joined by two other figures steathily creeping toward the campfire.

"Maybe they're friendly," Pa said. "Maybe they want food."

Old John cautioned, "Everyone stay where you are. There'd be more than three if they planned to fight."

Friendly? Were they really friendly? Maybe they were. Surely if they were bent on evil they wouldn't come so boldly into the circle. Not a word was said as the three intruders warily circled the group about the fire. Then they saw Emma Susan and moved toward her. The Indians were grinning in friendly fashion as they stood by Emma Susan. One reached out and stroked her hair. Pa waited breathlessly, ready to spring to her defense.

Then with a sudden swoop, an Indian had whipped

out a knife and pulling one of Emma Susan's golden curls from her head had cut it off. Then he yanked another away from her head and cut it off and then another. Each of the braves had a curl and they grunted and disappeared into the night.

Old John had laughed. "Whadaya know? All them braves wanted was a good luck charm. I've heard they're mighty taken with long blond curls."

All joined in merry laughter of relief. All but Emma Susan who ruefully felt the three short stubs where her curls had once dangled. Those curls would flap from the belts of three Indian braves! Lavender used to peer into a mirror and hold up three curls to the top of her head to see how she looked without three of her long blond curls. It was such fun to pretend she was Emma Susan.

That is, it was fun until the day Pa told her what happened to Emma Susan. It seemed it had started to rain. It rained so long and so hard that the wagon train was mired in mud. Emma Susan came down with a fever. It was a bad time for the wagon train. Everyone holed up in their wagons. Pa had looked out across the forsaken countryside with its rolling hills and its prairie grass blowing in the storm and sighed.

Old John had fixed an onion poultice and put it on Emma Susan's chest. Emma Susan's mama did nothing but cry, sure that Emma Susan would die. "We'll be digging a grave in this sea of mud," she predicted. "We'll be leavin' our little Emma Susan out on this prairie." Leave little Emma Susan out here in this prairie with the rain and the sun beating down on her grave! With the dried grass waving eternally above her. Pa prayed as he had never prayed before.

He remembered a night not too long before when he and Emma Susan had been looking at the stars together. They had twinkled so brightly, like diamonds against black velvet. So close he felt he could reach up and pluck a few for Emma Susan. Emma Susan had asked him, "If this side of heaven is so beautiful and sparkling with diamond stars, what do you suppose the other side looks like . . . the side that faces God?"

Now would Emma Susan find out about that other side, the side that faced God? The days passed, the storm raged and Emma Susan put up a valiant fight for her life. Then when the rain stopped and the sun shone and those in the wagon train were sure that things would take a turn for the better, including their prayers being answered, Emma Susan closed her blue eyes forever.

Old John scooped out a huge log for the coffin and Pa, with tears running down his cheeks, wrapped her thin body in a quilt and they buried her. There was a short service but everyone was so heartsick with grief and sobbed so that Old John's words from the Bible were buried in the sobbing.

They ran the wagons over the grave. No one knew quite why only Pa had suggested it and it seemed the thing to do. "It's to keep her safe," Pa told himself. "Only the angels know where she is, only the angels and God." He did not know if it was true but years before he had heard that Indians or animals might dig up the dead. He could not chance that, not while he was not there to protect his little Emma Susan.

Lavender tried not to think of that lone grave out on the prairie but she was sure Pa thought of it many times when he sat before the fireplace thinking. When she was

107

little she would persuade him to tell her of his soddy. At least then he would not be thinking of Emma Susan. She liked to hear of his building a soddy near the Platte River. And she heard this story so often she was sure she could build a soddy if she had to.

"You cut two or three foot strips of sod," Pa explained, "and lay them like bricks, one upon the other, to form the walls. It's a heavy job. Openings are left for the door and windows. You had to use quilts at the windows cause there ain't no glass. Rough poles and a matting of small branches supported the overlapping sod strips on the shedlike roof. There was a partition through the center dividing the house into two rooms."

"What about the walls, Pa?" the young Lavender had asked.

"Had to smooth them down and plaster them with mud. The floor was dirt."

"And that was your home, Pa?" Mint had asked.

Jacob was more interested in how long Pa lived in the dirt house as Pa called it.

"Only stayed a year or two. That winter was turrible. Snow up to the roof and strong winds where you couldn't even catch your breath. It was lonely too. That was before I met your mama. I gave up and came back to Westport Landing."

"You and Mama got married and settled down here," Lavender prompted.

The three children never tired of hearing Pa's tales of his journey by covered wagon to the Platte. They felt they too had felt the hot winds that parched Pa with feverish breath. They felt the dreary pelting rain and smelled the odor of clover and the rich pungent smell of newly-turned loam and felt the heavy darkness. And he

108

told them of spring on the prairie with the teal flying out of the coarse grass, with the willows and the cottonwoods bursting into green beauty, with sweet-William and blue phlox and wild indigo coming up through the heavy sod, and the white clouds scudding low with the wind. He glossed over the reality of the frontier where the simple act of existing was most often a bitter struggle. The frontier was one of plagues, drought, storms and epidemics and extremes of heat and cold.

He did not tell them that many of the first settlers lived in dugouts cut into a hillside. Corn meal, sorghum and salt pork were staples and gunnysacks were men's pants and the women were lucky to have a calico dress. Snakes, mice and bedbugs flourished in the soddies and in the dugouts as did smallpox, cholera and typhoid fever. There were few if any doctors and they were ill-trained and most likely alcoholic. And always there was danger from blizzards, prairie fires, tornadoes and Indians. Grasshoppers sometimes swarmed across the plains, hiding the sun, devouring everything.

He did tell them that when he came back to Westport Landing, he hung a sign on his wagon saying, "In God I trusted, And am going home before I'm busted."

In those days when Lavender was recovering her strength she would look at Pa and try to remember him as the hero of her little girl days. Now he looked like a shriveled old man. He complained constantly about the railroads, the new-fangled ways the people had taken up, and about the way President Ulysses S. Grant was running the government.

"He's a drunk, that's what he is," Pa declared.

"No, Pa," Lavender said. "I heard he drinks hardly anything. It's just that some people can't stand to take even a swallow. Some people seem to get drunk when they even look at a bottle of whisky."

"I guess he was a good general but as to being a good president that's something else again."

"He's a smart man, Pa," Lavender said. "I read in a newspaper where he said, 'In America you won, and you lost, and you kept on moving ahead!'"

Moving ahead? The words stuck in her mind in the days following this conversation. She would have to move ahead. She couldn't just sit there day after day and listen to Pa's ranting and complaining. Mama kept telling her to rest and get her strength back. She didn't want her to help with the household chores.

She asked Pa one day why he continued to use oxen instead of horses to plow his fields.

"The old ways are the best ways," he said stubbornly.

Well, there was no use trying to change Pa, she conceded.

On July 15th, 1871, Tad Lincoln died in Chicago. The country had loved little Tad when he was growing up in the White House. They loved him in death. Pa had idolized Abraham Lincoln. He did not like Mary Lincoln, wife of the late President.

"That woman ain't no good," he ranted. "If she'd of stayed put instead of roamin' all over the world that little boy would be alive."

"Pa," Lavender said. "That little boy is eighteen years old and he was always a sickly boy. It's not poor Mrs. Lincoln's fault he died."

But there was no use convincing Pa of anything, and again she thought of President Grant's words, "Moving ahead."

"Mama," she said one day when Pa was out in the

110

fields. "Mama, I think I'll go visit Mint."

Was it her imagination that Mama looked relieved? She supposed she was an embarrassment to Mama and Pa. A woman who came home without a husband.

She heard Mama and Pa whispering about it that night.

The next morning at breakfast, Pa said, "I hear you're aimin' to visit your sister, Mint."

Lavender looked at him and in her heart begged, "Pa, tell me not to go. Tell me you want me to stay here with you and Mama."

"I think that's a right good idea. You can see firsthand how she's makin' it and what kind of a scoundrel she married up with."

On August 1st, 1871, Lavender Younger boarded the train at Independence, Missouri. There was only a two hour train ride. She would have to go the remaining ten miles by stage or wagon. She was excited, eager to be on her way. She had a new dress of dark blue cotton piped in white. There was a tiny bustle in the back from which pink roses peeped. She had regained her figure and her waist was small and her breasts curved alluringly beneath the blue cloth. The high neck was trimmed with a bit of cream lace with a cluster of the same pink roses. On her golden curls a brimmed hat of blue with a white ribbon was perched. She was beautiful and knew it.

Pa was angry because she was going to go by railroad. Even to go part way was sinful, he thought.

"Thank you, Mama and Pa for my new dress and bonnet," she said gratefully.

"We couldn't let you go visitin' lookin' like a tramp. That dress you wore was a sore sight," Pa complained.

"It was the only one I had big enough, Pa," she said frowning. She wished he wouldn't say things that made her think about the baby Rose.

"Are you rouged?" Pa demanded looking at her closely.

Mama bristled, "You know Lavender ain't rouged. Mint nor her ever had to rouge. I seen to it they took care of their beautiful skin. I made them always wear a sun bonnet when they were goin' to be out in the sun."

Pa was glaring at the engine which was belching smoke. "Goodbye, Mama. Goodbye, Pa," Lavender said giving them each a kiss.

She was anxious to be on her way. If Mint didn't want her she would go somewhere else. She was just glad to leave Mama and Pa and begin living again.

She enjoyed the train ride and was sorry when the conductor called her station, "Marysville."

There was an hour wait for the stagecoach. It was a short run stagecoach, the man in the station explained, since the railroad had come through.

"Where you goin', Miss?" he asked.

"I'm going to visit my sister, Mrs. William Ruggles."

"Oh," he murmured and looked at her strangely.

"Is something wrong?" she asked quickly. "Do you know Mr. Ruggles?"

"No," he said but she noticed he cast furtive glances at her when he thought she wasn't looking.

The stagecoach presently arrived and she saw the driver and the man who ran the way station looking at her and whispering. Another passenger told Lavender the two were brothers and had a right thriving business. Lavender wished now that she had written Mint that she was coming for a visit. Well, if Mint didn't want her

112

to visit she could always go back to her Ozark cabin. If Cole came looking for her that is where he would go. What if he came and she wasn't there? She felt heartsick at the thought.

Presently the driver called down to her from his perch. "The Ruggles place is just around this next bend."

When he stopped the stage and helped her alight and gave her her carpetbag, he said very low, "Miss, are you sure you want to get off here?"

"Yes," she answered. "Why shouldn't I want to get off here?"

He tipped his hat respectfully, "That, Miss," he said sadly, "is something I cannot tell you."

Lavender went toward the cluster of trees at the end of a winding road wondering what he had meant. There had been something like fear in his voice when he had talked to her, something like a warning. She came now to a clearing in the midst of which sat a shack. She must be at the wrong place, she thought, walking slowly forward. Mint couldn't live in such a hovel. There was sagging lean-to connected to the shack. A huge stone served as a step.

Lavender stepped up on the rock and knocked. No one came to the door and she knocked harder. The place wore such an air of desolation she was sure it was deserted.

She decided she would go around to the back of the shack and if no one was there she would have to go back to the road and start to walk back toward Marysville. She wondered again about the stagecoach driver. Why had he acted so mysterious?

Chapter 9

When Lavender rounded the corner of the shack she saw Mint. She was bent over a washtub and scrubbing on a washboard. Her hair straggled down her back. She was a forlorn and pathetic figure. Lavender stared in unbelief. This slatternly looking woman couldn't be Mint, her lovely, dainty sister!

She thought of Pa and how he would rant if he could see this sorry looking creature. Lavender went forward slowly, picking her way through the high weeds.

Mint looked up from the washtub and saw Lavender. She pushed the hair away from her face and stared for a moment as though she couldn't believe her eyes.

"Lavender, is it really you?" she cried and rushed toward her. They hugged and the tears ran down Mint's face.

"Lavender, I can't believe you're here," Mint said over and over again.

"I'm here," Lavender said ruefully looking around at the desolate surroundings.

"It's pretty awful, isn't it?" Mint faltered and flushed.

"You eloped?" Lavender questioned. "Tell me all about it."

"I eloped with Will Ruggles," Mint said slowly, almost bitterly. "Why? I can't remember why. I must have been crazy."

"You're not happy?"

"Happy?" Mint snapped. "I wish I was dead."

"Oh, Mint, don't say that. Don't ever say that."

They went to sit on the big stone that served as a step to enter the back of the shack.

"You're tired from your journey," Mint said. "You don't want to listen to my sad tale now, do you? Would you like to rest?"

"No, I'm not tired. Just tell me what happened?"

"I don't rightly know. I must have been bewitched."

"I know," Lavender agreed. "I was bewitched too by a knight, all shining and bright and riding a white horse."

"Brandy?"

"Yes, but his name wasn't Brandy Wells at all. His name was John Younger."

"One of the Younger brothers," Mint breathed in awe.

"None other, and when I was going to have a baby, he just rode off on his white horse and I haven't seen him since."

"You were going to have a baby? Where is it? What happened?" Mint cried.

"I went home to Mama and Pa. My baby was born dead. My baby had a face like a tiny white rose. I named her Rose."

"Oh, Lavender, I'm so sorry."

"Don't be sorry, Mint. Pa says it was God's will. But I can't believe that. Why would it be God's will for my poor little baby to be put in the wet, weeping earth?"

Mint sighed and began to cry, "Oh, Lavender, we were those pretty Mueller girls. Everyone thought we

115

would make such good matches and look at us?"

Lavender smiled. "We're young, Mint," she said firmly, hopefully. "Only God knows what the future holds."

Those had been words spoken by Cole. She would tell Mint later all about Cole but not now. If Mint was so bitterly unhappy, they would leave here. Mint was talking. "It was spring, Lavender, and I was jealous because you were married and I wasn't and I was a year older than you and I should have been married first."

Lavender laughed. "Oh, Mint, that's silly."

"No, it isn't silly. There was Pa makin' fun of me 'cause I was an old maid. I thought maybe Charlie Engleman would propose but he didn't. Then one day I was out in the orchard and wishin' for a real beau and Will came wanting a drink of water."

She was silent a moment then went on, "I remember the pear blossoms were blooming. They were so beautiful being tossed about on the spring breeze. I remember thinking they were like hoop skirts tied with green velvet ribbon."

"You always had a way with words," Lavender said admiringly.

"Well, those yellow-hearted blossoms were sailing across that blue sky like white butterflies and I looked to see this man coming across the yard. He was so handsome. He's got dark eyes with black eyelashes that curl up and make him look like he's always smiling. He's got black curly hair. Lavender, I never saw anyone as handsome."

Lavender listened silently.

"I was so happy," Mint went on slowly. "So very happy. I would meet him on the sly. I knew Pa wouldn't like him."

Lavender sighed, thinking back to those first magical days after John Younger had bought her box at the box social. She could see that box yet in her mind's eye, the box she had prepared so lovingly with its twist of leaves. She remembered each bright day and now thumbed though each one glowingly. Life had been so wonderful. She shut her eyes and it was as if time turned back. She could remember the rapture, the joy. She could remember how John waited for her at the turn of the road. Their eyes would meet, their hands link, neither would speak for a long moment. And then she would be in his arms and the whole beautiful day would seem to burst into a fountain of light as he kissed her forehead, her nose and chin.

She had been so thrilled, her senses whirling like windmills, her whole body weak with the joy that flowed through her. Then promising to meet him again the next day she would walk home through the sweet twilight whispering into the gloom, "Oh, I am so happy."

She remembered how she would lie in her bed at night, her pulses beating high with anticipation and joy. She would stretch her slim body, thrilling with delight, thankful for her young beauty. It was too good to be true! It had happened just as she had known it would happen someday. A young handsome man had come riding out of the West to claim her. She had thought his name was Brandy Wells but it was really John Younger. The memory of the time when he told her his true name came back to haunt her now.

She had mounted her horse, Manna, and had met Brandy for a ride. His horse was wheeling and nervous and they were away and enjoying the excitement of the ride over the wide flat prairie. After a while, they walked their mounts slowly side by side. The ride had been hot and her golden hair lay in flat ringlets near her face.

"You're beautiful," he had breathed looking at her.

Lavender remembered she had never been so happy before. And then he told her that his name was John Younger and not Brandy Wells. They had talked it over and decided not to tell Mama and Pa and Mint or Jacob his real name. It seemed strange to her now to remember that they had talked this over because after that John was so silent about everything.

She brought her wandering thoughts back to Mint now. "Oh, Mint, I know exactly how you felt. It isn't fair for love to make one unable to think. Maybe if Pa had been different. Maybe if we could have talked to him. But nobody can talk to Pa. Mint, he even said my baby would have murderer's blood in it."

"No, Lavender, I don't think anyone can reason with somebody in love. I just wanted to be with Will and when he looked at me with those beautiful eyes, I would have followed him to the ends of the earth."

"You're right, of course. No one could have talked me out of marrying John. All I could see was myself in a white dress and veil and carrying a bouquet of daisies." she said.

"I couldn't believe this handsome man wanted to marry me," Mint went on. "We finally eloped and were married by a traveling preacher. Then we came here."

"If you're unhappy, Mint, why don't you leave?"

"He would kill me," Mint said very low. "I am afraid of him. Besides there's Ma Ruggles. She's inside," she nodded. "She's sickly and needs care. I think that's why he married me."

"To care for his mother?" Lavender asked, stunned.

Mint shrugged. "He wishes she was dead. He's always saying that to her. The poor thing is weak and dyin'. I like her. I keep thinking I'll leave when she dies but I guess it's just a way of putting it off."

"Will he be angry that I've come to visit?" Lavender asked.

Mint looked at her sister for a long moment. "No, he'll like you because you're so beautiful. He'll be charming to you. That is, unless he's drinking and then I never know what to expect. Maybe a beating. Maybe kisses. I'd rather have the beating."

"He beats you?" Lavender cried shocked.

"I told you, I'm afraid of him. He's a mean man, Lavender."

"He better not lay a hand on you when I'm around," Lavender said darkly.

"Come on in the house," Mint said getting up from the step. "I'll get you something to eat and feed Ma." She glanced toward the washtub. "I'll have to finish the washing too before Will comes back."

"Does Will farm or what does he do?" she asked suddenly remembering the expression on the way station master's face and the stagecoach driver's face when they knew where she was going.

"He doesn't work," Mint said shortly. "Come with me and meet Ma."

They went into the shack and Lavender was appalled. The chairs were rickety, the table propped up with a stick. The furnishings were sparse. The floor was packed dirt.

An old woman sat in a rocker by the fireplace. Mint went to her and patted her gray hair and tightened the shawl around her thin shoulders.

"Ma," she said. "This is my sister, Lavender, who has come to visit us."

"Welcome, lass," the woman said, peering up at her. "You are a pretty lass and so is your sister, Mint."

Mint smiled, pleased. "I used to think I was pretty," Mint said, bending over to kiss Ma. "I was so proud of my white skin. Now look at it. It's all sunburned. But I have to work out in the garden and a bonnet doesn't seem to do much good."

"Remember how Mama always made us wear a bonnet," Lavender said smiling.

"We didn't have to spend hours hoeing."

"Mint, let's make some of that recipe for soft white skin. You know the one with lily bulb juice and part of a honey-comb," Lavender cried enthusiastically.

"Let's do. We'll make it tomorrow. I have to finish the wash now but first I'll give you and Ma both a bowl of chicken soup. It's been simmering all morning," Mint said going to the fireplace. A black pot hung from a rack near the flames.

After she dished up the soup, Mint went out to the backyard and Lavender helped Ma sip her soup, carefully guiding the spoon into Ma's lips.

"I didn't see any chickens," Lavender remarked.

"There's a henhouse out by the barn," Ma said. "We should be livin' in the barn instead of this shack. My husband, Henry, built that barn and that henhouse and a nice house. Henry died three years ago and a tornado took down our house. Will ain't like his Pa. He's lazy and does nothin' but tear around the country with a bunch of no gooders."

Lavender finished her soup and told Ma she would lie

down for a while. The trip had been tiring.

"This shack was our tool shed. 'Taint fit for livin' in but Will isn't about to care how we live. He isn't here all the time. I don't see how he got a sweet purty gal like Mint to marry up with him."

There seemed nothing to say to this and Lavender flung her self across the bed and napped. When she awakened, Mint was hanging the last of Ma's nightgowns on the line. She came into the house now, her face pale with fatigue.

Lavender commanded her to rest a while. She said she would take Ma out to sit on the back step and visit. Ma agreed wholeheartedly, warming to the thought of a fresh audience.

When they were seated, Ma began to talk, "I remember the spring Henry and I came here. Such a long time ago. We were just married. We had met at the Weeping Willow Methodist Church over at Weeping Willow Hollow. That's 'bout eight miles west of here."

Lavender looked closely at the woman and was amazed at the beauty of her dark eyes. They were wide eyes, of a darkness like brown velvet and with sweeping dark lashes. They were set wide apart. Her skin was like porcelain, white and translucent. Lavender thought her beautiful and realized in that moment if Will's eyes were as breathtakingly lovely as his mother's, no wonder Mint had been spellbound and hypnotized with love for him.

Ma said softly, "Lavender, I was but a wee girl when my folks came to Weeping Willow Hollow. I had a bleached bone dressed up in calico for a doll. I was proud of it and carried it everywhere with me."

Lavender listened attentively as the old woman continued to talk, her eyes dreamy with memories. "My Pa put crops in before he took time to build a house. We lived in a dugout. Then, as so often happened in those days, there was a prairie fire and the flames devoured everything. The sound of that fire cracking and hissing was awful to hear as it roared across the plains. We were safe only because we were able to get in the center of a green field."

"It must have been an awful experience," Lavender said.

The woman nodded, then pointed to a cluster of lilac bushes growing in the weed-infested yard.

"See those lilac bushes," she said. "My Uncle James came out from Virginia in 1854 to see my Ma. He brought those bushes from his home as a birthday gift. When Henry and I got married, Ma had my pa dig them up and plant them here."

"What a lovely wedding present," Lavender said.

"My Uncle James didn't stay long. He wasn't used to frontier life. He came by covered wagon, you know, and it almost killed him. When he went back East, he wrote that he would never be the same again. And I guess he wasn't. He died a long spell ago."

Poor Uncle James, Lavender thought. Well, there were some who could take this rough life and some who couldn't.

"You know," Ma went on, "it was in 1854 that President Pierce signed the Kansas-Nebraska Bill creating the territory of Kansas. It was on May the thirtieth that he signed it. Pa wanted Ma to move on to Kansas but Ma didn't want to. This was home, she said and she was like the tree planted by the waters."

Lavender nodded.

"My ma often went without a cool drink herself so her lilacs could have water. Then the grasshopper hordes came. They could be heard coming long before they came in sight. Ma tied up one bush in a quilt and covered the other with a big buffalo robe. The grasshoppers were so thick they blackened the skies like a storm and they ate their way through everything. Hours later, Ma went out to find everything gone, buffalo robe, quilt and bushes. There was only bare stumps left in the earth. But the next spring the lilacs came up from the roots more beautiful than ever."

Lavender patted Ma Ruggles' hand gently. Later Lavender asked Mint when Will would be returning.

Mint shrugged. "I never know. He comes and goes. Sometimes he brings food and sometimes he doesn't. I have a flock of hens and a few roosters and there's two cows so we're not going to starve."

Jays were looping the air with blue and gray in a final burst of activity in the dying day as Lavender went with Mint to the barn to milk the cows.

"Ma Ruggles is a sweet woman," Lavender said.

"I love her very much," Mint said. "She is failing. It's her heart. Did you notice that her skin is so white and she is very weak?"

"Yes," Lavender agreed. "She seems very weak."

"Will is cruel to her," Mint said. "Oh, Lavender, I hope God will forgive me for saying this but I hope Will gets his comeuppance. He fancies himself a Quantrill and has a few followers and rides around stealing. Everybody in the countryside is afraid of him. He's mean when he's drunk. I hate him, Lavender."

"You've got to get away from here," Lavender said.

"I can't leave Ma," Mint whispered. "She's been good

123

to me. She tries to protect me when Will beats me."

"Isn't it strange to know that the love you felt for someone is all gone?" Lavender asked. "All that radiance and glowing happiness is all gone! You wish you could go back but there is never any going back. You and I can never go back and laugh and giggle together and know that love is out there waiting for us to claim it. We can never go back. I can't understand why it had to happen to us." And Mint looked at her and sighed. There was no answer.

Chapter 10

A week went by and Will did not return. The strained haunted expression left Mint's face and she began to relax.

"Maybe," she told Lavender hopefully, "maybe he won't come back."

They were making the lily bulb concoction Lavender had spoken of before.

"I think I remember the exact measurements," Lavender said. "one ounce white wax, two ounces strained honey and two ounces of the juice of lily bulbs. We melt this."

Mint smiled. "I remember we thought it was a magic potion."

Ma was watching with interest.

"It is," Lavender promised. "It will make your skin like cream."

When the mixture had presently cooled, Ma looked at it dubiously. "It looks so sticky," she said.

"It is sticky," Lavender laughed. "But it will take all that redness out of Mint's skin and her skin will be as pretty as a white lily petal."

"Keep your eyes shut," Lavender later cautioned, deftly quickly spreading the amber liquid over Mint's face. "Think beautiful thoughts while you're sitting here."

Mint's eyes opened and she looked straight at Lavender. Lavender knew what she was thinking. How could she think beautiful thoughts when she was on edge, fearful of her husband's return?

"Try, anyway," Lavender whispered. "Close your eyes and try."

Ma spoke up now. "Thoughts are like people you've known in the past. Sometimes they haunt you. Anyway they are always with you. But the happy times are nice to remember and a great comfort in time of despair."

Lavender had marvelled before at Ma's vocabulary and Mint whispered now, "Ma had schooling. Will's father could not read or write and he didn't care if Will had schooling or not."

Ma began to talk and Lavender knew she was living again in the past. "My grandmother," she said, "started out with us on the long trek to our new home. She was old. I can remember yet how thin and tiny she was. We loved her so. As we followed the trail which led to the Mississippi River, she died."

"My face feels strange," Mint put in now.

"Keep your mouth shut," Lavender commanded firmly. "I'm going to spread it over your face again and put more on your neck."

Ma went on talking now, "The wagon train stopped and the men cut down a big tree. There was no coffins, you know. They did the best they could. They put Grandmother's best dress on her and tenderly put her in the shell. Then they nailed the slab back on the log and buried her. My ma cried and cried. There were many Indians around in those days and the men ran the wagons back and forth over the grave so wandering Indians would not be able to tell that anyone was buried there."

126

Lavender thought about the little Emma Susan who had been buried in a hollowed out log on the prairie. She wondered how many such graves there were. Only God and the lonely prairie knew! Ma was talking again, "My ma stood at the back of the wagon staring back toward the place where Grandmother was buried. She stood there for hours as we rattled on across the prairie."

That evening, Lavender told Mint she looked like the lovely Mint Mueller again.

"You are beautiful," she complimented with enthusiasm.

"I'll never be as beautiful as you, Lavender," Mint answered sadly. "I remember how everyone made over you all the time. With your blonde curls and big blue eyes you look like a fairy princess."

"Brown hair and brown eyes are beautiful," Lavender said firmly. "You are my lovely sister, Mint, and I love you."

"I love you too," Mint said sincerely. "And I love you for coming to this forsaken place and I love you now for trying to help me."

"It will all work out," Lavender said but she knew now how Mint felt about leaving Ma. She, too, had learned to love the old woman in this week she had been there.

The following day Lavender was humming happily as she gathered eggs, holding those that were yet warm to her soft young cheek, brushing the wet feathers from the shells. In the early sweetness of the fall morning, the air was as clear as crystal. Moisture lay heavily on the nearby fields that had been burnt to a crisp. It had been a dry summer and the fields looked brown and parched.

Only a few trees stood green, the rest had changed the color of their leaves for autumn finery and a few were already bare.

Lavender looked at the barn and sighed. It was silvered with age and wore the hood of neglect. There was so much repair work to be done on the old barn. The timbers should be strengthened. She looked at the grape arbor. The poles there needed to be replaced. They sagged in the middle.

She walked to the place where the house had once stood. It must have all been beautiful years ago when Ma's Henry was alive. No wonder Ma lived in the past when life had been a sweet song of happiness.

That evening, the three women lingered at the supper table. It had been a good day. Mint and Lavender had remembered happenings when they were young girls and Ma had enjoyed their tales, joining in with their laughter. They heard the sound of horses' hooves at the same time. They looked at each other and Lavender saw Mint gasp and whisper in terror, "Will."

Lavender thought sadly, How terrible it must be to dread your husband's coming, to feel cold and frightened at the thought of him sharing your bed!

Lavender was always to remember that meeting with Will Ruggles. He stamped into the room and looked at the three women at the kitchen table. He seemed to fill the room with his bold dark eyes staring at them.

Lavender had thought his eyes would be like Ma's eyes but they were different. They were large and luminous and oddly tip-tilted at the outer corners. His ebony black hair was sleek. Strange, she thought now, that she should remember the crow that had haunted her in the Ozarks. Both were evil. This handsome man and that crow that had harassed her through so many long days! His hair rose in twin peaks above his ears like horns. He looked, she thought now, exactly as Satan did in Ma's family Bible.

Will was tall, his shoulders wide, his hips slim. The effect should have been perfection in appearance but it was not. The twist of his thin lips and the cruel hard lines marking his face gave him a sinister appearance. He swaggered toward them, his dark eyes appraising Lavender.

"And who is this beautiful lady?" he asked.

"Will, this is my sister Lavender," Mint introduced them. "Lavender, this is my husband, Will."

Lavender acknowledged the introduction.

"There's some rabbits in that bag on the back step," he said to Mint. "Go clean 'em."

Lavender bit the words back. She wanted to tell him that was man's work but she felt the warning in Mint's quick glance as she went obediently to do the man's bidding.

"First give me some victuals," he commanded.

He ignored his mother as he turned his attention now to Lavender.

"Mint told me she had a sister but she didn't tell me how beautiful you are," he said.

"She's told me much about you," Lavender said.

The man looked at her sharply but Lavender's face was as innocent as a baby's.

Ma spoke now, "Will, I'm glad you're home. Mr. Cartwright came by two weeks ago and . . ."

Will cut in snarling, "I told that old man to stay away from here. I don't need him to tell me the barn is goin' to fall down if I don't fix it."

What a disagreeable person you are, Will Ruggles, Lavender thought to herself! Ma's voice wavered but she went on, "You know it's almost time for the Fall Roundup and Barbecue. Mr. Cartwright came by to see if we could go. I told him I'd ask you when you got back."

"You're damn right you better ask me. I ain't carin' if you women folk go. I ain't goin'."

Good, Lavender thought and was afraid for a moment that she had voiced the word. No wonder Mint was afraid of this brute.

When it came time to go to bed, Lavender went to her pallet in a corner of the room. Ma slept in the lean-to on a sort of cot, wide enough for only one person. Lavender remembered that winter when Cole and Melon and Ruby had slept before the fireplace. She knew there had been love in that room but here she could almost feel the vibrations of hate. She was ready to doze off when she heard Mint cry out in pain. There was silence for a moment and then grunts from Will as the corn shuck bed creaked from his strenuous action. She heard Mint weeping softly.

Will's strident voice awakened her again toward morning when he commanded Mint to turn over. There was more rooting and grunting and Lavender's heart sank. Poor Mint! How could she endure such treatment! She heard Will's curses and a sharp slap.

As she drifted off to uneasy sleep, Lavender thought, We'll have to leave here even if we have to take Ma with us.

In the following days, Mint and Lavender were up at dawn doing the chores while Will slept the day away. Then he would yawningly drag himself to the kitchen table and demand to be fed. Then Mint or Lavender must stop whatever they were doing to fry eggs, make biscuits and cut strips of pork.

Lavender had taken over the task of milking the cows and on this late fall day she went, with the buckets, to the barn. It was almost dusk. The sweet smell of hay and lingering odor of milk made the place seem warm and cozy.

She put her slender hands on the cows' spotted heads and scraped knowingly at the soft place between their horns. The cows shoved their great warm heads close to her affectionately. She put her stool and pails down and then seated herself, sweeping her skirts aside, her forehead almost touching the cow's big flank. Milk began to stream into the bucket, filling it to the brim in a foam-covered cap.

She heard someone come into the barn and turned her head, expecting to see Mint. But it was Will. He stood in the doorway filling it. Then came to where she sat, milking.

"Did you come to do the milking?" she asked, her voice edge with sarcasm.

"Hell, no," he laughed. "I came to look at my beautiful sister-in-law."

"It seems to me," she said boldly, "that you could help with the chores."

"That's women's work," he growled.

"Mint works too hard."

He laughed. "She can work herself into the grave and I won't give a damn. I'd rather have you." He put his hands on her arms and lifted her from the stool.

She was like a wildcat, clawing him, running her fingernails over his face. She felt blood and scratched the harder. The bucket of milk had been sent sprawling and the cow mooed in terror.

"Wildcat," he exulted. "I like 'em wild."

"I'll kill you," she cried and brought her opened hands over his face again. The blood spurted and he let her go with a vile curse and stalked out of the barn.

She quieted the cow and looked at the spilled milk ruefully. She was trembling as she milked the other cow and went presently into the shack with one pail of milk.

Mint looked at her and asked, "Lavender, are you all right?"

"Yes, I'm all right."

"I was afraid this was going to happen. Will came in all scratched up, and mad as a hornet. He left to meet his gang. I hope he'll be gone for a month this time."

"Me, too," Lavender echoed. "If I never see him again I'd be happy."

Autumn time was Fall Roundup and Barbecue time in Weeping Willow Hollow. When the leaves hung scarlet and gold and purple and the crisp twang of coming winter was in the air, country folk would gather and talk of the days and the old times that were gone forever. Ma loved barbecue time. There was singing and square dancing and gaiety. She looked forward to it all year as the highlight of her existence.

Mr. Cartwright, an old admirer of Ma, was to come for them to go to the affair. Lavender and Mint had dressed Ma in her Sunday best and they were getting ready now. Lavender had brushed her hair until it shone like golden flax. Her beautiful eyes sparkled with the anticipation of actually going to a party. She had put on the dress she had worn on the journey to visit Mint.

Mint, too, was dressed in the dress she had worn when she eloped. She had tucked a bit of goldenrod in her light brown hair and looked lovely.

Mr. Cartwright pretended to be speechless with admiration when he saw the three of them lined up awaiting his arrival.

"My three American Beauties," he said gallantly.

Ma rode in the front of his buggy and Lavender and Mint in the back seat. It was a happy day for all three women. It was nice to be with a pleasant admiring man for a change.

Lavender whispered to Mint, "Mr. Cartwright seems right taken with Ma. Why hasn't he courted her? His wife has been dead quite a while, hasn't she?"

"His wife died several years ago. He came to see Ma off and on but Will ran him off with a shotgun. Rather than cause trouble, Ma told him not to come back," Mint explained.

"What a shame! You can see he adores Ma."

"And she adores him," Mint said sadly.

The ride was only too short but when they arrived at the Hollow, eager hands reached for the reins and Ma was greeted with love and enthusiasm. Lavender and Mint left Ma in the capable hands of Mr. Cartwright and they were free to drift toward the music.

The fiddlers were in fine form and Grandpa Kopp was swinging his hands and shouting with glee,

"Old Dan Tucker, he got drunk. . . ."
(Swing your partners)
Fell on the fire and she kicked up a skunk!
(Skip light, ladies!)

Lavender's feet beat time beneath her skirt. How exciting! How wonderful!

And then the dance was ended and she was the center of attention. Everyone wanted to shake her hand, to greet the newcomer, to make much of her.

She and Mint joined in the square dancing and enjoyed every moment.

Presently they drifted to the side yard where clusters of older men and women were gathered talking. The good talk immediately became more animated when Mint and Lavender joined the group. The men, anxious to impress such lovely listeners, plunged into their stories with enthusiasm.

Mark Kampmeyer was talking now and his beady black eyes glistened. "It was back in 1840," he said. "I had gone to town for supplies. It was a long perilous journey of two days, one day going and one day coming. When I returned, God help me, I saw a glowing pile of embers where my cabin had been. I ran here and there calling for my Sarah and my children, Peter and Rebecca. One by one, I found their bodies. They had been murdered with their scalplocks torn away." Some of his listeners had heard the story many times but they wept as they listened.

Bertha Smith chimed in to tell of her trip from Iowa by covered wagon. She told of the herds of buffalo that dotted the plains. Hides sold for a dollar and Bertha told how she could look out of the cracks of their cabin on a moonlit night and see the coyotes sitting in the snow.

And always, always, the conversation would go back to the Big Blizzard. They relished the telling of this perilous time. Even though it had taken place some five

years ago, they talked of it as if it had happened yesterday.

"We brung them mules into our soddy," Lizzie White
said. "It was that or have them frozen stiff. We laid the
wagon box in between and put the mules on one side and
we 'uns on the other. For five days we lived like that.
The worst of it was the wonderin' if we'd ever get out of
there alive."

Eliza Baker's shrill voice swelled loudly, "The snow
blew in around our only cow until she nearly smothered.
I knew the children had to have milk, so I up and moved
that cow into the house with us. Stayed with us for a
whole week."

"And I moved our cow into the dugout with us,"
Esther Borne said. "Mathilda was born during that blizzard. We still lived in the dugout. Pa had just started
the house that fall. He had gone out after a load of wood
and when that wind started to howl, I was afraid. He
made it back in time. We always called Mathilda our
blizzard baby."

There were exciting stories of prairie fires and
grasshopper hordes that blackened the sky and covered
the sun. Grasshoppers four inches deep!

"Everything would be stripped," Frank Andrews
chimed in. "Every green thing would be gone. After a
grasshopper raid, I would pick up buffalo bones and
haul them to sell to buy feed for the team and food for
us."

The good odor of barbecued meat filled the air now
as the heartbreaking stories of death and birth came to
an end. Women had borne babies in covered wagons
with no one to help but their husbands. They spoke
proudly of unendurable agony that was somehow en-

dured, and wept as they mentioned loved ones who had died and were buried along some lonely forsaken trail.

They told of frozen fingers that had to be amputated without the aid of a doctor, of infected teeth pulled by the owner, of coughs that lingered due to exposure, of earaches that were remedied by blowing hot smoke into them. These stories were all told, Lavender was surprised to find, with much relish. It was as though they rejoiced to look back on suffering and privation and know they were strong enough to survive in face of tremendous odds.

When they had all eaten their fill of the barbecue and drank the sweet cider, a few hymns were sung and the Weeping Willow Roundup and Barbecue was ended.

"Goodbye, goodbye," they called to each other in parting. "May God be with you."

Chapter 11

The memory of the good time they had had at the Barbecue was with Lavender and Mint in the coming days. It brought wings to their feet and a song to their hearts and high sweet color to their beautiful faces. Ma had been pleased too and talked incessantly of Milo Cartwright.

"We won't have to go off and leave Ma alone," Lavender said struck with a brilliant idea. "It's plain to see that Milo Cartwright is in love with her."

Mint shuddered. "Oh, no, Lavender. Will would kill Ma and Mr. Cartwright in a minute if we left Ma with him."

Milo Cartwright came regularly to see them. He brought two of his hired men to lay in an ample supply of wood for the coming winter. He brought a slab of bacon and a smoked ham.

"We shouldn't accept these gifts," Mint told Lavender. "But how can we refuse? We would starve if it was up to Will to provide for us. And these offerings are gifts of love for Ma."

The days faded into weeks, the weeks into months and Will did not return. A heavy snow blanketed the countryside and Lavender, Mint and Ma huddled close to the fireside trying to keep warm. They moved Ma's bed close to the fire so she would be warm at night. It was a struggle to survive.

"If we can just get through this winter, things will be better," Lavender and Mint told each other over and over.

Mr. Cartwright checked on them regularly to see they were all right. He suggested they move to his warm home but Mint refused.

"I wish Ma could go," Mint told him. "But you know how angry Will would be."

Yes, Milo Cartwright knew.

Lavender was glancing at the newspaper in which he had brought them potatoes from his earth cellar. The ad jumped up at her, catching her attention, and bringing hope to her heart.

"Wanted," it read. "Woman to care for invalid. Must be young and willing to work. Write Major Edmonds, Box 784, Malvern, Arkansas."

She sat right down and wrote a letter glowing with details of her talents as a nurse. She did not mention she would be accompanied by her sister. "After all," she told herself, "a man who was a Major could well afford to employ two nurses."

Christmas came and went. Lavender brought a seedling pine in and they strung popcorn on its stubby branches. She showed Mint the tiny wood carving Cole had made for her last Christmas and which she had brought with her.

"Is Cole Younger as handsome as they say?" Mint asked.

"He's more than handsome," Lavender said, dreamily. "He looks like an angel."

"You're in love with him," Mint accused.

138

"He's sweet and kind and compassionate and a gentleman," Lavender said.

Spring came early that year. Almost overnight, soft sweet breezes, fragrant with the scent of earth and fresh growing things swept over the prairie. The woods were star-studded with dogwood blossoms and trees pregnant with buds. Ma's lilacs were fountains of purple buds. The pear trees were ready to burst into giant snowballs of white blossoms.

And with the coming of spring, Will came back. He burst into the shack on a cool spring evening and sneered, "Nothin's changed."

His glance rested on Ma. "Thought sure you'd be gone by now. Gone to that heaven you used to talk about."

Shocked speechless, Lavender and Mint could only stare at him. He swaggered up to them as they sat by the fireside and jerked Mint to her feet.

"Listen, woman, when you see me, you snap to attention. And you," he looked at Lavender, "when I tell you to jump, you jump. You might be a wildcat but I'll tame you."

"Will, Will," Ma murmured cajolingly. "Don't talk like that."

"Shut up, old woman," he barked.

The coming days were days of sheer hell for the three women. Will was drinking heavily and staggered around the shack, barking orders at Mint who scurried to do his bidding. Lavender stayed out of his way as best she could. She knew he had not forgotten their encounter in the barn when she had scratched his face. She felt like a helpless bird and he was a cat waiting to pounce on her.

She rode over to the Cartwright place and told Milo Cartwright that Will had returned. She asked him to be on the lookout for a letter she expected when he picked up mail at the General Store. He promised. She could tell he was worried about Ma.

"Mint and I are taking care of Ma," she told him. "We'll see that no harm comes to her."

This was easier said than done. Will took delight in tormenting Ma. And he took delight in telling them of his adventures during the past winter. He and his gang had collected quite a bit of loot and had been holed up in a region known as Tombstone Valley. He had a woman named Flame.

"She's a flame in bed, hot as fire," he bragged. "Not like you," he said to Mint. "She knows how to please a man."

As the days went by, Lavender wondered how much longer Mint could put up with his cruelty. Sometimes he would pinch her as she poured coffee or brush against her heavily trying to knock her off balance. He had taken to smirking at Lavender and whispering to her and patting her shoulder. She hated his touch and marvelled that Mint could crawl in bed every night with him. He was an animal, she thought in disgust. If only the letter would come!

When Will had drunk his fill of whisky and would fling himself across the bed to sleep the afternoon away, Lavender would ride to the Cartwright place. On one such day, Mr. Cartwright handed her an envelope. It was from Major Edmonds. The job was hers. He would await her arrival.

She told Milo Cartwright of her plan.

"You know I will care for Ann," he assured her.

"I'll talk to Mint about it. We'll try to work something out."

The letter in her pocket was like a living thing as she rode back. It spelled hope. They would be away from Will and safe. When she got back, Will had awakened and was in a vile mood. It had started to rain and the shack was cold and damp.

"Dammit," he yelled. "When I tell you to build up the fire, you build up the fire."

Mint cowered away from him. He had whipped off his belt as he talked and began to beat her unmercifully.

"You're a hell of a wife," he screamed. "You're a nothin' in bed. I need a woman like Flame. She's all woman."

Lavender sprang to Mint's defense, trying to grab the belt from his hand.

"Oh, the wildcat wants some too," he laughed, bringing the belt down again and again.

"Will, Will, stop that," Ma cried hurling herself at him. He twirled around and with all his strength pushed his mother against the stone-edged fireplace. She sank to the floor, blood oozing from her head, staining her gray hair with red.

"You've killed her," Lavender cried. "You've killed your mother!"

"Good riddance!" he snorted, and staggered out of the shack.

Lavender and Mint tenderly lifted Ma to the bed and Lavender hurried to get water and a cloth. They spoke lovingly and tried to bring her around but she did not open her eyes.

"We need help," Lavender said to the weeping Mint. "I'll ride to the Cartwrights' place."

When she galloped up to the Cartwrights', Milo Cartwright was instantly on the porch when he heard the sound of horse's hooves. It was as though he had expected this.

"There's no doctor within miles but Lucie, the darkie who is my housekeeper, is as good as a doctor. I'll hitch up the buggy. I'll bring a couple of my men too in case Will returns. I should have known this would happen. The man is an insane brute. I'll report this to the law," he said getting ready for the trip to the Ruggles. He called Lucie and told her to bring her medicines and sent word for two of his men to accompany them. Lavender tore back and Milo Cartwright and his party came shortly after her return. The men stationed themselves, one at the front door and one at the back. They were ready in case Will returned.

Ma never regained consciousness. She lay in a coma for hours and then quietly slipped away.

Milo Cartwright was inconsolable. He blamed himself for putting the rough stones around the fireplace. "I wanted to make it pretty for Ann. She thought it was so pretty. She loved the native stone."

"You brought joy into her life, Mr. Cartwright," Lavender assured him. "She looked forward to your visits and she did so enjoy the Roundup Party and Barbecue."

It was decided to have the "wake" at Milo Cartwright's. "There's no room here for all the people that will be coming," he said definitely, looking around the dingy room. "It's fitting that Ma's friends pay their respects. Lucie will be there to oversee the 'spread.' "

Mint and Lavender, with Lucie's help, dressed Ma in the dress she had worn to the Barbecue.

"I wish Ma could see how beautiful she looks," Mint said.

Mr. Cartwright's men had spread the word of Ma's death and people came from miles around for the funeral. Ma would be laid to rest at Weeping Willow Cemetery beside her Henry and her mother and father.

The mourners came with fried chicken and ham and potatoes for the "spread" that always followed a burial. Reverend David Lykens, the preacher at the Weeping Willow Church, was on hand and spoke of the shortness of life and that Ma, being a good woman, tried and true, was now with her Maker.

The "spread" was a solemn affair. Everyone talked in muted tones befitting the sad occasion. They spoke lovingly of Ma and predicted a no-good end for that no-good son of hers, Will. No one knew exactly what had happened. Mr. Cartwright thought it best to let the law take care of Will and not make the funeral a time of planning for revenge by Ma's neighbors. When the last mourner had departed, Lavender and Mint prepared to go home. It was then that Lavender told Mint about the letter from Major Edmonds.

"Maybe he won't want both of us," Mint said.

"Of course, he will. Besides we don't have to stay there very long. It will give us a chance to decide what to do. Neither one of us want to go home to Mama and Pa. I don't want to spend the rest of my life listening to him rant and rave."

"No, that would be terrible," Mint agreed.

They told Milo Cartwright of their plan and he agreed that now was the time for them to leave. He offered to drive them to the railroad station the next day.

"Perhaps you should stay here tonight. You'll be safe here," he suggested.

"No," Mint said. "I'll want to pack a few things. And Lavender has a carpetbag."

"We'll be ready when you pick us up in the morning," Lavender said kissing him. "We're so grateful for your kindness to Ma."

"Perhaps I should send a couple of my men along with you in case Will comes back tonight."

"He's probably heard about Ma and he'll be scared to come back," Lavender said. "I just hope the law takes care of him."

"I'll report this to the United States Marshal at Marysville tomorrow when I take you to the train station," he promised.

Back home, they flew around packing after doing the chores.

"I'm too excited to sleep," Lavender said.

"Me, too," Mint said beginning to cry. "Lavender, I miss Ma so. If Ma hadn't tried to protect me when Will was beating me she'd be alive."

"Ma is with her loved ones," Lavender said definitely. "Just remember how happy she was at the Barbecue. And remember how frightened she was of Will."

When they were in bed and trying to sleep, they heard the clatter of horses' hooves. Someone was coming. Lavender grabbed the gun over the fireplace and waited.

They both recognized Will's heavy step on the stone before the door burst open. He was so drunk he wobbled as he staggered to the bed and flung himself on it. Lavender stared at him a moment then commanded Mint to get dressed. When they were ready and their carpetbags at the door, she rushed out to the barn and returned with a rope.

144

"Get on that side of the bed," she instructed. "We're going to tie this monster up and then we're going to give him the beating of his life."

"Dare we?" Mint whispered, frightened.

"Indeed, we dare!"

They passed the rope between them, over and under, over and under, over and under and then Lavender tied the two ends carefully.

She made another trip to the barn and returned with a horsewhip.

Crack! She brought it down as heavily as she could. Crack! Crack! Crack! He screamed. He ranted. He raved. He cursed. And still the whip found its mark. Again and again and again. When Lavender's arm was so tired she couldn't raise it another time, she handed the whip to Mint.

"It's your turn," Lavender said.

Mint took the whip and a change came over her. Gentle, quiet Mint became a demon of rage.

"This," she cried, "is for Ma. Ma who you murdered!"

He was threatening to kill them. Then his threats turned to wails of agony. When Mint was exhausted, Lavender took the whip again and said quietly, "Ma loved you and you treated her like a dog. Thank God, you can't hurt her anymore."

And she beat him again.

They jumped on Will's horse, which was still saddled and with carpetbags flapping at their side, hurried to the Cartwright place. Milo Cartwright was pleased when they told him what had happened.

"And he's all tied up just waiting for the law?" he asked in deep satisfaction.

* * *

Later, at the train station, he kissed Lavender and Mint goodbye. He promised to see that Mint's livestock and chickens would be taken care of.

"You'll need money," he said getting out his wallet.

"No, I have the ticket the Major sent and enough money for Mint's ticket," Lavender protested. "Pa gave me money when I left home."

"I want you each to have fifty dollars. I couldn't do anything much for Ann but you loved her and took care of her," he said sadly. "I want you to take the money. Please make an old man happy and take it. Too, if things don't work out, you'll have money to leave this Major Edmonds."

He made them promise they would drop him a letter when they were settled. "Then I can write and tell you if Will got the rope or life imprisonment," he said.

He kissed them goodbye again and with tears in his eyes said, "I'll see that there are always fresh flowers on Ann's grave."

Chapter 12

Lavender Younger lay on the high walnut carved bed at Windcrest. Major Edmonds had insisted she rest after her long journey. The Major had been most gracious when she and Mint had arrived unannounced. He had apologized for not having met them at the train station. If he had known they were arriving he would have been there, he assured them over and over again. It would not have been necessary for them to hire a conveyance to bring them to Windcrest.

Lavender was still dressed in the blue dress with white piping in which she had arrived. She had taken her shoes off and lay relaxed, thinking. She was impressed with the Major. He used such big words and seemed so charming. He must be very rich, she thought now to have such a mansion so far from civilization. It must have cost a fortune to haul all the building material out here on the edge of nowhere.

She thought she would take a brief rest as the Major had instructed and then she would find Mint. He had insisted that Mint rest in an adjoining room. Her last waking thought before she drifted off to sleep was one of thankfulness that she and Mint were safe from Will's cruelty. And poor dear Ma was free of him too.

She was awakened by heavy footsteps entering the

room and opening her eyes saw it was the Major. She rubbed her eyes, fluttered her lashes and smiled at him.

"No, no," he said quickly as she started to sit up. "Stay where you are. You must rest, my dear. I just wanted to tell you again of my delight that you have arrived. I have looked forward to your coming."

"Thank you," she said, smiling at him again. "My sister and I are glad to be here."

"You will meet my mother this evening at dinner," he said as he moved a chair close to the bed and sat down. She looked at him questioningly. Then she decided he evidently just wanted to talk, to perhaps tell her what her duties would be in taking care of his mother.

She relaxed and waited. She saw that his florid heavily-jowled face was moist and flushed. The years had not been kind to him. His hair was gray. His mustache was also gray and stained at the corners a dark brown. His pale blue eyes glittered at her as he put out a fat-padded hand to caress her blonde hair.

"You are so beautiful," he purred.

She jerked back from his touch.

"I'm sorry," he apologized. "Your hair is like spun gold. I couldn't resist touching it. I am sorry."

His manner changed and he became very businesslike as he outlined her duties. She listened attentively, then assured him his mother would be well taken care of. She intended to live up to his expectations.

"I'm sure you will," he said.

She complimented him then on the beauty of Windcrest. He was pleased. "Wait until you see the rest of it," he boasted.

She looked around at the mirrored walls, the thick red carpet and the gorgeous crystal chandelier. "All this beauty away out here in the country," she breathed in awe. "I've never been in a room like this before. I never dreamed Windcrest could be so beautiful."

She wondered suddenly how he had acquired all his wealth.

"Why don't you call me Mark when there is no one else present?" he asked.

She hesitated a moment before answering. "If you wish."

"I do wish," the man said definitely. "I think we are going to be very good friends."

She looked at him sharply. He had emphasized the word "friends."

Thinking to change the subject, she asked, "Major, I'm sorry, I meant Mark, I want to ask you something. I asked a man on the train if he had ever heard of Windcrest."

"You what?" he snarled, his face flushing an ugly red and anger thick on his full face. He was glaring at her and making a visible effort to control himself.

"He had never heard of Windcrest," Lavender hastened to say. "He didn't know a thing about Arkansas."

He relaxed but his face was mottled and he was breathing heavily.

She got up from the bed and ran her stockinged feet beneath the bed for her shoes. "Mark," she said sweetly, "I never saw anything as pretty as Windcrest when we drove up through that stately row of poplar trees."

She found her slippers and stood up. "What are all those cabins way in back of the mansion?" she asked curiously.

"It takes a great many hands to make Windcrest the

showplace it is," he answered smoothly.

"Do you have much company?" she asked, anticipating parties and carriages driving up the winding tree-lined road to the wide veranda. In her mind's eye, she saw herself in a billowing white dress with strawberry-red streamers being part of a gay crowd. But then maybe the Major would prefer her not to mingle with his guests. After all she was in his employ. He might consider her as one of the hired help.

She was thinking these thoughts when he stepped close to her and put his big hands on her shoulders and pulled her close. His wet mouth crushed down on hers. She gasped for breath and squirmed to free herself.

Then suddenly, across the stillness of the late summer afternoon, a piercing scream, wild and agonizing in its intensity, rang out. Lavender froze in the Major's arms. She saw his eyes narrow with something like anger as he abruptly released her and stalked toward the door.

"What is it? Someone must be hurt," she cried following close behind him. At the door, he turned and shoved her backwards. She heard the click of the key in the door and the Major's retreating steps.

She hurried to the window and looked out but could see nothing but the vast sweep of carefully kept lawn and the row of poplars flanking the winding drive. She was trembling yet at the brusque way the Major had shoved her back into the room. It was as if he didn't want her to find out what had happened to cause the unearthly scream.

She tried the door but she knew he had locked it. There was another door leading to an adjoining room. Perhaps Mint was there. She put her head close to the door and called, "Mint, Mint, are you there?"

No answer.

She knocked hard and called again.

Still no answer.

Well, there was nothing to do but get ready for dinner. She went to the dresser and sat down before the mirror and stared at her reflection. She smiled at her reflection and felt better. The Major had said she was beautiful and she guessed she was. Everyone seemed to think so. Even Cole. She combed her hair carefully with a pearl-handled comb that was on the dresser. There was a bottle of cologne there and she used it lavishly. She would smell like a rose.

She was waiting when Jock, the butler, unlocked the door and invited her to follow him to the dining room. The staircase was lined with portraits of uniformed men each in a gilt frame. Their eyes seemed to follow her as she came slowly down the stairs. The Major was waiting at the foot of the staircase.

"My beautiful lady," he murmured, putting one of her hands to his lips. She dimpled.

They went then into the long chandeliered dining room. Lavender stared completely fascinated. She had never seen so many candles before. There must be thousands, she thought in awe. The crystal on the table dazzled with all colors of the rainbow.

"Do you like it?" he asked, pleased at her wide-eyed admiration.

"It's beautiful," she breathed.

She saw they were not alone. A woman sat, at the far end of the table, watching them. She was an elderly woman with white hair pulled back from a thin mulish face.

"This is my mother," the Major said crisply. "Mother, this is Lavender Wells."

"I'm happy to meet you," Lavender said.

The woman grunted in reply.

"Isn't Mint going to eat with us?" Lavender asked. "Where is she?"

"My sister, Virginia, is visiting from the East. She wanted Mint to dine with her in her room. I thought this would give you a better chance to get acquainted with Mother if we were alone," he said smoothly.

He pulled her chair back from the long table for her to be seated. As she did so, she caught sight of her reflection in a mirror at the far end of the room. She knew she had never looked lovelier than she did at that moment. The candlelight turned her hair into a halo of gold. This was the way life should be, she thought happily, exciting and luxurious.

The dinner was delicious, a hearty vegetable soup followed by roast of beef, potatoes, garden peas, beets and great hunks of angel food cake. It was served by two men-servants who rolled their eyes at her in a strange manner. There was something insolent in their manner when they served her. She would have liked to ask the Major why they looked at her so oddly but she dared not.

Once she intercepted a glance exchanged by the Major and his mother. Why, they hate each other! she thought to herself. Mrs. Edmonds spoke only once and that was to ask her how old she was.

"I'll be eighteen next month," Lavender said.

"A child," Mrs. Edmonds said sadly and began to chew her meat loudly. The Major scowled but said nothing.

When the meal was over, the Major escorted Lavender from the room to the wide porch in front of the mansion.

"Your mother is not very friendly," Lavender said. "But when we get to know each other I'm sure she will like me."

"She's a cranky old wench," the Major growled.

"Perhaps she doesn't feel well."

He shrugged indifferently. Suddenly without warning, he jerked her close to him, pressing her mouth to his. She felt his free hand caress her bosom, lingeringly patting her breasts.

"Please," she breathed and tried to free herself. He released her so suddenly she almost fell.

"There is time," he said crisply. She knew he was angry but he said nothing as he escorted her up the stairs to her bedroom door and bowed low over her hand.

"Goodnight, my dear," he said softly. "Sleep well."

"Major Edmonds, I mean Mark, I want to see my sister before I go to bed," she said firmly.

"She and Virginia are together," he said bluntly. "You can see her tomorrow."

He was gone, shutting the door with a violent slam. She heard the key turn in the lock. Something is all wrong, she thought as she undressed. Perhaps it was the sullen manner of Mrs. Edmonds or the way the Major's hands had cuddled her breasts or the way the menservants had ogled her. She had to talk to Mint. But where was Mint? She hadn't seen her since the Major had escorted her to a room to rest. Well, she would demand to see her sister tomorrow. A strange sense of foreboding swept over her and she felt her eyes sting with tears and her throat thicken with fear.

Chapter 13

He was at her door bright and early the next morning. He was in a jovial mood.

"My dear," he greeted her. "Come, there is much to be done today. Dress quickly, my beautiful Lavender."

"I want to see Mint," she said firmly.

"All in good time, my dear," he said tenderly. His eyes glistened like blue marbles. "You shall see her all in good time. I will leave you now. Your breakfast will be brought to your room."

"But . . ." The sentence was never finished. He was gone. Breakfast was brought to her room and later, luncheon. When Jock picked up the luncheon tray, she told him to tell the Major she wanted to see him immediately.

"I will tell the master," Jock grinned at her.

She was pacing the floor when he came to her room. "I came here to take care of your mother," she cried. "How can I take care of her when you lock me in this room?"

"Such a temper!" he chided her.

"I want to see Mint. What have you done with her?"

He ignored her question. "Quit your babbling," he commanded harshly. "If you ever want to see your sister again you will do exactly as I say. Do you understand?" She could only stare at him. The black cloud of foreboding she had felt the night before returned now. She had to find Mint and get out of here.

"Today you will be my beautiful bride."

The man was crazy! she thought wildly. He was stark raving mad!

"I'm married," she said. "It's against the law to be married to two men at the same time."

"Law?" he questioned sarcastically. "There is no law but my law here at Windcrest."

He left her then and again the key was turned in the lock. She was a prisoner and there was nothing she could do about it! He had threatened to harm Mint. It was all her fault they had come to Windcrest. Mint had finally been free of Will and she, Lavender, had led them like trusting lambs, lured by the Major's ad, into this trap. It was late afternoon when Jock brought her a huge white box. "With the master's compliments," he said. When she lifted the lid, she found a beautiful satin dress trimmed with lace and sewn with thousands of seed pearls. There was a veil too, gauzy and frail and exquisite.

Well, there was nothing to do but get dressed and watch for an opportunity to outwit the Major. She dressed carefully and as she dressed, she thought of another wedding day. The day she married John Younger. How innocent she had been! And so young! She felt herself to be much wiser now, and she was definitely older. Older and wiser? She knew only that she was frightened. And worried about Mint.

It was almost twilight when Jock came to summon her. She followed him downstairs to a room she had not been in before. The Major was waiting with a man dressed in a black suit. She supposed he was the minister. For a moment she had an impulse to appeal to the minister. But she stifled the impulse realizing it would be futile. No, she would have to bide her time.

The Major was beaming at her. He introduced the dark-suited man as the Reverend James Janson. Jock and another servant were called in to serve as witnesses. She was surprised his mother was not present. She looked at the four men and burst out, "Where's Mint?" she cried. "I'm not going to be married without Mint being with me."

For an answer, the Major stepped to her side and jerked her arm roughly. She cried out in pain but no one seemed to notice. It was a very brief ceremony and as soon as the Reverend Janson had pronounced them man and wife, the Major ordered her to her room.

Jock followed her up the stairs. "Take the wedding dress off and I will return it to the master," he said coldly. "I will return for the dress shortly."

Again she heard the key turn in the lock.

She glanced at her reflection in the mirror before taking off the veil. She really did look beautiful, she thought sadly. When she slipped out of the dress she noticed there was a stain under one of the sleeves. It's been worn before, she thought in surprise. Puzzled, she put the dress and veil in the white box. She dressed in her blue dress and waited for Jock to return. When he came, he was accompanied by the Major. Jock took the box and left. The Major frowned when he saw her. "You're dressed!" he exclaimed making the simple words an accusation.

"Aren't we going to have dinner?" she countered. "I'm hungry."

"Hungry!" he snarled. "You prattle about being hungry on your wedding night!"

She stared at him as he began to unbutton his fancy-tucked white shirt. Her throat thickened and her temples throbbed. Her temper was rising. She really was hungry as she had not eaten since noon.

"Get undressed," he rasped as she stared at him angrily. How dare he order her around!

He belched a loud oath as he saw her staring at him and making no move to obey his orders.

"Take off your clothes before I tear them off," he shouted.

"You can't talk to me like that," she flared angrily. He came to her and jerked her forward as if she were a doll. With one hand he jolted her upright and with the other, he grasped the front of her dress and ripped it from top to bottom. She stared at him in angry amazement as the dress fell to the floor and billowed around her legs like the petals of an inverted peony.

"Undress," he commanded and she knew that, at least for the moment, she was bested. She slipped out of the torn dress and stood in her undergarments.

"Do you want those torn off," he asked sarcastically.

She slanted her blue eyes at him, now almost purple with suppressed anger. He would pay for this! He let out a string of vile words and turning his back on her began to finish undressing. She got the nightgown she had worn the night before from its place under a pillow on the bed. She took off her undergarments one by one and hastily slipped the gown over her head.

He was watching her and although she was trembling with nervousness and fright, she tried to act as though she was not afraid. She sat down before the mirrored dresser and took the pins from her hair. His fat figure reflected in the mirror made her sick to her stomach. She was afraid she would vomit.

She was brushing her hair when she saw him loom up behind her. His pale eyes were upon her as with a quick lunge, he bent over her, swooping up the mass of curls and pulling her straight up off the chair. With the other hand, he grasped the front of her gown and ripped it from top to bottom.

She screamed in terror.

He slapped her smartly across her open mouth and commanded, "Get in bed."

In bed, she cringed with fear that he was going to kill her. An hour later, she wished he had killed her. He had pounced on her and crushed her and mangled her. Laughing with sadistic delight, he twisted her breasts, tweaking them until she screamed in agony.

She was sure he would tear her asunder when he plunged brutally in her. Once he whispered, "You are wondering why I bothered with the wedding ceremony? It is because I cannot lie with a whore, only a wife."

He tried a dozen acts of perversion.

Finally he slept and she lay bruised and dazed. Presently she fell into a kind of stuporous sleep only to be awakened by the Major roughly taking her body again. After that, she dared not close her eyes. She braced her body for another merciless attack.

Dawn finally came and long golden fingers of light crept stealthily into the room making the mirrors dazzle with radiance.

The man got up, dressed and left the room. Lavender wondered if she had the strength to get out of bed. She ached all over as she dressed. She was surprised to find the door was unlocked.

She went down the winding stairway to find Mrs. Edmonds sitting alone at the dining room table. The woman looked at her but said nothing.

"Good morning," Lavender greeted.

The woman did not return her greeting nor did she smile. "It's a beautiful day," Lavender went on. She thought to herself, I must make friends with her. Maybe through her, Mint and I can escape. One of the servants came now with eggs and a slice of ham for her. There were golden butter and creamy light biscuits.

"Have you seen my sister, Mint?" Lavender asked Mrs. Edmonds. For an answer, the woman looked around fearfully. She's afraid, Lavender thought. That poor old woman is afraid! After breakfast, Jock escorted her back to her room. She asked him about Mint and he ignored her question.

The days passed in dreary monotony. She was a prisoner in the beautiful mansion on the hill. No one came and she went nowhere. She would stare out the window hoping a carriage would drive up through the poplars but no one came but the ruffians who took orders from the Major. She begged the Major to let her see Mint. He, like Jock, ignored her questions. She begged him to let her care for his mother and he pretended he did not hear her. The nights were each alike, filled with pain and shame.

She ate her meals with Mrs. Edmonds who sat there like a wizened waxen statue saying nothing. She was either too stupid, Lavender decided, or too frightened to want to be friends. As the days went by, Lavender knew she must either escape or lose her sanity. But she did not intend to go without Mint. Perhaps, she thought, if I could get to one of those cabins in back of the mansion I could get a horse and escape and get help and find Mint. She planned a thousand ways to escape but none of them materialized.

One day it had been raining since early morning, pattering on the windowpanes and at times beating in great swirls of water against the mansion. Coming from the dining room after a silent meal with Mrs. Edmonds, the Major had not joined them, for which she was thankful, she went to the door to look out.

She was surprised to find that Jock was not there to see that she returned to her room. She looked out at the storm and saw the trees bending beneath gusts of wind. She started to go out on the veranda when a man barred her way. One of the Major's guards, she thought angrily. He was standing there like a sentinel when she heard him say, "Lavender!"

Her first thought was that she was going crazy like the Major. She could have sworn someone said, "Lavender."

"Lavender!"

There! She did hear someone say her name!

She looked at the man and she thought, I am mad. It can't be . . . it can't be Cole Younger!

Chapter 14

Cole Younger! Lavender looked at him and thought, I am going crazy like the Major. I've lost my mind and I'm imagining Cole is here!

"Lavender! What in God's name are you doing here?" he said.

"Cole! Is it really you?"

"Yes. Don't say anything, Lavender. Here comes Jock."

Cole Younger! She could hardly believe her eyes. She stared at him. Cole! She had dreamed of him so often, dreamed that he was here talking to her, loving her and here he was!

"Oh, Cole, Cole," she murmured.

Jock came up to them.

"I didn't let the little lady on the veranda," Cole said to Jock. Jock was pulling her away from the door and guiding her up the stairs to her room.

She wanted to shout for joy, to dance, to cry out that Cole had come to rescue her. But she went meekly to her room wondering, with every step she took, what Cole was doing here? Had he followed her? But no, he seemed as surprised to see her as she had been to see him.

Although she looked for him every day after that first meeting she did not see him again for a week. When she did, he was in a hurry; he had a message for the Major. He brushed past her, hardly giving her a glance. She wanted to cry out to him, to tell him that she had to get out of here, that the Major was a devil, and she would go crazy if she had to go to bed with him much longer. She bit her lip to keep the words back.

He was being careful, she told herself. It would never do for him to reveal the fact that they were friends. The opportunity to talk to him came two days later. They met in the hall. Jock had disappeared into the kitchen. They were alone.

"We've only a minute to talk," he said.

The words bubbled from her lips, "Cole, have you seen Mint?"

She did not wait for his answer, but rushed on, "We came here together. I answered an ad to take care of the Major's mother. I never saw Mint again after that day we arrived. The Major is mad. I told him I was married but we went through a wedding ceremony. I hate him. Try to find Mint for me."

"I will, dear," he promised. "I love you."

"Oh, Cole . . ."

"Someone's coming. My job here is almost finished. We'll find a way out," he said very low. And he hurried away.

The next morning at breakfast, Mrs. Edmonds spoke out of a deep silence. They were alone. "Does he give you a bad time?" she asked.

Lavender looked at the woman warily, not quite trusting her. Then she shrugged and answered frankly, "Your son is a brute."

"Son!" the woman snarled the word. Then, frightened and trembling, retreated behind her customary shell. What did she mean by that? Lavender thought in wonder. It was easy to tell that the woman lived in mortal fear of the Major.

But there were so many things happening at Windcrest that made her wonder. Mrs. Edmonds was always tense and nervous but when the moon was full it was as though she became wild. She would squirm and roll her eyes. Too, when there was a full moon she could hear the sound of drums beating and savage loud music coming from the row of cabins. It seemed as though the Major's band of ruffians would converge at Windcrest at that time too. There were other chilling sounds. Screams emanating from the cabins. Screams like the screams she had heard on her first day at Windcrest.

In those first weeks of her stay, she had been delighted when she heard a flurry of horses' hooves coming up the winding drive. Company! They were going to have company!

But there was no company, never any visitors. The horsemen went only to the cabins. The horsemen, she came to realize, were the Major's bands of ruffians. He's like Will Ruggles, she thought, only on a grand scale.

On an evening when the screams rang out, she went early to bed and pulled the covers over her ears. It was very late when Mark Edmonds came to her bedside. His face was flushed and his eyes wild. She braced herself for his usual brutal onslaught but tonight he said simply "Come."

His eyes gleamed like blue slate. She was sure he was a maniac as he motioned for her to follow him. She got out of bed and trailed him down the hall, watching as he inserted a key in a door at the far end of the hall.

Maybe, she thought in a wild surge of hope, he was going to take her to Mint!

They entered a room that was brilliantly lighted by many candles in sconces on the walls. The brilliance was reflected in the mirrored walls of the room. The furniture was early French, dainty and beautiful and white and gold. The carpet was so thickly velvet that her bare feet sank into its softness.

Mark said, "You are like a Dresden goddess. I would admire you."

He sat down, straddling one of the dainty chairs.

He spoke slowly, as one drugged, "Disrobe."

She undid the satin ribbons on her dressing gown and let it fall to the floor. She slipped out of the nightgown. How she hated him! He ogled her naked body for a time. He did not touch her and for that she was thankful. She suspected that he had participated in some kind of orgy at the cabins and having spent his passion, was taking delight in looking at her body in the candlelight. She was positive now that he was raving mad.

Day followed day and she did not see Cole. No doubt he had been sent out with the Major's band of ruffians. She was sure the Major was engaged in many devious activities. How else would he have the money to maintain such an establishment as this? She had heard rumors of military officers who were alleged to have made off with gold during the Civil War.

Suddenly Cole was back. She was standing at the window of the dining room looking out when he was beside her, speaking softly. They stood close together for a moment, her beautiful golden hair touched his cheek. He cleared his throat and said huskily, "There has never

164

been another woman as beautiful as you."

"Do you know anything about Mint?" she begged.

"I'm trying to find out," he whispered; and she felt he was concealing something from her. There was no time to say anything else. They heard footsteps approaching. He hurried away and she went to her place at the table.

They had a chance meeting a week later. There had been some kind of disturbance in the kitchen. Jock and the menservants left her alone when Cole came to the dining room table. He spoke quickly and very low. Mrs. Edmonds sat like a shriveled elf picking at her food and looking around in fright.

"Don't pay any attention to her," Lavender said.

"I'm finding out strange things about this place," he whispered. "Quantrill sent me to find the Confederate gold confiscated by the Major. Don't give up hope. It won't be much longer."

"Did you find out what happened to Mint?"

"Not yet, but I will, my darling."

He was gone and she looked up to see Mrs. Edmonds staring at her. She said simply, "Be careful."

Lavender looked at her and felt for the first time a kindred feeling for the woman. I think she likes me, Lavender thought and she was pleased.

When they had finished eating, Lavender pushed her chair back to go to her room when Mrs. Edmonds came to her side, and said quickly, "He's kept you longer than anyone else. The Major tires of his wives very quickly but you evidently please him."

Back in her room, Lavender pondered the woman's words. Please him? She had no desire to please him. She endured him because she was determined to survive his brutal passion; she was determined to endure until she was free of him. How she despised him!

In October, the Major left Windcrest. He told Lavender he would be gone for a while. The usual rules would prevail he informed her icily. She was not to wander outside.

"Jock will see to that," he informed her coldly.

"Where are you going?"

He ignored her question. She did not really care. She cared only that she would be free of him. Perhaps there would be a chance to see Cole again. But in the months the Major was gone, she did not see Cole and she surmised that he had been forced to accompany the Major on his trip. She asked Mrs. Edmonds if she knew where the Major had gone.

Mrs. Edmonds shrugged. She did not know nor did she care. She, like Lavender, was glad he was gone.

The monotonous days went by, one like unto the other. She ate and she slept. She would sometimes creep to the other end of the long hall and look out toward the row of cabins and wonder if Mint was there. Perhaps the screaming she heard was Mint. She couldn't bear to think about that.

She overheard Jock and one of the menservants talking about Mexico. Well, if that was where the Major had gone no wonder it was taking him so long. But what was he doing in Mexico?

Winter finally passed. Spring came with a rush of green and flower fragrance. And with spring, Mark came back. Evidently his trip had not been entirely successful. He was irritable and mean.

He was sadistic in his love-making and she was black and blue from his pummeling. There were times when she was sure he was going to tear her apart with his brutal penetration of her body. She felt terrible. She felt ill and bloated and miserable. She ached with pain when she went up and down the stairway. When she felt she could not longer endure his brutal love-making, she told him she was sure she was going to have a baby. She was in bed when she blurted out this information.

He had been undressing, unbuttoning the elaborately ruffled shirts he wore and he came now to stand beside the bed.

"Are you sure?" he asked, glaring at her.

"Yes."

His face flushed red with anger and he raised his fist as if to strike her.

"Unclean," he hissed, and stalked from the room. Lavender lay, seeped with joy. She had heard of men who felt revulsion for a pregnant woman. She wished she had told him that before.

Two days later, she found her symptoms of pregnancy had been false. She did not tell the Major that she was not going to have a baby. He was sleeping elsewhere and she saw him only occasionally at dinner. He said nothing to her.

She was on the lookout for Cole. She wanted to tell him what had happened and that she felt the Major was going to dispose of her in some sinister manner..

Chapter 15

She wondered what the Major was waiting for. If he was going to kill her and kill the unborn baby he thought she was carrying, why didn't he do it? It was almost full moon time. She could feel Mrs. Edmonds's growing nervousness, her fear.

Lavender waited for the clatter of horses' hooves up the winding road as they galloped to the cabins in back of the mansion. It had been a long time since he had shared breakfast with the two women but this morning he came to the table.

When they had eaten, he looked at Lavender and said coldly, "You are of no further use to me. Pregnant women sicken me. You will go to The Shadows today."

"The Shadows?"

He jerked his head toward the back of the mansion. So that's what the row of cabins was called. The Shadows! Perhaps, she thought, it would be easier to escape from there. She packed her carpetbag and was surprised to find the door was unlocked. She went down the stairs.

Mrs. Edmonds was waiting for her at the foot of the stairs. "Run, run," she whispered. "Run for your life." Lavender looked at the woman, a wizened figure in black. She took the woman's hand and held it. "Don't be afraid," Lavender said gently.

"Run, run," the woman said again.

"Tell me why you are so afraid of your own son?"

"Son!" the woman spat the word. "He's not my son. He's my husband. He married me and took my money. He discarded me and sent me to The Shadows." She began to cry. "He said it was my punishment because I wanted to go to the law. I live but I wish I was dead."

Lavender gave her a hug.

"This was my home. My father built Windcrest. The Major has my money. My family is dead. I live because it is more convenient to have me alive because of Windcrest."

"I knew my marriage to him was a farce," Lavender said. "I told him I was already married but he paid no heed."

"He makes his own laws."

"How many women do you suppose he has gotten married to?"

"I've lost count but there have been many. You lasted the longest. They all end up at The Shadows. He is a devil."

"What is The Shadows?"

"It is hell," the woman said slowly. "It is a hell where women are kept for the pleasure of the Major's band of ruffians. It is a whorehouse waiting for the men at the full of the moon. That is when they get their reward for doing the Major's bidding."

"I heard screams," Lavender said.

"I told you it was hell."

One of the burly servants came now and told Lavender to follow him. Lavender gave Mrs. Edmonds a parting hug and a kiss and followed her guide out of the mansion. It had been so long since she had been out-

169

doors, she wanted to dance over the velvety grass. She stood a moment drinking in the beauty of the outdoors and looking up at the azure sky.

"Come," her guide barked at her.

"My carpetbag is heavy," she said. "Why don't you carry it for me?"

For a moment she thought he was going to refuse but he picked it up and she followed him silently. She wondered where Cole was. Perhaps he had heard of her plight and had horses ready and Mint waiting and they could escape. They came now to the row of cabins and he stopped before the first one, opened the door, stepping aside and gruntingly motioned her to enter. The room was inky black but she could hear someone breathing heavily. She went forward slowly as her guide left the cabin.

She heard a whimper and asked, "Is someone here?"

"I'se here," a soft voice said.

"Speak up," Lavender commanded. "I can't understand you."

"I'se Wren," the voice said. "An' I'se 'fraid."

Lavender's eyes were getting accustomed to the darkness. There was a shaft of light coming in through a crack in the wall.

"There should be a lamp in here," Lavender said as Wren continued to cry brokenly. Lavender went to the door and turned the knob. The door was bolted on the outside.

"We's locked in," wailed Wren. "They's goin' to kill us. I heard tell 'bout de Shadows."

"It'll be all right," Lavender said gently.

"Dey's somebody on de floor," Wren said, "but dey don' say nothin'."

Lavender saw a figure on a pad in a corner near the door. When she drew near, she saw it was a girl with reddish hair billowing around her face. She was naked and she lay completely lifeless.

"I think she's daid," Wren declared knowingly.

"She's not dead. She's breathing," Lavender said bending down.

"She was here when de man brung me here. I dunno what's de matter wit' her." Wren shrugged. She had white teeth that shone like pearls against her velvety black skin. "She 'pears to be daid."

There was a long drawn out moan from the figure on the floor.

"Well, she wouldn't be moaning," Lavender said, "if she was dead. I wish we had something to cover her up."

"Deys nothin' heah," Wren said.

Lavender opened her carpetbag and took out her dressing gown and put it over the woman on the floor. She knelt beside her.

"Are you all right?" Lavender asked.

"Oh, my head," the woman moaned putting her hands on each side of her head and trying to raise herself.

"Tell me what happened to you."

"I hurt."

Wren began to cry again. "I'se 'scared. Dat Major Edmonds done bought me."

"Oh, no, Wren," Lavender said. "There is no more slavery."

"Dey is, Missy. Dey is," Wren cried. "My massa sold me to de Major an' he say he let my mammy go free effen he kin sell me. I'se a virgin, I is." The last was said proudly.

The woman on the floor spoke now in a quivering voice, "I answered an ad. It sounded so exciting. I lived in a Mission near Westport Landing. But when I got here, I didn't want to stay. I told Mr. Brannigan that I was leaving. He's in charge. He became very angry and told me he would show me what happened to those who disobeyed."

Lavender and Wren listened silently.

"He took me to a cabin," she continued, "and there was a girl there tied to a post. She was naked. A man had a whip and Mr. Brannigan told me to watch. He said she was going to get ten lashes to keep her in line. He said I would get the same if I wasn't careful. When the man with the whip got through, she was all bloody. She screamed and screamed and screamed."

The screaming! Lavender remembered the many times she had heard the unearthly agonizing screams.

"Then Mr. Brannigan made me go with him to another cabin, a long one, and there were many women there. They all looked terrible. He told me to take a good look at them. Then he slapped me hard again and again and made me take off my clothes. He said so I'd get used to being naked. And he laughed and laughed. He left me here," she finished.

"Is we gonna die?" Wren asked sadly.

"I hope not," Lavender said hopefully. But she wondered what lay ahead. If only Cole would come!

They waited in silence. Presently the bolt was pulled back and Jock stepped into the room. He carried a lamp and set it on a low table in a corner of the room. Lavender had not noticed the table before but now she could see there was a single chair and two other pads on the floor.

"We're hungry," Lavender said.

"Food will be brought," he said and looked at Wren. "Come with me."

"Where are you taking her?" Lavender demanded.

"The master wishes to see her," Jock said as he grabbed Wren roughly and shoved her out the door. Poor little girl, Lavender thought sadly. She won't be a virgin when he gets through with her and she won't ever be the same again.

The woman told Lavender her name was Angela. They looked at each other in silence wondering what was ahead for them. Lavender sat on the chair and Angela lay on her pad.

"We'll probably never get out of here," Angela said bitterly.

"How did you say you got here?" Lavender presently asked. It was better to talk than just sit here and wonder what would happen next.

"I answered an ad."

Me too, Lavender thought sadly. Oh, if only she could go back to the time when she and Mint had gone to the railroad station with Mr. Cartwright! If only they had taken a train eastward — or how much better if they had gone home to Mama and Pa.

Angela went on talking, "I had no kin and when I was grown I stayed at the Mission to help. The Mission was on the main trail. I'll never forget the ragged men in uniform stopping to rest in the Mission gardens after the War."

"Don't think about anything connected with the War," Lavender said softly. "It's better not to look back."

"The Methodist Mission was strict and when my friend Mary Ann Williams and I found the booklet we were

173

almost afraid to open it. It had two bold black words on it, 'The Exchange' and under that it said in smaller letters, 'Devoted to the Interests of the Unmarried."

Angela wiped her eyes before continuing. "Mary Ann and I thought we were so smart. There were pictures of men and women in the booklet, pictures of people who wanted to get married or maybe just wanted a job. Some of the people told how lonely they were. I picked out Mr. Brannigan's picture. I dreamed dreams. I thought he would give me a job and I would fall in love with him and we would be married and live happily ever after."

She fell silent and Lavender waited. "What a starry-eyed little fool I was!" she said bitterly.

There was a noise at the door and both women looked at each other. Angela hurriedly slipped on Lavender's dressing gown. The bolt jerked back and when the door swung open, Jock entered the room. He said simply, "Come."

"Where are you taking us?" Lavender asked.

He did not bother to answer but herded them ahead of him into a much larger cabin. Lavender saw women of all ages, shapes and sizes lined up against a wall. Lavender looked for Mint.

Could Mint be in this bunch of tired looking, beaten women? Not lovely Mint with her golden-brown hair, big dark eyes, fresh lily-white skin! She did not see Mint as Jock steered her and Angela into the line of women.

Suddenly there was a flurry of heavy boots and a laughing jostling pack of men came in. They were dirty and looked as though they had been on the trail for a long time. Jock was speaking, "Take your pick, boys, and remember, the Major takes mighty good care of his men. If you ain't satisfied, just come back and get another one. And if you get a fighter, there's plenty of whips to tame 'em."

Chapter 16

The men swaggered down the line looking at the women. They ogled. They touched and drooled. The leader of the group was first. He was a robust squarely built man with a red face and big hands.

"I get first pick," he yelled and dared anyone to dispute his words. The others fell back while he made his choice.

Lavender searched the group of men for a glimpse of Cole.

"I'm Big Bill Brannigan," the leader announced belligerently. "I want a woman who's all woman."

He stalked the length of the room staring at the women until he came to Lavender.

"Think you can satisfy me?" he bellowed at her. She stared at him insolently.

"I asked you a question."

She looked at him but said nothing. For all her outward bravado she was quivering with fright in her heart. She felt this uncouth man would be even more brutal than the Major! The women on each side of her were looking at her with admiration and something like awe. Here was someone standing up to Big Bill Brannigan! And yet there was fear in their eyes.

"Guess maybe you need a good dressing down," Big

Bill said, motioning to Jock. "Give her a couple lashes and see if she can talk."

Two of the band stepped forward and stripped her of her clothing. Jock came with the whip.

"This cat-o'-nine-tails is goin' to tear open that white skin," Big Bill laughed. "Give her three." This last was said to Jock.

The big brute stepped forward and brought his arm into position.

"One," Big Bill shouted.

Lavender cringed. This couldn't be happening to her! Not to little Lavender Mueller who wanted nothing more than to marry a knight on a white horse! Well, she had married that knight and here she was standing naked before a group of tough men and desolate women!

The whip with its nine leather thongs danced through the air and caught her squarely across her waist. It was like a livid firebrand and she screamed in agony.

"Two," Big Bill's voice rang out.

Lavender braced herself for the pain that was coming. But this time the whip did not crack.

She glanced back to see a big blond man holding Jock's upraised arm in an iron grip. Cole! It was Cole!

"That's my woman," he was saying in a steely voice. "I saw her in the big house. She's mine."

There was a deadly silence. Then Big Bill spoke, conceding ungraciously. "A man would be a fool to cross you. I seen you hit a dove from a mile away. I don't aim to have a shoot-out with you."

The men had tensed. Some had edged toward the walls fearful of a shoot-out between Big Bill and the blond man they knew as Blaze Bingham. Cole picked up Lavender's clothes from the floor and pushed her ahead of him to a nearby cabin.

"Oh, Cole," she collapsed in his arms when they were alone. She was shaking like a leaf.

"Be calm, dear," he cautioned. "Don't crack up."

"I've been beaten. That Big Bill could have had me killed and you tell me not to crack up!" she cried hysterically.

"I know, my darling," he soothed her. "It's just that we have to keep our wits about us. The Major is sending Big Bill and the boys out on a job tomorrow. There'll be only a few left here as guards. Lavender, I have a good idea where the Major has hidden the Confederate gold and I aim to get it when he leaves."

"We can't leave without Mint."

"Mint is dead," Cole said gently, holding her. "She was killed right after you came here."

Lavender cried bitterly. "It's all my fault, Cole. I brought her here."

"Don't say that and don't think that," he said. "Mint wanted to come here, just as you did at that time. If you had the same moment to live over again you would do the same thing."

"What can I tell Mama and Pa?" she sobbed.

"You won't have to tell them anything if we don't get away from here tomorrow," he said practically.

"Why don't we leave tomorrow and not bother with the gold?"

"No, I came for the gold. I aim to get it and take care of the Major at the same time. He's a thieving, no-good bastard. Stealin' from the Confederacy he had sworn to protect. We'll have to kill him, Lavender. He'll hunt us down and shoot us like dogs if we don't."

She thought suddenly of Wren. She told Cole about the youngster who had so proudly proclaimed that she was a virgin.

"She's dead," Cole said bluntly. "I heard some of the men talkin'. They buried her out back."

"Dead!" Lavender was shocked.

"The Major finished her off."

"Oh, Cole," Lavender whispered. "She was only a little girl."

"You ought to know she's better off dead," he said. "No, no, my darling, I don't mean you'd be better off dead after all you've been through. No, no, I know it's a miracle that you lived through that hell."

"I used to wish I could die."

"Before I knew it was you in the big house, I used to hear the men talking," he went on. "They talked of the golden-haired beauty. They had bets on how long you would last. No one ever lasted long in his hands. He was more considerate of you, Lavender, than the others, or you would be out in the graveyard in back."

"Is that where Mint is?"

"Yes. She's at rest, Lavender."

He held her tenderly in his arms.

"When I saw you that first time in the big house, I couldn't believe my eyes," he said. "I had looked everywhere for you. John went off to Mexico to set up headquarters for Quantrill. I thought that was strange as he intended to be gone a long time. I went to your cabin and you were gone."

"John rode off and never came back," she said. "I was going to have a baby. I went back to the home place. I went home to Mama and Pa. My baby was born dead. It was so beautiful, Cole. It had a face like a white rose. I named her Rose."

"My poor brave Lavender."

"I got tired of my pa always ranting and complaining and I went off to see Mint who had gotten married."

She told him then of Will Ruggles and of sweet Ma Ruggles and kind Milo Cartwright and how she had found the ad and it had seemed like an answer from heaven.

"I went to your home place searching for you," he said. "I remembered you talked of your home that winter I was at your place. Your pa wasn't too cordial. He refused to tell me where you had gone. I looked in the nearby towns. I went back to your cabin."

"Oh, Cole."

"I'm going to get some salve for your back and then we better get some sleep if we're going to hit the trail."

He left and she waited in fear and trembling. What if something happened and he didn't return? He returned in a few moments and made her stretch out on a pad on her stomach. He tenderly smoothed salve over the welts on her back. She winced and he whispered lovingly, "My brave darling. My brave sweetheart."

He had locked the door and came to lie down beside her holding her close.

"Cole, I keep remembering that little Wren saying, 'I'se a virgin.' "

"Don't think about Wren. Don't think about the past. All we have is this moment and what we can take in the future. I think the men remaining here will help us. They all hate him but they're scared as hell of him. He'd as soon kill them as look at them."

"He's mad. I used to see that awful gleam in his eyes. I knew he was crazy."

She told him about Mrs. Edmonds.

"I knew about her," he said. "The men talked of her. Called her an old witch."

Lavender was indignant. "She is not an old witch. The Major bilked her out of Windcrest."

"Well, when we do away with him, she can have Windcrest back again."

He had draped her clothing over her when he had finished applying the salve. Now he pushed the clothing aside and turned her toward him.

"Oh, Lavender, my beautiful darling."

"No, Cole," she protested but he smothered her face with kisses. She felt his rising passion.

"How I love you!" he marvelled. "My brave Lavender."

"I was brave to stand up against Big Bill, wasn't I?" she asked proudly. "That's why he had me beaten."

"My darling."

She trembled in his arms as she felt desire for him flame through her body.

"Love me, love me," she whispered.

Perhaps this will be the last time, she thought. Perhaps this will be the last time we can belong together. Perhaps we will be dead tomorrow.

"My sweetheart," he murmured taking her in a wave of ecstasy.

Chapter 17

They heard screams, wild and terrifying, during the night and Cole cuddled her tenderly. In the early morning hours, they heard the men leaving. Cole went to get food for them and when he returned he was jubilant, "Most of the men have gone with Big Bill. There's about eight left. They want to take the house now."

"I'll hurry and get dressed," she said.

"I've promised them they could have whatever they want. We'll storm the house before long."

"Be careful, Cole," she begged. "I want to go with you. Wait for me."

"You'll have to stay way back of the men in case they have to fall back. But I don't think we'll have any trouble from the inside men. They hate the Major's guts."

Lavender wondered what would become of Mrs. Edmonds when Windcrest was stormed. She would surely have enough sense to stay out of the way. They crept across the wide back lawn. There was no activity yet in the big house. They moved stealthily through the back door and into the wide hall and up the staircase. Cole led the way.

"Jock, is that you?" the Major called. "Dammit, I told you not to come pussyfooting around this early in the morning."

181

Then there was silence. The band led by Cole waited in the wide upstairs hall. They heard the Major grunt and they heard a woman's low moan.

"Shut up," the Major rasped. "Turn over here."

"Oh, please," a sad little voice begged. "Don't hurt me again."

Lavender, remembering the countless times she had endured pain at the hands of the Major thought, That woman will soon be free of the Major. When all was quiet again except the moans of the woman and while they waited breathlessly, there was a rustle on the steps and they turned to see Mrs. Edmonds rushing up the steps and opening the door of the Major's bedroom.

They hurried after her into the room. The Major let out a roar when he saw the intruders.

Nettie Edmonds rushed straight up to the Major and thrust an old cap and ball gun straight into his face and fired. The report was shattering and left the Major a ball of bloody flesh. Lavender watched as she saw the band of men, including Jock, dashing around the room rummaging through drawers and grabbing gold candlesticks and whatever they could lay their hands on.

Lavender saw Cole rummage under the bed and pull out a chest. Apparently it was the Confederate gold, she thought. He seemed satisfied and motioned for her to follow him. Lavender had recognized the woman in the bed as Angela who lay in shock spattered with the Major's blood. Lavender pulled her out of the bed and jerked her to her feet.

As they went down the stairway, they could see the men ransacking the house. This was too bad, Lavender thought sadly. These treasures really belonged to Mrs.

Edmonds. But they were a small price to pay for their freedom. She saw the woman still carrying the gun wandering about in a daze.

Lavender had wrapped a sheet around Angela but she seemed too weak to hold it around her body. It kept slipping off and making her trip.

"We'll have to get my carpetbag," Lavender told Cole. "There's a dress in there for Angela."

As they started to leave the back entrance, they smelled smoke.

"Old Mrs. Edmonds set the place on fire!" someone yelled. There was a mad scramble to escape the flames and smoke. Safe on the lawn, Lavender turned to look up at the big mansion and she saw Mrs. Nettie Edmonds' figure silhouetted against the dancing orange flames. Poor Mrs. Edmonds, Lavender thought sadly. The Major destroyed her and she destroyed the Major. How she must have hated him!

One of the group named Sam laughed, "Big Bill and his men are gonna be surprised when they come back. How about that, Blaze?"

"Damn right," Cole answered. "Serves 'em right."

"Won't be nothin' here but ashes," another put in.

"And we'll be gone."

"What about the women?" Lavender asked.

"We'll let them out," Sam said.

The group trailed to the cabins, the men staggering under their loads of loot. Cole and Lavender with Angela retrieved her carpetbag and Lavender helped Angela dress. She seemed incapable of thought and moved woodenly.

Cole went to get saddlebags and transferred the coins from the heavy chest into the bags.

"We'll have to guard these bags with our lives from those bastards," Cole told her.

"What about the women?" Lavender asked.

"There's plenty of horses," Cole said. "The strong ones will survive, the weak won't."

"Oh, Cole," Lavender murmured.

"Which way you headin'?" Sam asked Cole.

"Down Texas way. Maybe to Mexico."

"Mind if I ride along a ways?"

"No."

"We'll have to take Angela," Lavender told him. "She's acting strange."

"It's seein' all that blood," Cole said. "You said she was raised in a Mission. She's not used to such goin's-on as seeing a man blown to hell in his bed."

They put Angela on a horse and she wobbled so that Cole had to tie her on. The group presently rode off southwestward.

"What's in them saddlebags?" Sam asked when they made camp that first evening. "Seems like you got an awful lot of saddlebags and extra horses to carry 'em."

"Those bags are my property," Cole said coldly.

"Don't mean to pry, Blaze," Sam explained, his beady eyes staring at Cole.

"Then don't," Cole rasped.

Lavender gathered firewood. Cole waited until she returned and then filled the waterbags that had been emptied that day. Sam left to return with two rabbits for their supper. When he was gone, Cole told Lavender, "We must guard these saddlebags. Sam suspects there is something valuable in them and he's not going to rest until he finds out what."

After supper, they sat around the campfire. Sam

edged over toward Angela who was sitting transfixed staring into the flames. She sensed his presence and screamed hysterically, "Don't touch me. Don't touch me."

"I ain't gonna touch you, lady," Sam said angrily and to the others he remarked, "Do you s'pose her mind is unhinged?"

"Sometimes a person's mind can't take in what has happened to them," Cole said.

Angela jumped to her feet, and started to run, then fell to the ground in a dead faint.

"Don't think she's gonna come around," Sam said. "Look at how wet her face is. I've seen lots of 'em like this."

Cole brought water and Lavender doused her face. Angela's breath was coming in gasps.

"She's dyin'," Sam said flatly.

"I'm sorry, God, for leaving the Mission," Angela whispered and was gone.

"But how could she die so quickly?" Lavender cried.

"Her mind couldn't take the terrible things that happened to her," Cole explained.

No, Lavender thought, marvelling that she had lived through the ordeal she had. Perhaps her encounter with Will Ruggles had toughened her. She thought of the Major. Men like the Major and Will were like bulls. She shuddered, remembering the countless times the Major had crushed the life from her bruised and battered body. They wrapped Angela's slender body in a horse blanket and buried her by moonlight.

They settled down for the night. Lavender saw that Cole kept his gun handy. The moon, now not quite full, shone on the lone grave. Lavender, listening to a coyote's mournful cry, shivered and groped for Cole's hand.

After a breakfast of cold rabbit, they were ready to hit the trail.

"Goodbye, Angela," Lavender whispered.

Day followed day. They rode steadily. Lavender was tired. Both men were good shots. Rabbit and squirrels were plentiful. There were fish for the taking in the streams. At night she would look up at the sky and think how beautiful it all was! Silvery moonlight and glittering stars against the black velvet sky. Crickets and the hooting of owls combined with other friendly night voices. The aroma of the campfire now burning low.

She told Cole, "The stars seem so big. They're like sparkling white lilies that I could pick and weave into a chain."

Sam snorted and laughed.

"I wonder," she said softly, "if this side of the sky is so beautiful and sparkling with diamond stars, what do you suppose the other side looks like?"

There was no answer to this.

One evening as they ate supper, Sam startled them with the announcement that although he had never bragged about it he was a friend of the James boys and the Youngers.

Lavender and Cole looked at each other and the dimples around Lavender's mouth danced.

"Yep, it's many a mile I've rode with them. That Cole Younger is a dead shot. Mean as hell though. That Jesse James! He's a killer too. Would as soon kill you as look at you."

"I've heard tell the James and the Youngers rob the rich and give to the poor," Cole said.

"Ain't never seen 'em do that. I was with 'em in February of 1866. We went into Liberty, Missouri about eight in the mornin'. I remember it was cold. There was ten of us. We went into the Clay County Savings and Loan. Four of us went in and cleaned the place out. We got away and a big blizzard moved in and covered our tracks."

"Heard tell there was a young boy killed," Cole said.

"Yeah. He got in the way."

"What did this Cole Younger look like?" This from Cole.

"Just like anybody else," the man said. "Nothin' outstandin'."

"You know the James and the Youngers ain't the bosom pals they make out to be," Sam continued knowingly.

"I heard they would die for each other," Cole remarked.

" 'Taint so," Sam scoffed. "I was with 'em too at Lexington. Let's see; that was in October of '66. We came ridin' down the main street of Lexington. It was about noon. The streets were deserted. We was right smart. Cole had a scarf tied about the lower half of his face and he asked the cashier to cash a fifty-dollar United States bond. The cashier aimed to do that. Cole cocked his gun. 'Empty that drawer, Cole said.' We got the loot and backed out. I yelled, 'Don't shoot or we'll blow out your brains!' "

"That's mighty interesting," Cole remarked dryly.

"When are you going to tell him you are Cole Younger?" Lavender asked when she and Cole were alone.

"When we get close to the border. I may need Sam before then."

The days went by. The sun was hot and the journey

187

monotonous. Sam continued to embellish their evenings around the campfire with tales of the Youngers and the James. Cole encouraged him and Sam elaborated on the exploits of the band of outlaws. Sam stressed that he was a confidant of Cole. Cole trusted him far more than he trusted the James.

Lavender would have liked to walk awhile so she could pick violets, the big creamy and yellow dog-tooths, primrose anemones and blue spiderwort but Cole insisted they had no time for such pastime. When they stopped to rest she would gather a bouquet of poppy-mallows and would look at the creamy blossoms with their red-striped petals and think that she would probably never pass this way again. Tonight the pale moon would look down on the spot where she had picked the poppy-mallows but she would be far down the trail.

"We'll be coming into the dry country soon," Cole told her. They saw fewer herds of buffalo now, and the rich black earth gradually took on the appearance of sand.

Cole had had a supply of lucifer matches.

"What if you run out of matches?" Lavender asked.

"I can always start a fire by putting a rag saturated with damp gun powder on the ground. Then sprinkling a little dry powder over it, I can take my gun placing the cone directly over the rag, explode a cap and the rag ignites. It always works."

One day when she complained she was tired of eating rabbit, squirrel and fish, Cole brought her some pemmican.

"Anyone who rides a trail always carries pemmican," he explained giving her a sample.

She took a bite and spit it out. "It's terrible," she said. Cole laughed. "It's not so terrible when you're hungry.

188

It's made from buffalo meat cut into thin flakes and hung up to dry in the sun. Then it's pounded between two stones and reduced to a powder. This powder is placed in a bag of buffalo hide. You've seen these bags, Lavender. The hair is on the outside. Melted grease is poured into the bag with the powder and the bag sewn up. What you just had is raw, but it can be mixed with flour and boiled and it ain't so bad. Beats starving."

Lavender doubted that and said so.

No more anemones or violets now. There was still grass. Tall waving grass but it was dried grass, not the lush green growth she loved. Lavender looked at the waving grass and felt fear clutch her throat. Her horse lurched, steadied and went on and Lavender felt the fear again. She wanted to see the green of the honey-locusts and the red and yellow and creamy whiteness of blooms along the trail, not this waving sea of coarse prairie grass.

Even sunflowers, wild plum and Indian currant were preferable to this waving brown sea of grass. The emerald beauty seen in the past had been shut out as if by a heavy brown curtain and now this oppressive veil of waving grass seemed to roll over her in waves like the rippling of sea waves. The grass! Would it ever stop moving? Would it ever stop waving? It had a kind of rhythm,

> *Blow grass blow . . .*
> *Blow grass blow . . .*
> *Blow wave ripple . . .*
> *Blow . . . blow . . .*

"How much longer, Cole?" she asked when they were

189

alone. "The grass makes me dizzy."

"I know, sweetheart," he answered. "Soon you'll wish you could see the waving grass. Soon we'll come into the desert."

"I'll be glad when Sam knows you are Cole Younger. I'm so afraid I'll forget and call you Cole instead of Blaze."

Cole laughed. "What was it he said about me? That we were riding pals. That I looked like everybody else."

"He's going to get the surprise of his life!"

The sun got hotter if that was possible. They had to rest frequently. Lavender decided the tall waving grass was preferable to the yucca plant. On and on they rode toward the Mexican border.

Sam's curiosity about the saddlebags grew. Cole was careful that Sam did not get too close to them. It was Cole who carefully lifted them from the horses' backs at night. Cole who led the four extra horses through the rough places.

"We'll be hittin' the border soon, Blaze," he said one evening after supper.

"Yes, that we will."

"I've been thinkin' maybe you'd let me see what's in those bags."

"Nope."

"You seen what I took from the big house. You seen them gold candlesticks and the eatin' forks and knives. Let me see what you took."

"Nope."

Sam scowled.

Later Cole told Lavender, "Sam is going to make a move any day now. It's lucky I'm a light sleeper."

Two nights later, as they slept, Sam stealthily crept

190

toward Cole who slept with the bags between him and Lavender. Cole was ready.

Lavender awakened and saw the creeping Sam. She tensed and waited.

Chapter 18

Sam made his move to open one of the saddlebags when Cole sprang to action. He was like a crouching tiger, flinging himself at Sam.

Sam, caught off guard, fell backwards. Cole pinned him to the ground.

"Now, Blaze, I was curious. Cain't blame a man for being curious."

"The hell you were! I told you those bags were mine."

"Cain't see why you won't tell me what's in 'em. I'd like to know what you're totin'."

"Get to your feet," Cole ordered. "Tomorrow you're leaving us."

"The hell I am! I ain't rode all this long way for nothin'. I don't aim to leave. I'm goin' all the way with you."

"Like hell you are! We'll be coming to the Rio Grande tomorrow and that's where we part company."

"Don't forget I rode with the Youngers and the James. I'm gonna tell them about these saddlebags you been carryin'. They'll be interested."

"Tell them," Cole said shortly.

"They'll be hot on your trail," Sam predicted.

"I hope they are."

"You might be a good shot but you ain't as good as Cole Younger. You'd be dead 'fore you could get that gun out of the holster."

Cole looked steadily at the man a moment. "I am Cole Younger," he said.

Lavender, watching, saw Sam stiffen with surprise and shock.

"Any of those stories you want to change," Cole challenged.

"How do I know you're Cole Younger?"

Cole's hand flashed to the gun in his holster. Sam slumped. "I believe you," he said.

"Go to bed," Cole commanded and Sam slunk to his place near the campfire.

Lavender could not go back to sleep. She turned over on her stomach and tried to shut out the events of the evening. What if Sam had succeeded in surprising Cole? What if Sam had shot Cole before Cole knew he was creeping up on him? She tried to shut the thoughts out.

Cole would never let anything happen to her. She would always be safe with Cole. What would happen now? When Sam left them they would be alone. The thought made her tremble with love for Cole. To belong to him again. They had not made love on the trail, mainly because Sam never left them alone long enough. And at night, Cole could not afford to be caught off guard. She smiled into the darkness. She could almost feel the fierce possessiveness of his lips on her mouth. She could hardly wait to feel his body claim her own.

When they came to the Rio Grande, Cole told Sam, "We part company here."

"Thought maybe you'd change your mind."

"Nope."

They watched as Sam turned to the left and rode close to the river bank. Cole and Lavender watched until he was out of sight.

"We'll have to keep a sharp eye out," Cole said. "He may try to surprise us."

"I'm glad he's gone."

"I'm glad too. And now we're alone, my darling," he said softly, taking her in his arms. "This has been a hard trip but you've taken it in stride. I'm proud of you."

"Cole, where are we going?"

"Quantrill has a camp just below the Rio Grande. He is tired, Lavender, and he's sick. He wanted the Confederate gold. He can't reconcile himself to the fact that the South lost the war. He dreams dreams of outfitting a new Confederacy."

"Oh, Cole, it would be terrible for the United States to have to go through another war with brother fighting against brother."

"He dreams dreams," Cole held her close, kissing her. "Don't worry your pretty head about it."

"You said we are going to Quantrill's camp," she said and then asked, "What if John is there?"

"We'll face him," Cole said. "We'll tell him we love each other."

"He'll try to kill you," she predicted, alarmed.

"We'll think about that later," he soothed her with more kisses. "Come. The water is not too deep at this point. We will cross here and the night will be ours. Before too long we will be in Quantrill's camp. He'll be glad to see us but he'll be happier to see the gold."

In his arms that night, she forgot about her dread of seeing John again. With Cole's lips on hers, and their willing eager bodies merged as one, she felt on fire with love for him. She wished this night of magic would last forever. She could hardly bear the ecstasy they shared. Oh, this is the way life should be, she thought happily.

A woman was meant to be filled with this radiant sense of glorious fullfillment. A woman was meant to make her man happy and she was making Cole happy and she rejoiced in that fact.

She breathed with him. Her body pulsated with his. She wanted only to be always with him, always to cherish him this night and for all the rest of their lives.

Chapter 19

She felt like a woman again. And she gloried in the feeling. She ran her hands over her body and was glad that her body, so satiny smooth, could give Cole so much pleasure. She was sure he loved her.

She delighted in asking him over and over, "Cole, do you truly love me?"

And his fervent "Yes, you know I do" thrilled her. These days as they rode stirrup to stirrup passed only too swiftly for Lavender.

Sometimes she felt as if she had been riding a whole lifetime. It had been a long journey from Windcrest to this dry, arid, parched land. But she dreaded the time when the journey would end, when they would come to Quantrill's camp. It was so hot. She pushed back the wet curls from her forehead and licked the dust from her lips.

"Do you think Sam will follow us?"

"Yes. He will catch up with us in a day or two. The thought of those heavy saddlebags will drive him crazy. He will throw caution aside and decide to follow us. He will try to surprise us, probably the night after next."

"Oh, Cole, I thought he would leave us alone. He seemed so frightened when he left."

"Yes, but the thought of possible gold in those bags will haunt him."

"You are so wise, Cole."

"I know how men think, Lavender. Especially the greedy ones." He laughed and went on, "As to women, I am not so smart about them."

"Cole, is it true you were in love with Belle Starr? John mentioned it before we were married."

"No, of course not. Belle started the story that we were in love."

They were seated near the campfire after their supper. Her head was on his shoulder and his arm was around her.

"She loved you," Lavender said dreamily. "No one could help loving you, Cole."

He laughed, but he was pleased. "Just so you love me, my darling."

"I will love you forever," she vowed.

"Let me tell you about Belle," he said.

"Was she as pretty as they say?"

"She had hair the color of a raven's wing and she wore scarlet velvet dresses and white plumed hats. She had two Navy Colts hanging at her shapely waist. She liked to be called 'Queen of the Outlaws.' "

"Shapely waist?"

"She had and still has a magnificent figure," he went on. "She was only a little girl when I saw her for the first time."

"And how old were you, Cole?"

"I was sixteen. It was at Carthage, Missouri. Belle was sitting on the ground, making mud pies. Her father had a hotel in Carthage. I went into the back yard and there she sat. 'Hi,' she said. 'My name's Belle.' I told her that I knew her last name was Shirley. She left off making mud pies and offered me her mud-splattered hand. She had a potato sack doll called Maggie."

197

"She must have made a real impression on you, Cole."

"She was a mighty sweet young 'un, but she got tough as nails through the years."

"What changed her?"

"It was the times in which we lived, Lavender. We had to get mean and tough to survive. I would like to think of Belle as galloping across the pages of American history on her golden mare, Venus, as a sweet and lovely heroine. But that is not the true picture."

He was silent a moment, looking back through the years. He presently continued, "Belle's brother, Edward, joined Lane's Bushwhackers and was killed at Sarcoxie, Missouri. Another brother, Prescott, ran away to Texas. Belle was so ashamed of Prescott, and burning to avenge the death of Edward that she took to hanging around the Federal camp. The men considered her a nice child. Belle could charm the rattles off a rattlesnake. The men teased her and let her follow them around."

"It sounds like you admired her, Cole," Lavender said wistfully.

"I was fond of her. Belle found out that the Federals were about to attack a Confederate camp and she was determined to warn them. However, her plan was discovered and the cavalry major ordered her held under guard until the Federal troops were gone a half hour from the camp."

"She sounds brave."

"Yes, Belle never lacked for courage. Well, the newspaper heard of the incident and they embroidered fact with fiction. The article spoke of the beautiful Belle Shirley sobbing, 'I'll beat the cavalry and warn the camp' as she vaulted in the saddle, courageously riding through the fields, erect as an arrow, her hair flying in the breeze. Belle outlined the article in heavy black pencil and sent the newspaper to me in care of my mother at Harrisonville, Missouri."

"She truly loved you, Cole."

"I guess she did," he admitted ruefully. "I guess she did."

"What happened to her after that?"

"Her father sold the hotel in Carthage and decided to go to Texas. They traveled the Old Settler's Trail. They traveled by ox-drawn Conestoga wagon. It was an exciting time for Belle, now almost fifteen years old. I had seen her through the years while she lived at Carthage. Her mother told me then that Belle talked constantly of me, that she was in love with me. I thought it was a joke."

"Did she like Texas?"

"She hated Texas. She kept a kind of diary of her trip there and later sent me the story of her trip. She told of the hot winds that billowed the canvas cover of the wagon. I remembered she had a crazy notion about time. She thought the wind blew and blew and it was like time, blowing away before one's eyes. She hated the wind. She was afraid the hot dry wind would turn her white soft skin into leather."

He stopped talking to put more wood on the fire and settled back to continue, "Belle wrote about the wagons on the trail, wagons returning to Missouri. Some had signs painted on their sides, 'Busted, it was worse than we thought' and she said one had a picture of a big bug painted on its side with the words, 'He won.' "

"How sad for those returning when they probably dreamed of a new life in the West."

"Yes. I forgot to tell you what happened in Carthage that made the Shirleys leave. It seemed that the Union soldiers were fond of tearing through the streets singing the hated song, 'Marching Through Georgia' at the top of their voices. Well, one day Belle was walking down Main Street when five Union soldiers swooped down the street singing. When they saw Belle they brought their horses to a slow walk and began to banter with her."

"Didn't they know she was for the Confederacy?"

"Sure, that's why they started to tease her and ask her how she liked their song. For answer, she smiled sweetly at them, told them that it was her turn now and she sang 'Dixieland.' "

"I'll bet they didn't like that!"

"That was like waving a red flag in front of a bull. During her rendition of 'Dixieland' a large crowd had gathered and they applauded with gusto. So Belle was just ready to swing into 'Yellow Rose of Texas' when her father appeared. After this escapade he decided to sell the hotel and move west. He reasoned that the War was lost and it was best to make a new start."

"Was Belle glad to leave Carthage?"

"Belle was ready for any new adventure. She was raring to go. Her folks were glad to go because they didn't trust Belle. With her daring and her red hot temper, they were afraid she would get them all in trouble. On the very day he sold the hotel, the news came over the wire that President Abraham Lincoln had been assassinated. Belle's father grieved. He had admired the president. He wore a black arm band to show his respect and Belle never quite forgave him."

"She sounds like a strange one."

He laughed. "She is a strange one," he agreed. "I

hope you can meet her sometime. There's only one Belle Starr."

"Where is she now?"

"She calls herself 'The Queen of the Outlaws.' She's got a little spread near Dallas. Like I told you she is a tough woman. She had a baby, swore it was mine. In fact, she called it Pearl Younger."

"Was it your baby, Cole?" Lavender asked.

"Hell, no. She thought it was smart to pass it off as my child. She married Jim Reed who had come to Texas from Vernon County, Missouri with a sheriff's posse at his heels."

"Pearl Younger," Lavender said softly. "That's a pretty name. I would like to have your baby. I would like to have a baby named Cole Younger Jr."

"Only God knows the future," he said.

"So Belle got married finally," she prompted.

"Yes, but it didn't last. Jim went off to avenge a brother's murder and when he returned he brought a full-blooded Cherokee with him. Anyway the law was on Jim's trail and they had to make a run for it. The last I heard she was living near Dallas."

"Would you like to see her again, Cole?"

"Hell, no."

"I'm jealous of Belle," she said as he fixed the fire for the night.

"Don't be. You have my heart, Lavender, and it will always be yours. I love you. I have never loved another woman in my life."

"Have you ever told other women you love them?" She could not help asking the question.

"Yes, I have told many women that. You are the only one I have told that to and truly meant it."

201

Later he told her they must be on guard in case Sam had trailed them. "You sleep and I will watch, then I will sleep and you can watch."

She slept fitfully. She was frightened and for the first time realized the dangers that befell those who rode the Outlaw Trail. She thought about Belle Starr and the Navy Colts hanging from her waist. What kind of a woman was Belle with her velvet dresses and her plumed hats? She must have truly loved Cole. But then what woman could resist loving Cole?

When Cole awakened her, she sat by the fire clutching a shotgun. Every night sound startled her. She was sure someone lurked in the shadows. She was sure Sam was creeping up on them ready to kill them and steal the saddlebags. When dawn finally streaked the sky with pink and gold she was thankful. They had made it through the night. Cole had said they should reach Quantrill's camp in about three more days.

The following evening they followed the same procedure. One slept while the other watched. Lavender had taken her place to watch as Cole stretched out. She was looking at the way the orange glow of the fire turned his hair to gold when she heard the strange noise.

Instantly she was alert. She cocked the gun and waited. She was completely calm. She was ready. She never knew if Cole heard the noise too or if her tense posture was revealed to him somehow as she had straightened her body in her desire to be ready. She saw him move and knew he was waiting too.

In a lightning-swift move he was on his knees and firing into the darkness. The report was deafening to Lavender.

"I got him," Cole said simply.

It was Sam.

Now that the waiting was over, Lavender trembled and began to cry. "He's dead," she whispered.

"You would rather he was dead than us," Cole said bluntly.

"I know but he was a human being."

"He was a murdering snake," Cole said as he set about to bury the man. "You'll have to toughen up. You must realize, Lavender, to survive here you have to be tough. The tough survive, the weak die."

She did not answer. She wondered if she would ever get used to Cole's life. When the job was finished, he said, "Come, my darling, we need not worry about Sam trying to kill us. We can love."

She obediently went to him. She must please him. Yet as their bodies joined in an ecstasy of passion she wondered what type of man he was that he could snuff out a man's life and so easily lose himself in exquisite mounting rapture.

Chapter 20

"We should arrive at the camp by nightfall," Cole told her two days later.

"What will it be like?"

"That will be up to you, Lavender. You can hate it or you can love it. It's a wild carefree sort of living. We eat, we sleep and we love."

"Is Kate there?"

"Kate Clarke? Yes, she's Quantrill's woman."

"She came to the cabin once. You weren't with the band."

"I heard about it later. Quantrill thought you were a beauty." He grinned at her and added, "Kate didn't think so."

"She wouldn't!" Lavender said dryly.

"She's jealous of you. Quantrill teased her, praising your golden hair and blue eyes. You know she is as dark as an Indian."

"Does he love her, Cole?"

"Of course not. I told you before that men like Quantrill do not love."

"What will he do with this gold you are bringing him?" she asked.

"He has wild dreams of setting up an empire but, Lavender, they are only dreams."

"Will you follow him always, Cole?"

"I told you before that Quantrill is tired. He is weary of the trail. He wants to settle down. I think he is going to appoint a couple of leaders who will take command of the Black Raiders. Then he will be free to dream his dreams."

"Will he appoint you?"

"I told him I do not want the command, Lavender. I, too, am weary. I want to get a spread and settle down. Would you like that?"

"More than anything in the world."

"We'll get this business with John settled."

"I hope he isn't in camp when we ride in."

"If he's there we'll face him together. He left you. He deserted you when you needed him."

"I want only to be with you always, Cole."

It was almost twilight when they rode into camp. Campfires were blazing. Men and women intermingled and were laughing and talking boisterously. It seemed to Lavender to be like a big party of merrymaking. Everyone wanted to talk to Cole, to make much of his coming. There were shouts of "Cole. Cole. Welcome back."

Quantrill, himself, emerged from an adobe hut to greet Cole with enthusiasm. He looked at Lavender clinging to Cole's arm and roared, "Ah, you have the beautiful one with you."

"Is John here?" Cole asked.

"No, he is gone with some of the boys to Louisiana. I have sent many out to spread the word. We will have one last reunion."

"One last reunion?"

"Yes, I have so planned it. You have brought the

205

gold. I expected you to bring the gold. I could always depend on you, Cole."

Quantrill was silent a moment then went on, "I am weary. I want time to think and plan for a great new empire. I want a new life. Charley Quantrill is dead. The new Quantrill, William Quantrill, will live a different life."

Lavender later told Cole, "He looks sick."

"Yes, I think Quantrill thinks he is going to die. He talks of one last reunion."

They were free now to saunter around the camp. Cole introduced her to many of the men. The women stared at her and hardly spoke.

"They do not seem too friendly," Lavender said.

"You are new to them and you are very beautiful. To them you are a rival for their men's affections. They will be friendlier when they find you are my woman and mine alone."

She asked about Melon. She had gone off with Trigger Malone to inform some of the band up Kansas way about the reunion, she was told.

In the coming days, Lavender found that the men who followed Quantrill were rough and tough and yet they seemed to have a sense of caring about each other. She asked Cole about this.

"We took an oath, Lavender. I cannot tell you what it is but the oath is sacred to us."

The camp, she found, was made up of adobe mud huts and shacks. The women did the cooking. The men hunted and at night, they loved. Lavender had supposed, remembering Ruby's words, that there was much interchanging of partners, that there would be open love-making for all to watch. But this was not the case.

She asked Cole about this. "It is different here in camp, Lavender. When a few are out on a job and the women are along there may be trading off. Ruby, of course, delighted in such goings on."

"I haven't seen Kate."

"Quantrill sent her off with Tom Hopkins and a group up Missouri way to spread the word of the reunion. They said she was mad as a hornet. Didn't want to go. Guess Quantrill wanted a rest. She's a real hellcat."

She became friends with a woman named Lacey. Lacey was a spirited redhead with a buxom figure. Lacey was in love with "Bloody Jim" Anderson.

"He's my man," she told Lavender. "I left my ma and pa to follow 'Bloody Jim.' Been with him now five years. Sure he does things I don't like but he's my man. I'd die for him."

"Is he good to you?" Lavender said.

"Can't say he is. He gets mean sometimes."

"Lacey, how come there aren't any children in camp? Don't the women get in the family way? Don't they ever have babies?"

Lacey laughed.

"Quantrill wouldn't have any squalling babies around. You ought to know that. They'd just be in the way when we had to have a quick get away."

"What happens when a woman thinks she's going to have a baby?"

"Do you think you're in the family way now?"

"I could be."

"Well, don't worry. I've got plenty of tansy root stashed away. Believe me, Jim would kill me if I told him I was going to have a baby."

207

"He doesn't like children?"

"Hates 'em."

That night when she and Cole were together in their adobe hut she cuddled close to him. "I love you, Cole," she whispered.

"I love you, sweetheart."

He took her then with wild abandon. And she thought, as she gave her body and her mind completely to him, that it was always as exquisitely beautiful as the first time. She always reached the heights of ecstasy when he caressed the inside of her thighs. With every accelerating tremor of her body, they rode together slowly, lovingly rising and falling together until they reached the peak of pleasure and love. Afterwards they would hold each other close in an afterglow of radiance.

Tonight she whispered, "Darling, when two people love as you and I do there is a very good chance we'll make a baby."

"You are a darling," he smiled in the darkness. "Make a baby! What a beautiful way to tell me you are with child."

"Oh, Cole, can you tell it? I want to have your baby. I'm not sure yet but Lacey and I talked about it today."

"I guess Lacey knows more about the subject than anyone else in camp," he said dryly.

"She said Jim didn't like children and that Quantrill didn't want any in camp."

"They would be in the way."

She sat up in the darkness and spoke earnestly, "Cole, you said you were going to get a spread and we could settle down. We can get married later on?"

He drew her down gently and put her head on his shoulder. "Our future is too uncertain, Lavender. Get tansy or whatever it is that Lacey uses."

Lavender was silent. She was thinking of her baby with its little face like a white rose.

"We don't want a bastard," he said definitely and she felt as though he had struck her. "Later on after we're married you can have a dozen babies for all I'll care."

The next day, she watched Lacy mix a half ounce of powdered tansy in water. She drank it and felt her insides on fire. Long after Cole had fallen asleep that night, Lavender wept silently.

Chapter 21

They came from every direction. All those who had ever ridden under the Black Banner of Quantrill were gathering together. They came with their women. They shouted, they shrieked with joy at seeing comrades with whom they had ridden stirrup to stirrup. They embraced. They gave the Rebel yell. They danced around the campfires at night and they drank much whisky.

The night of the Reunion came. The women were herded together to be taken away. Some screamed they didn't want to go. They didn't want to miss any part of the celebration. Quantrill laughed and said to be generous in supplying the women with whisky. And also generous with the barbecue. And so they were herded off.

Lavender went willingly. She wanted no part of the men who had ridden into camp. There must be at least five-hundred of them and many looked like ruffians. Kate had come too, as had Melon. Melon was delighted to see Lavender. Kate glared at her.

They were taken a distance of at least a mile away to await the end of the festivities at camp.

"It's so good to see you again, Lavender," Melon said over and over. "I often wondered if I would ever meet up with you again."

Lavender told her of John's desertion. She told her of her love for Cole.

"You are a lucky woman, Lavender," Melon said softly. "I, too, love Cole. I think all women love Cole."

It was a full moon. They sat around the campfire. They ate of the barbecue. Kate was walking around the group.

"She thinks she is our queen because she is Quantrill's woman," Melon whispered to Lavender.

"She does not like me," Lavender said.

"She is jealous of your beauty."

"I'm afraid of her."

"Don't be afraid of her. She wouldn't dare hurt you. She's too afraid of Cole. Just stand up to her."

Stand up to this vicious uncouth woman? Lavender thought.

"Our men will want us back before long," predicted Goldie, a woman with long dirty blonde hair. "My man can't do without me."

"And you can't do without him," Kate sneered. "I wonder . . . I wonder," she stopped talking to stare at Lavender, "I wonder how that one can please Cole. He's used to a real woman."

"Pay no attention to her," Melon said very low to Lavender.

"She tries to be so lily-white and pure." Kate went on. "She won't please our Cole very long. Cole is all man."

As she talked, she was drinking from a tin of whisky.

"She'll get drunk and pass out before long," Melon said.

"I want to watch the Reunion," Melon whispered to Lavender presently when true to Melon's prediction, Kate was sprawled on the ground passed out.

211

"They would kill us if we watched," Lavender whispered.

"They won't know it. Come."

Lavender followed Melon as she led the way. It seemed to Lavender they had walked a far distance when Melon whispered, "Here we are. We can watch from here."

Lavender sank to the ground exhausted. They were behind yucca plants which shielded them from view of those below participating in the festivities. She smelled the barbecued pig and scarcely breathed as she watched the activities below. She saw a blazing orange and gold campfire and the shadowy figures eerily silhouetted against the flames.

Quantrill stood alone on a rise. He looked handsome and stood erect. Quantrill! Looking at him she knew why his very name held magic! He was like a god as he stood there. She knew now why the men who had ridden under the Black Flag would face death for him. Even from the distance where she watched, she felt his magnetic power.

They are like they are under some kind of spell, she thought, watching the hundreds of men. Their rapt faces stared at Quantrill.

"Welcome, welcome," they cried as if with one voice. "You are our leader."

The old rebel yell rang out as Cole Younger, the firelight turning his blond hair to gold, stepped forward. Quantrill began to chant and Lavender realized she was witnessing the oath known as The Black Oath.

Cole had said he could not tell her about the oath, only that it was sacred to the followers of Quantrill. Quantrill's voice boomed out over the gathering. He spoke easily, confidently, majestically.

"The oath is given only in the dead of night," Melon whispered. She wished she hadn't come. If they were caught Cole would be furious and Quantrill would demand their death. There were to be no witnesses to the oath, only participants and they were bound by secrecy.

A hush fell over the audience as Quantrill said, "And to succor one another at all hazards, we have pledged ourselves most sacredly, and are bound by ties much stronger than honor can impose."

Two men stepped forward now. Evidently they were candidates who were to be initiated. They were escorted by four men clothed in red and black suits and wearing hideous masks over their faces.

Lavender recognized Cole's voice now. "With this understanding of what will be required of you, are you willing to proceed?" They were going through the ritual, Lavender realized.

Quantrill spoke now, "In the name of God and Devil, the one to punish and the other to reward, and by the powers of light and darkness, good and evil, here under the black arch of heaven's avenging symbol, I pledge and consecrate my heart, my brain, my body and my limbs, and swear by all the powers of hell and heaven to devote my life to obedience to my superiors that no danger or peril shall deter me from executing their orders, that I will exert every possible means in my power for the extermination of Federals, Jayhawkers and their abettors, that in fighting those whose serpent trail has winnowed the fair fields and possessions of our allies and sympathizers, I will show no mercy but strike with an avenging arm, so long as breath remains."

Melon murmured, "I wish we hadn't come."

But wild horses couldn't have pulled Lavender from the spot now. She strained to hear Quantrill continue, "I further pledge my heart, my brain, my body and my limbs, never to betray a comrade, that I will submit to all tortures the cunning that mankind can inflict and suffer the most horrible death rather than reveal a single secret of this organization, or a single word of this, my oath."

"Let's go," Melon whispered.

"No, I want to hear more," Lavender answered.

"I further pledge my heart," Quantrill boomed, "my brain, my body and my limbs, never to forsake a comrade when there is hope, even at the risk of great peril, of saving him from falling into the hands of our enemies, that I will sustain Quantrill's Guerillas with all my might and defend them with my blood, and if need be, die with them. In every extremity, I will never withhold my aid, nor abandon the cause with which I now cast my fortunes, my honor, and my life. And before violating a single clause or implied pledge of this obligation."

He paused. There was absolute silence before he went on, "I will pray to an avenging God and an unmerciful Devil to tear out my heart and roast it over flames of sulphur, that my head may be split open and my brains scattered over the earth, that my body may be ripped open and my bowels torn out and fed to carrion birds, that each of my limbs be broken with stones and then cut off, by inches, that they may feed the foulest birds of the air."

Quantrill paused and the air rang with the Rebel yell.

"And lastly," he spoke slowly now, "may my soul be given unto torment, that it may be submerged in melted metal and be stirred by the fumes of hell. And this punishment be meted out to me through all eternity, in the name of God and Devil. Amen."

The voices rang out again, "Amen. Amen. Amen."

Lavender listened and marveled at Quantrill's delivery of the ritual. His memory was incredible! Not once did he falter, and it had been some time since he had ridden at the head of his men. There had been something majestic and yet sad about him as he stood there. He realized, no doubt, that this would be the last time he would address his followers. Tomorrow his two lieutenants George Todd and Bill Anderson would take over. The Quantrill Raiders would fade into history.

As Lavender and Melon crept away from the camp, she was thankful that Cole had turned down Quantrill's offer of leading half of the band.

John had not returned for the Reunion but Cole had told her Frank and Jesse James were there. Cole loved Frank and hated Jesse. He had told her that fact often in the days they had travelled the trail together. He said Frank could be trusted but Jesse would betray his own grandmother for gold.

Lavender and Melon rejoined the women now. No one had noticed their absence and they joined a group around the campfire.

Some were getting restless. They wanted to go back to the big camp and join in the festivities there.

"You know you can't go until you're sent for," Melon said.

"Well, if my man don't send for me soon, I'm goin' to him."

"I would rather stay here all night," Lavender told Melon.

"Me, too," Melon agreed. "They'll all be drunk and some of 'em get mighty mean. Might be a killin' or two."

Presently a messenger came to summon the women back to camp. He hoisted the drunken Kate on his horse and rode off into the night.

"I'm not going," Lavender told Melon.

"Cole might be angry," Melon warned.

"I'm going to stay here."

Some went eagerly and some went reluctantly.

"My friend, Abbie, came to no good end at one of these reunions," a woman told Lavender. "The men all get drunk and not knowing what they're doin'. They kilt her. About ten of 'em passin' her around one to 'nother. I don't want to go but my man would kill me if I don't."

"These men can tear a woman right in two if they want," another put in.

Several of the women lingered behind and joined Lavender at the campfire.

"I'm not goin'," one of them declared. "I'm not goin' and get all bruised up. Some of 'em are like animals. They don't care what they do to a woman."

"I ain't goin'," another spoke up. "I reckon my man will come after me but I'm not goin'."

Lavender looked in the flames and wondered if Cole would take another woman. The thought was unbearable but she could not force herself to join in that drunken wild orgy. Presently they heard the sound of galloping hoofbeats. A horseman was tearing into camp.

Lavender braced herself wondering if it was Cole. Had he come for her?

The horseman had jumped from his horse and Lavender saw it was a lean tall man with a sunburned leathery face. He seemed angry and his voice was slurred as he approached the woman who had declared she wasn't going although she reckoned her man would come after her. Well, he had come after her. He let out a volley of oaths and curses as he jerked the frightened woman to her feet.

He slapped her across her face as he clutched the front of her dress. She was like a rag doll as he battered her back and forth, slapping her, hitting her. Then he put her on the horse, jumped on in back of her holding her on. Her face was beaten to a pulp and she was moaning as they rode off into the darkness.

"God help her," one of the women whispered. "He'll kill her for sure before he's through."

The others around the campfire were silent. Presently they looked at each other and decided they had best go back to camp. All but Lavender. She sat alone.

Chapter 22

Cole came for her late the next morning. He was cheerful. He kissed her and hugged her and complimented her on staying away from the big camp.

"It was rough and it was wild," he said simply.

"Did you have a woman, Cole?" she asked. She had to ask. She had to know.

"Frank and Jesse and I talked. We did not take a woman. Not that there weren't plenty available. We talked until dawn, Lavender. They are riding with us to Belle's place at Scyene."

"Belle Starr?"

"Yeah. We're going to Belle's place. Belle's been doing pretty good. She got thirty thousand dollars in gold from a wealthy old Creek Indian in his house on the North Canadian River. Tortured him until he told them the hiding place."

"We're not going to stay there, are we, Cole?"

"No. It'll be a good stopping place for us as we go back to Kansas or maybe Missouri."

She met Frank and Jesse James that very day. And she never forgot the meeting. Frank was cordial and overly friendly. Jesse stared at her with cold blue eyes which blinked, and said simply, "You're Cole's woman?"

Melon clung to her. "I hope," she said tearfully, "that

our paths will cross again. I love you, Lavender."

The trip to Scyene was uneventful. Jesse said little but sometimes his blue eyes were fixed on her and she felt herself uncomfortable under his intense gaze. Frank was friendly. Frank and Cole were close friends. Jesse was always aloof.

They arrived at Scyene and went directly to Belle's which was known as the Shirley Place. She took one look at Cole and melted into his arms.

"You are my love, Cole Younger," she cried. "You are my love. I told you that when I was a young 'un and you just stared at me with those big beautiful eyes of yourn. But you are my love."

Cole laughed easily. "Oh, come, Belle, that was a long time ago. A lot of things have happened since then."

"But nothin's changed my love for you, Cole. I would die for you."

The Shirley place was a barren farm. It showed signs of neglect. The barn was falling down, the house needed repair. Belle seemed oblivious to the neglect of the place. Her eyes sparkled as she told of the hauls they had been making.

"We been makin' out real good. Hope you'll stay and join us. You, Cole, and your friends, Jesse and Frank James, will be a big help to us." She ignored Lavender.

"Where's Pearl?" Cole presently asked.

"I toted her and baby Jim over to my ma's. Ma says I ain't a fittin' mama. She can have the care of 'em for all I care. I ain't got no use for kids."

She presently asked if the visitors would like to ride into town and take a look around. The saloon had a piano which she liked to play. They could have a real good time! Lavender begged off. She would rest, she said.

Just before they went out the door, Belle, splendid in a creamy white Stetson with a flowing ostrich plume, said to Cole, "Guess you heard what happened to your brother John?"

"No."

"Well he was in Dallas not so long ago. He took to braggin' that he was your brother. He took to wearin' six-shooters and boasting of his markmanship. One day last winter he persuaded a drunken old bar fly to let him shoot the pipe out of his mouth at ten paces. The old man, so drunk he could hardly stand, agreed for the price of a drink."

Lavender listened and wondered if John was dead. She waited breathlessly for Belle to continue her story. "John aimed and fired. The pipe and part of the old man's face disappeared."

"That crazy John!" Cole said.

"So did John disappear. A warrant was sworn out for John and Deputy Sheriff Nichols of Dallas County came here to serve the warrant. John was waitin', his finger hot on that trigger. He kilt Deputy Sheriff Nichols. I hid him out and then sent him on to Missouri."

"I'm thanking you for what you did for my brother," Cole said.

"The only reason I did it was for you, Cole. I never did take any hankerin' for your brother, John. It was just for you."

They left then and Lavender, watching them go, wondered how much longer they would stay. She sensed Jesse was anxious to move on. Cole had told her Jesse was in love with his cousin Zerelda Mimms and he was anxious to get back home.

220

"Did Jesse and Frank James take women at the reunion?" she asked.

"I told you we talked. We had no time for women."

"Was that the only reason?" she asked wistfully. She wanted him to say he loved her. She wanted him to say he neither wanted nor needed another woman.

"Yes," he said gruffly, dismissing the subject.

Lavender watched as Belle, with the plume flying and her long hair flowing in the breeze, leaned from her saddle to talk to Cole.

The days went by. Lavender saw Cole basking in the admiration of the charming Belle. Jesse was plainly bored. He did not enjoy the daily visits to the town's saloon to hear the boisterous Belle pound on the piano.

Cole enjoyed galloping into town with her. She made a colorful picture as with her long red velvet dress draped over one arm, she would call loudly for whisky or sit down at the nearest faro table. She played with the sky the limit. She had plenty of money. Her fierce and wild temper made her someone to be careful not to cross so when she rode through the town whooping and firing her guns, she was never arrested. Windows crashed and signs were splintered and men ducked behind wagons and into alleys. But no one ever tried to disarm or arrest her.

"That hellcat is going to get herself killed and us with her," Jesse complained one evening after a wild time in town.

Cole laughed indulgently. "She's just a high-spirited gal."

"We've been in some tight places together," Jesse said to Cole and Frank. "We've come through because we're plenty smart. We use our heads. But I ain't goin' to get

221

killed on account of some of her crazy shenanigans."

"You ain't scair't," Belle blazed.

"Hell, no. I'm gettin' out of here tomorrow," he said to Cole and Frank. "If you all want to stay, you stay. This woman's crazy as hell."

"It's time we were movin' on," Frank said. Cole said nothing. Lavender looked at him. His handsome face was expressionless.

"When we shot up a town, Cole," Jesse said earnestly, his blue eyes blinking as they did when he became excited, "it was for a purpose. We didn't just do it for fun. I don't see any sense in cracking windows just for the kick of it."

Frank nodded. Cole said nothing.

"Remember that robbery of the stage between Austin and San Antonio? Five of us, all masked, went up the road and met the stage, presented our pistols and ordered a halt. The driver asked us what we wanted. And I told him we aimed to hold him up."

Frank laughed, "I remember. You said, 'goddamn you! Keep your mouth shut or we'll make you!' "

Jesse continued, "One of the passengers was Bishop Gregg of the Episcopal Church. 'Do you mean to rob us?' the Bishop asked. And I told him I intended to relieve him of his surplus funds and useless jewelry. He could call it robbery if he wished."

"And he said he was a minister of the Gospel," Frank took up the story. "He wanted to keep the watch. He said it was a gift from a friend."

"I told him the disciples didn't have watches. I told him we'd take his money too for he was commanded when he travelled to take no purse or scrip. If he wanted to live by the Book, he had to abide by it!"

"I remember it all," Frank said. "We cut the mail bags open and cut out the two lead horses from the stage team and left them to drag the four-horse coach with two horses."

"Those were exciting days. We can have more of such good happenings when we get back home. I aim to go tomorrow. Just told you about the robbery to remind you there's more to livin' than staying here in this dry forsaken land."

Cole spoke now. "Belle would like for us to stay and join up with her. She plans on moving up to 'The Nations,' which is the Indian-held section of Oklahoma. We would headquarter there."

Jesse stared at Cole for a long moment before he spoke. "You ain't serious, Cole! You can't be thinkin' of joinin' up with that woman. She ain't nothin' but a horse thief. Cole, we're big time."

"There isn't any call to talk mean about Belle," Cole said quickly.

"I aim to leave tomorrow," Jesse said curtly.

Lavender looked at Cole. His face was unreadable. What was he thinking? Oh, please, please Cole. Let's leave tomorrow with Jesse. For a moment she thought she had spoken the words aloud but she sat silently waiting.

Chapter 23

Long after Lavender had gone to bed, she lay awake wondering what Cole would decide to do. She slept on a pallet in a corner. Cole slept next to her but in these weeks since they had come to the Shirley place, he had made no effort to make love to her.

Her body ached for his touch. She would reach over and pat him lovingly just to let him know she loved him but he did not reciprocate. It was as though he wanted to display no emotion in front of the wild and tempestuous Belle.

He and Belle sat at the table and whispered long after she had gone to bed. The lamp light made Cole's hair shine like gold and revealed the love light shining in Belle's eyes as she talked. Lavender wondered what they were whispering about. Were they making plans to meet later on? Or was she persuading Cole to stay with her now?

She finally fell into a troubled sleep. She did not know what time Cole finally came to bed but shortly after dawn, he prodded her awake.

"We're going," he said simply.

Belle was belligerent as she served them coffee and a bit of side pork and biscuits. One of her hands, the men who followed her and whom she called her "jolly lads," had made the biscuits and they were as hard as rocks.

"I don't want you to go," Belle said over and over to Cole. "You belong here with me. You ain't even seen Pearl this trip. 'Tain't right for you to go ridin' off like this. You and me belong together."

"Jesse and Frank and I got a big job comin' up soon and we got to make plans," Cole answered.

Belle was still pouting when they were ready to leave. She grabbed Cole around the neck and held on for dear life.

"I love you. I love you," she cried. "You will always be my love, Cole Younger."

When presently they were on the trail, Jesse said, "I never saw a crazier woman in my life."

"She's just high-spirited," Cole defended her.

"High-spirited, hell!" Jesse said.

Lavender said nothing. She was glad they were on their way back home. She hoped she would never see Belle Starr again. They were going home by way of the Ouachita Mountains, Cole told her. They had gold buried in a cave there. They would pick it up and if luck was with them they might try robbing a stagecoach or two.

Jesse grinned. "There's easy pickin's. All those rich city folks goin' to the Springs for the baths. The train goes to Malvern, the transfer point and from there the rich bitches have to take the Concord stagecoach."

"And we'll be waiting for them at Gaines Place, about five miles from Hot Springs. They stop there to water the horses," Cole explained.

It was a cold damp day when they arrived at Gaines Place. Lavender thought with longing of the luxurious hotels at Hot Springs where she might sink her weary body into the hot mineral water. They waited shivering, shielded by giant pines, for the stage to come into view.

"Here it comes," Jesse yelled.

"Stay back," Cole cautioned Lavender.

It was all over in a few moments. The unsuspecting stagecoach driver was trapped as were the fourteen passengers. Jesse courteously notified the passengers that all that was wanted was their money and jewels.

One passenger, badly afflicted with rheumatism, was allowed to remain in the coach. The others were ordered out. The male passengers were arranged in a circle so they could be watched. The women were permitted to seat themselves on handkerchiefs while a methodical search for valuables was conducted. Lavender, watching, shivered.

One man with a decided southern drawl said he had been a colonel in the Confederacy under General Stonewall Jackson. He was permitted to retain his purse and was treated with great respect. Cole bowed to the man and told him they would not take the money of any man who had fought for the Confederacy. Cole then apologized to the group for having robbed them and assured them they, the bandits, needed the money and jewels more than they did. They broke open the mail bags that had been put on the stagecoach at Malvern and searched the registered letters. They then rode off.

Safe in a cave in the Ouachita Mountains, Lavender began to cry. Cole held her safe and assured her she had helped them.

They divided the loot four ways. Jesse glared at Cole when Cole said Lavender was to receive a fourth. Frank agreed with Cole and that was that!

The rain was coming down in torrents now, beating

against the curtain of pines that shielded the entrance way to the cave. Inside it was cold and damp and water oozed from the rock formation towering above them.

"This is my castle," Jesse affirmed gaily.

"Damned cold in here," Frank said. Their breath came in spurts of cold air.

Jesse was looking around the familiar cave when Frank said, "I saw a picture not long ago of a family gathered around a fireplace. The mama was roasting chestnuts and all the children had little bowls and . . ."

"Hell, Frank," Jesse cut in, "you wouldn't be satisfied sitting around the fire eating roasted chestnuts."

Frank shivered. "It would be better than being here where it's cold and damp and we could catch pneumonia."

"You're getting soft in your old age," Jesse scoffed and went into the adjoining cave where he flung himself on one of the damp pads and went fast asleep.

He laughed about it later when he awoke thinking it was a great joke but Lavender, shivering in the dampness of the cave, did not laugh. She was weary and still frightened and trembling from the experience of watching the holdup of the stagecoach. Cole slept close to her that night while Frank and Jesse were in the adjoining cave. They loved with wild abandon.

"It's like it used to be," she whispered.

"I love you," he said simply. "We'll go home now."

"I'll be glad to see Mama," Lavender said. "But it's going to be hard to tell her and Pa about Mint. Oh, Cole, so much has happened."

"I know, dear," he comforted.

"They won't understand about Mint," Lavender predicted. "It's going to be just terrible to try to tell them."

But she wrong. Pa was dead. He had passed away quietly in his sleep the preceding winter. Mama had cancer and was so ill she seemed hardly to recognize Lavender. There was no need to tell her of Mint. Mama had but one thought and that was to join Pa.

"My darling Lavender," Cole said kissing her tenderly, "I will leave you here with your mother. I will go to the home place and see what I can find out about John. You'll want to nurse your mother back to health, sweetheart."

He left then and Lavender wondered when she would see him again. The days went by. The doctor came and went. Mama lay like a wax doll, wanting only to die.

"She has the eatin' disease," the doctor said. "It's eatin' her."

"Why don't you come out and say she has cancer?" Lavender asked.

"We don't talk about that," the doctor said meekly. "There is only one thing to do and that is operate."

He operated on Mama. The operating table was the kitchen table and her blood spurted to the ceiling. She died and Lavender looked at the doctor and asked, "You knew she would die, why did you put her through this torture?"

He was evasive. "We do what we must do," he said.

Lavender wrote Cole that Mama was dead.

Two weeks later, Lavender had a visitor. She had expected Cole, but it was Jim Younger, Cole's brother.

"Lavender," he said quietly, taking her hand in his. She had not seen too much of this brother of John and Cole's. He was the quiet brother who stayed always more or less in the background.

"Cole sent me," he said. "I'm so sorry about the death of your mother. Cole sends his sympathy."

Lavender stared for a moment not comprehending. She was very pale but she was never more beautiful as she repeated his words, "Cole sends his sympathy."

"He's sorry but he couldn't get away right now."

Lavender wanted to cry out, wanted to ask Jim Younger what was more important than Cole coming to her now when she needed him? But Jim was so concerned, so sympathetic she could only invite him into the house.

"Lavender, perhaps I shouldn't tell you this now. I know you are heartsick about your mother's death," he said and stopped talking, groping for words.

"Has something happened to Cole?" she asked. Yes, she thought, that must be it. Otherwise Cole would be here.

"John is dead," Jim said bluntly.

"Dead!"

"It was at Monegaw Springs in St. Clair County, Missouri that it happened, Lavender," Jim went on. "John was staying at the home of a friend, Theodorick Snuffer. There was a detective from Chicago and a St. Louis detective and a deputy sheriff rode out to apprehend John at the Springs."

Lavender felt an impulse to shriek, "Don't tell me about this," but she listened as he went on.

"The three man-hunters spent the night at Roscie and early the next morning, March 17th, they started for the farm home of Snuffer. When they arrived there, John was inside eating. Always suspicious of strangers, he remained in hiding. The man-hunters asked Snuffer directions to a certain point but when they didn't follow those directions, but took a different route, John followed them."

Poor John, Lavender thought, poor suspicious John. John, with the hate always bottled up in him.

"Snuffer told me this, Lavender," Jim went on. "John caught up with the man-hunters and the man Allen drew his revolver and shot John in the neck, severing the jugular vein. Although mortally wounded, John fired both barrels of his shotgun into Allen's chest, dropped the gun, drew his own revolver and chased after the other two who had fled. John drew close and fired and killed the one man. Almost simultaneously the other shot John."

Lavender, staring at Jim as he talked thought, I'm a widow. Her mind could not grasp that fact. She couldn't be a widow. All the widows she ever knew were old and wrinkled and had white hair. She was too young to be a widow. And yet with this thought, came the sudden realization that she was free now. Free to marry Cole.

And then on a June day when the world was shining and singing in summer splendor and beauty, Lavender had another visitor. Leaves gleamed on the poplars and elms, and lilacs nodded everywhere and varnished daisies lined the paths. Larks trilled sweetly above in a blue, blue sky as Lavender sat on the back porch hulling peas.

She felt rather than saw someone come around the side of the house. When she looked up expectantly, a squarely built man was standing there, smiling at her. It took Lavender a moment to realize it was Cole. Cole Younger!

"Cole," she whispered setting aside the pan of peas

and going instantly to him. Deep peaceful waters seemed to be reaching her heart. Through the heartbreak and sorrow of losing her mother, the surprise news of John's death, she had thought constantly of Cole and now he was here.

"My darling," he whispered.

Tears flooded her beautiful eyes. "Cole," she cried. "You're back."

They went to sit on the porch and he said, "Lavender, my sweetheart, you haven't been out of my mind for a minute since we parted. I came back wondering if you could possibly be as beautiful as I remembered. And you are much more beautiful."

And Lavender, looking at him, knew that her hours of memory had not distorted him or changed him. His gray eyes were the same, his fair hair the same and his fine friendly smile the same. All as wonderful as she remembered.

"It seems so long," she murmured.

"I've come to take you with me."

"We can be married now," she said dreamily.

"No, you'll want a mourning period before we are married," he said smoothly.

"But . . ."

He stopped her words with a kiss. "My two aunts, Aunt Mary and Aunt Martha, are living on the Younger homestead. I want you to stay with them."

"But Cole, we will be married?" she had to ask the question.

"Of course, my darling."

"I'll be Mrs. Cole Younger," she breathed happily.

"If only I could offer you a name unstained and unsullied. True, I have done some things of which I am ashamed such as the burning of Lawrenceville. And several other things. But Lavender," he said earnestly, "I am blamed for much that I did not do."

"I know, my darling," she comforted. "We'll go away. We'll make a new start."

They made plans as she prepared to go with him back to the Younger homestead. He was preparing material for a book to be published the following spring. And he talked of another project he and the James boys were working on. "With the money from the book and this last big job, we can get us a real spread out West," he said eagerly.

"Tell me about your aunts. Will they like me?"

"They are going to love you. Their names are Aunt Mary and Aunt Martha. Just like in the Bible. And like the Mary and Martha in the Bible they are very different although they, too, are sisters."

"How are they different?"

"Just like in the Bible, Mary enjoys life. Martha is a real drudge always worrying about trifles."

"They do sound as though they are different from each other."

"Remember where it says in the Bible that Martha is troubled by many things? Well, that is the way my Aunt Martha is. She's always worrying for fear the table is cluttered or the floor not swept to perfection."

"I'm sure I will love them both," Lavender said gallantly.

In the weeks to come, Lavender was to think often of Cole's words. Aunt Mary and Aunt Martha were very different from each other, both in appearance and temperament. Lavender found it hard to believe that they were related. Lavender loved Cole's Aunt Mary.

She made life such fun. And Aunt Mary was beautiful. Her eyes were pale blue, widely-spaced and her skin was lily-white and soft and unwrinkled.

Aunt Martha was jealous of Aunt Mary, jealous of her beauty and her bubbling personality. And she scoffed at Lavender's open admiration of Aunt Mary. Lavender noticed how the men gravitated toward Aunt Mary who had buried two husbands. Aunt Martha had never been married.

And Lavender thought, as she had thought so many times before, that there are two types of people in the world, the kind you love and the kind you endure. She guessed that was the way Cole felt about Frank and Jesse James. Frank, he loved and Jesse, he endured.

Cole had told her of how Jesse had tried to get him killed by telling George Shepherd that Cole was gunning for him. He said, "George was just out of a Kentucky prison for a bank robbery at Russellville. Jesse told me that George was gunning for me. Luckily, Frank told me of Jesse's scheme and nipped the whole thing in the bud."

She loved to hear Cole tell of his adventures, but his many narrow escapes saddened her.

Aunt Mary was an incurable romanticist and liked to tease Cole about Belle Starr's love for him.

"Lavender knows there isn't a word of truth in it," Cole would laugh. "It's just a fairy tale. How the 'Cherokee maiden fell in love with the dashing captain!' And, as a matter of fact, Belle Starr was not a Cherokee."

"I'm sure Belle isn't as pretty as our Lavender," Aunt Mary put in.

"Lavender can vouch for that," Cole said. "We stayed over at Belle's place. Lavender can tell you all about the wild and impulsive Belle."

Aunt Martha snorted, "Belle Starr indeed! She's nothin' but trash!"

Cole grinned. "Come now, Aunt Martha, she's just a poor woman trying to make it through this old world. Life hasn't been too good to her."

"She's a liar," Aunt Martha declared vehemently. "I heard how she tells that girl of hers named Pearl is yourn."

"If it gives her pleasure to tell that lie, let her," Cole laughed.

"I don't think it's right for her to pass herself off as Mrs. Cole Younger," Lavender said indignantly.

"No, I don't like her doing that," Cole admitted. "But, honey, there's so many tales out about the Youngers, I guess she figured one more wouldn't make any difference."

Lavender was curious about Cole's relationship with Jesse James of the blinking blue eyes. "What year did you meet up with Jesse?" she asked now.

"In 1866 if I remember rightly. It was just a year after Jim was ambushed while riding with Quantrill near Smiley, Kentucky. Jim expected to be executed on the spot when captured but much to his surprise was confined to the military prison at Alton, Illinois and was released the latter part of 1865."

"I remember that was when your Ma came back here to the home place," Aunt Mary said.

"Yes, we were all anxious to make a new beginning. Father's fortune was gone, scattered far and wide as a result of the War. We thought we could return to the farm and rebuild the family fortune, but it was not to be. Sectional feelings ran too high in Missouri with too many border disputes."

"Those were sad days," Aunt Mary said wistfully.

"We were the target," Cole went on soberly, "for too many hatreds nourished by the people. It was then a band of self-appointed Vigilantes took John to the barn and hanged him. Each time he lost consciousness they revived him and repeated the act. But he refused to divulge one word about where I was. Finally, they took the rope from his neck, dragged him down the road and left him half-dead by the road."

And Lavender listening, thought again of John being as two people. One cold and hard and at the other times, kind and loving. Not, of course, as Cole was loving. She looked at Cole now and marvelled at her love for him. She smiled into his gray eyes and flashed him a message, "I love you. I love you. I love you."

At night, she lay in her soft warm bed listening to the night sounds, the cicadas humming through the evenings. She could hear Cole in his room down the hall. He would be pacing back and forth, back and forth. She knew he wanted her as badly as she wanted him. She ached for the feel of him in her. She wanted them to be as one. They were one in heart and soul. It was not right for them to be apart now. She had to cling to the bed. Otherwise she would run down the hall to Cole's room and fling herself at him.

But it was fear of stern Aunt Martha that kept her from doing this. Aunt Martha occupied the room between them and Lavender imagined the woman lying awake all night listening, waiting for them to try to get together.

They could meet in the orchard during the day. This was small comfort to her aching frustrated body but she must be satisfied with his cuddling her and kissing her eager lips. She could feel his passion mounting in him as he held her close.

"I want you, my dearest darling," he would murmur over and over.

"Sweetheart, I want you too."

"It is only a little bit longer. We will soon be together always."

Chapter 24

Cole's book was coming along beautifully. He had always kept a diary of his activities and the book was a long narration of the wrongs visited on him and his family during and after the War. He told in vivid detail of the happenings of those years between 1861 and 1865 up to the present time. He wanted to write frankly of Quantrill. He told Lavender of his admiration for the man and yet like John, Quantrill was really two different people.

"He had an unbelievable streak of cruelty in him," Cole told her. "This sadistic streak made him do things that even revolted his loyal followers. He could not stand the sight of a cat without destroying it. He could not stand to see a snake without nailing it to a tree and watching in delight as it tore itself to shreds trying to escape."

"How horrible!" Lavender breathed.

"He had his worst fight with his lieutenant, 'Bloody Bill' Anderson, because Quantrill saw a fluffy gray cat in a little boy's arms and made the boy leave it go and he shot it in the head. 'Bloody Bill,' as tough as he was, was plenty mad about that."

"How can you admire him as you do?" Lavender asked.

"Because of his leadership. Lavender, he was a born leader. He was of the caliber of a Napoleon. He was as great a leader as George Washington or would have been if it hadn't been for his insane streak of jealousy and cruelty."

"Jealousy?"

"Yes, he resented it if anyone spoke admiringly of someone's leadership qualities. He would become angry."

"He sounds like a very strange man," Lavender said.

"Yes," Cole agreed, "he was a very strange man. Do you know that he never once sent his mother money and she was always in desperate circumstances? I heard, not too long ago, he had given Kate Clarke gold to open a whore house."

They days went by. Cole was often gone now to hold meetings with the James' brothers.

"Our plans are coming along just fine," he told Lavender. "We plan this one last big job. Then you and I will have plenty of money to go westward and make a new start. The book will be finished by then and it should bring in a tidy sum. Our future is bright, my darling."

And now men began to come to the Younger place in the dark reaches of the night. She would hear them come stealthily into the house. She could hear their whispers.

"We are making plans, my darling," Cole would tell Lavender later. "There must be much planning in an undertaking of this kind. We must have trusted men."

"I'm frightened. We don't need the gold from this job. Let's just leave now. Your book is practically finished."

"No, I've promised Frank James. I can't go back on my word. It will soon be over, sweetheart."

But Lavender felt a cold premonition of fear. Like a fingertip of ice it touched her heart and was ever with her.

"I wish Cole would forget about this one last job he talks of," she told Aunt Mary.

"Men are strange creatures," Aunt Mary said wisely. "There are things they feel they must do."

"I've tried to tell him to forget about this job but he ignores me."

"Lavender, you are young and there are some things you must learn. Never try to talk your man out of something he has his heart set on," she advised. "Let him do what he must do."

"I can't bear the thought of his being hurt or worse yet, killed."

"Cole is well aware of the chances he must take. He has always come through unscathed. I always said he leads a charmed life."

"You comfort me, Aunt Mary."

"Come, let's mix some honey and the juice of lily bulbs and put it on our faces and think beautiful thoughts," Aunt Mary suggested.

Aunt Martha, who came into the room in time to hear her words, scoffed. "It's better you learn how to make pea hull soup and salve and cockleburr cough syrup than that syrup to put on your face."

"We want to be beautiful," Aunt Mary said, smiling.

"Humph," Aunt Martha rasped.

The men came and went at night, talking and planning. It was summer now. Lavender knew the big job Cole was so mysterious about was planned to take place in August or September. His book was almost finished. The last chapter would be written after the big job.

"It's been a long sad story, the story of my life," he told Lavender. "It was in the fall of 1864 that I joined the tattered gray riders. Now in the fall of 1876 the last chapter of the story of my life will be told."

"Don't say that," Lavender cried. "You make it sound as if it will be the last chapter of your life. It isn't the last chapter. It may be the last chapter of your life as a Younger outlaw but then you will start a new chapter. A glorious new chapter with me."

At night when she lay in her lonely bed, she tried to think only of that future that could be so near. But her thoughts were often interrupted by the sounds of heavy boots in the kitchen below. And one unforgettable night, there was another sound besides that of footsteps and men's voices. A woman's voice!

Lavender sat up in bed. She had heard that high screeching voice before. She was sure of it. And then it came to her. That voice could belong to none other than Belle Starr! Lavender was rigid with anger. How dared Belle come here? How dared she follow Cole to his home? How dared she?

She strained to hear but all she heard was the intermingling of voices and now and then the strident voice of Belle ringing out. Finally she heard Belle screaming and ranting and then there was the sound of a flurry of horses' hooves leaving the farm. And then the low murmur of those left in the kitchen, and finally silence.

She asked Cole about it the next morning. She had to know. He admitted quite frankly that the voice she had heard belonged to Belle Starr. She had heard of the big job planned by the Jameses and Cole and was determined to take part. She had been accompanied by Eagle Joe Lang, who had ridden with the Jameses on previous occasions. Jesse had sent word to Eagle Joe. Jesse had admired Eagle Joe's ability to shoot and he wanted a few more sharp-shooters. The fact that Eagle

Joe had divulged this information to Belle angered Jesse.

"You have a loose mouth," he stormed at Eagle Joe.

"Belle made me tell," the man whined. He appealed to Cole. "You know how Belle can talk a man into doin' anythin'. You know Belle can talk so good she can make butter melt in an ice storm."

"You men need me on this job," Belle asserted now. The plume on her hat danced in the lamplight.

"Like hell we do," Jesse said and let out a volley of curses. Frank agreed with Jesse, as did Cole.

Belle and Eagle Joe stormed and begged to be included. "I'm 'Queen of the Outlaws,'" Belle yelled.

"You're queen of nothin' but a band of horse theives," Jesse had yelled back. "Get goin' and be quick about it."

Jesse pulled out his Navy Colt and they scurried.

Aunt Martha was horrified when she heard that the infamous Belle Starr had been in her kitchen. Lavender thought it strange that Aunt Martha could pretend that men did not come and go from the farm. She simply ignored that fact.

While Lavender and Aunt Mary worried about the impending "happening" that Cole was involved in they did not mention anything to Aunt Martha. Let her live in the belief that nothing exciting was about to happen to all of them. Because it *was* exciting. Lavender was surprised now when Jim and Bob Younger came home. Cole told her it had been decided that there would be fewer men taking part than they had first planned.

"What is it, darling?" she asked. "What are you going to do?"

"It is better that you do not know any of the details. Then if anything happens, you know nothing about it."

"Please, Cole, please let's just go away. Aunt Mary said I shouldn't ask you but I must. I couldn't bear it if anything happens to you."

"Nothing is going to happen," he soothed her. "We'll be safe and back home before you know it."

"Oh, Cole, my dearest dearest darling."

"We have got to be together before I leave, my sweetheart."

"Dare we?"

"Now that Bob is home, I'll have him and Jim drive Aunt Mary and Aunt Martha over to see their old friend Mandy Griggs in Sugar Hollow."

"Oh, Cole."

"I've got to have you, to possess you. I love you so much."

"And I love you. I'll love you forever and always."

Chapter 25

Lavender could hardly wait for Jim and Bob to harness the horses to the buggy to drive Aunt Mary and Aunt Martha to see Mandy Griggs in Sugar Hollow. Aunt Martha was fuming as usual but Aunt Mary winked at Lavender and whispered, "I'll see that we stay the day."

When they were out of sight, Cole picked her up and she pillowed her head on his chest, feeling the warmth of him. How she loved him! She fastened her arms around his neck and his strength and his warmth enfolded her. He undressed her tenderly, letting his hands linger on her breasts.

"I've wanted you so much," he whispered. "There were nights when I felt I had to brave Aunt Martha's wrath and come to you."

"I know, my darling. I felt the same way."

"We will have this last time to remember until I return."

"Don't let's think about your going away. Let's just have this perfect time together," she said, tracing the outline of his features, smoothing the golden hair, touching his eyelashes lovingly.

In bed now, she watched as he shed his garments. Then he lay beside her, their naked bodies touching, clinging. Her fingers strayed to his neck, lingering there at a pulsating artery, then creeping further down, now touching and tweaking his paps. She felt a fury suddenly possess her. She wanted him to know that she was as fiery as Belle Starr. She wanted to match Belle as a bed partner. In her heart, she believed that he and Belle had had a torrid love affair and though he might deny it, she wondered if Pearl Younger wasn't the result of that flaming affair.

Well, no matter. What mattered now was that Cole was hers alone. And she intended to satisfy him. And give him a memory of today to carry with him when he left tomorrow.

"Love me, love me, Cole," she begged.

She touched him, she loved him, she felt his firm white skin, ran her hands over his firm belly and felt delight. There were no barriers, no reservations in their love today. She felt natural, uninhibited, worshiping and adoring him. Her body was his to do with as he wished. Today, there was a complete communion of their flesh, their minds and their hearts. She felt herself to be one with him. When it was over, they lay close together and whispered endearments and vowed undying love. Again, they took each other with complete abandon, thinking only of the other one.

Late afternoon shadows were creeping into the room when they got up and dressed. They knew, this would probably be the last time they would be completely alone before Cole left tomorrow. She clung to him.

"I'll be back home again before you know it," he promised.

"And we will be married? And you do promise that we will go away, far away from here, and start a new life together?"

"I promise," he said solemnly.

At dawn the following day, she watched Cole ride out. And watching him, she felt a part of herself riding in the saddle with him. There were eight men in all. Eight men astride the beautiful prancing horses. Eight men riding two by two. Eight men all dressed in linen dusters. She could not tell in the misty early dawn who led the group. She thought it was Cole and Frank. But she could not be sure. They wore dusters to hide their heavy revolvers and ammunition.

Watching them go, she hoped she would never again have to watch Cole riding away at dawn.

She knew their names. There was Cole, Jim and Bob Younger, Clell Miller, Bill Chadwell (alias, William Stiles), Charlie Pitts, (whose real name was Sam Wells) and Jesse and Frank James.

The days went by. Long days filled with wondering and waiting. Aunt Martha kept asking when Cole and Jim and Bob would return from their hunting trip.

"Any day," Lavender would answer. "Any day."

Chapter 26

Lavender, waiting anxiously in the old Younger farmhouse for Cole's return, tried to busy herself with other things. But her mind was on Cole. Where was he? She had once heard the word Mankato whispered but had dismissed it as her imagination. Mankato was so far away.

She kept seeing, in her mind's eye, the image of the handsome Cole erect in the saddle, in a white duster riding away in the early dawn.

She had her carpetbag packed in case they might have to flee before a posse.

"Do you think he'll be all right?" she asked Aunt Mary over and over.

"The angels watch over our Cole. You know that," Aunt Mary assured her. "Just you be ready in case he needs you. He may send word for you to meet him some place. Just be ready."

"Oh, I am ready, Aunt Mary. But I am so worried about Cole."

"He'll be all right. Don't worry."

The nights were the hardest to bear. She remembered that last unforgettable day with him. The ecstasy she had felt lingered with her. How she loved him!

Lavender was not to know until days later what happened to Cole and the others. She did not know that the eight riders she had watched leave the Younger farmhouse so confidently, had split up into three divisions. The three Youngers and Clell Miller were together, the two James brothers were together and Charlie Pitts and William Chadwell made up the other group.

They had travelled leisurely, passing through cities, towns and small hamlets. All were well-supplied with money and spent it freely. They were all well-dressed and made a favorable impression wherever they went. They were well-mounted and equipped. Each man carried a carbine strapped to his saddle and two Colts hidden under his long linen duster.

Each division put up in different place at night. Some stayed at boarding houses or nearby farmhouses. Another group, at a hotel. When asked their business they said they were civil engineers, railroad men, cattle merchants or horse buyers. They introduced themselves under various names, all made up at the moment.

Lavender was not to know until later that when she heard the name Mankato whispered, that that had actually been the destination of the band. They had intended originally to rob the bank there but when they arrived at Mankato they found a large group of citizens standing near the bank. They believed that in some way their plan had been discovered. Actually, it was just a group watching construction work next to the bank.

One of the bystanders had pointed in admiration to Jesse's horse and the Jameses were surely they had been recognized.

They rode out of town hastily and revised their plans. They would go to Northfield, fifty miles east. They decided on Northfield because Bill Chadwell knew something of the farming country of Minnesota and he maintained the bank at Northfield was one of the richest in the north, and besides, it had the payroll of the flourishing Ames & Company flour mill.

The band decided to regroup about fifteen miles from Northfield. There, they laid their plans carefully. They knew the business section centered around Bridge Square, so named because of the iron bridge which spanned the river. There was the Scriver Block, a two-story brick and stone building on the southwest corner. Scriver's General Store and Lee and Hitchcock, a furniture company, occupied the first floor.

The First National Bank was located at the rear end of the building a few feet from the corner. On the second floor were offices which were reached by an outside iron stairway. The Wheeler and Blackman drugstore was directly across the street from the bank entrance and next to it was a small hotel, the Dampier House.

The bank had a back door which opened on an alley giving access to Bridge Square. The Scriver Block made up one side of the alley. On the other side were two hardware stores.

Lavender found out later from the newspaper accounts that Cole and Clell Miller rode into town and rode slowly around the square. It was a warm drowsy afternoon. It was September 7th, 1876.

Cole loosened the duster carefully so as not to reveal the guns at his waist. Leisurely, they trotted back to the Cannon River where the others waited.

"Everything is ready," Cole reported, "and waiting for us."

"Even the women," laughed Bob.

Cole looked at him sharply. "You've been drinking,"

Cole accused him angrily, "and you, too, Frank. You've had too much."

Frank grinned confidently. "You know whisky always makes me think better," he said.

Cole shook his head. He knew whisky slowed Bob up and it made Frank James not only trigger-happy but belligerent. But there was nothing else to do but go on with their plan.

The plan was carefully gone over for the tenth time. Jesse and Frank James and Charlie Pitts would be the "inside" men. These three would go into town and have lunch and then wait at the corner of the Scriver Block for the others to come racing into town popping their guns and giving the old Rebel yell. Bill Chadwell and Clell Miller were to come in from the south and Cole and Jim Younger from the west. When the clock in the belfry of the Lutheran Church struck one, it would be the signal for the others to come sweeping into town, timing it so they would reach Bridge Square within minutes of each other.

Shortly before twelve noon, Jesse and Frank and Charlie entered town. They walked their horses across the Division Street bridge and tied them to a hitching rack in front of the Scriver Block. Their manner was so relaxed that no one gave them a second glance. Charlie casually asked a passerby about a good place to eat and then they went to Jeff's Restaurant, a few doors up the street.

There, they unbuttoned their linen dusters but did not remove them. They spoke cordially to the proprietor. They told him they intended to head west to look at farms near Mankato. They ate hearty meals, paid their bill and strolled down the street, sitting down on a wooden packing case outside of Manning's Hardware Store. Charlie lit up a cigar.

Lavender reading this detailed account in the newspapers could visualize Charlie throwing away his cigar as the church clock struck the hour of one. The three casually walked to their horses and examined the riding gear.

Then the sleepy afternoon silence was broken by Bob Younger, Bill Chadwell and Clell Miller storming into town, shrieking like savages, their guns roaring.

At about the same time, Cole and Jim thundered in from the west. The startled and surprised citizens were stunned and ran for cover. Jesse, Frank and Charlie charged into the bank. On the street, a Swedish boy, seventeen years old, understanding no English, started across the street and was instantly shot. All bedlam broke loose as the citizens raced for their guns.

Bill Chadwell was weaving in his saddle from a bullet that stunned him and now another bullet got him through the heart. Bob Younger's horse was shot out from under him and he leaped from the animal and ran to the foot of the iron stairway, climbing the outside wall of the Scriver Block.

Cole, too, had been shot in the shoulder and now realizing how thoroughly they had underestimated Northfield, Cole rode up to the bank yelling, "Come on. They're killing us! We've got to get out of here!"

Inside the bank, all was confusion. Two tellers lay dead. The remaining teller stood with his face to the wall and his hands up. He was not harmed. Ironically, the door to the vault was unlocked and if Jesse had tried it, it would have opened easily.

Usually sharp as to such details, today he was apparently unnerved by the noise outside. He and Frank and Charlie scooped up the cash in the counter tills and stuffed their pockets. When they reached the street they saw that they were in real trouble. Clell Miller and Bill Chadwick lay dead. Cole's face was a smear of blood. Part of Jim Younger's face was shot off and both shoulders were shot up. Bot's arm hung uselessly and he was trying to shoot with his left hand. As he climbed into his saddle, Frank James was hit with a bullet between the knee and thigh. Jesse alone remained unhurt.

Bob Younger, afraid the others meant to leave him behind, came from his hiding-place on the stairs, pleading, "Don't leave me. I've been shot."

Cole, bleeding, turned his horse around, and got Bob up on his horse behind him. Eight men had ridden into Northfield, Minnesota. Six men rode out. There wasn't time to cut telegraph wires. They realized they had to move and move fast. They rode west.

Back in Northfield, the telegraph operator put the news of the holdup and murder in the streets on the wire. The entire state was alerted in short order. By dusk, three-hundred armed men were on the trail. Posses were formed everywhere. And suddenly the warm weather changed to torrents of rain.

Lavender, reading these facts in the newspapers, agonized over each word, trying to read between the lines.

"Cole, my dearest darling," her heart cried, "where are you?"

Chapter 27

It was weeks before Lavender was to know of the hardships endured by the six surviving members of the gang who had ridden so lightheartedly away on a misty August morning. She did not know that as they hobbled along through the rain, Jim Younger's mouth wound was so profuse that a trail of blood was left behind, quickly obliterated by the pounding rain. He was so weak that Cole and Bob had to ride on each side of him to hold him up.

She did not know that the 13th of September found them floundering through swamps and mire, tired and hungry and harassed.

And it was much later when she heard that Jesse had turned to Cole saying, "Cole, we are in a bad fix and there is only one way out. Jim cannot live. Look, he is hemorrhaging. And we can't make any time with him hanging on. We'll be caught sure as hell. Let's get rid of him now. He can't live anyway. With him out of the way, we can travel faster and escape."

The six men had looked at each other. Five of them stared at Jesse. They could hardly believe their ears. Here was Jesse, whose life had been saved numerous times during the war and after by valiant efforts on the part of his guerilla companions, coldly proposing to kill one of them to save his own skin!

Cole, his face bloody from buckshot, his wounded shoulder throbbing, hissed, "Damn you, Jesse. To kill my own brother! I'll stay with him and fight until the very end, and then carry him on my shoulders until I, myself, fall. Be off with you and any of you who wish to go. Take your own paths, and I hope we never meet again."

Back in Missouri, Lavender waited. The farmhouse was surrounded by the law. The curious rode by in buggies and wagons to stare in awe as if expecting the Younger gang to come riding up to the house at any moment.

Aunt Martha snorted and Aunt Mary did her best to comfort Lavender. And Lavender waited and waited for word that did not come.

Cole, of course, could not send word. The remaining members of the gang were burdened by the fact that the territory was unfamiliar to them. William Chadwell, who knew the territory, was dead.

At first, they were lucky. They rode to Dundas, three miles south of Northfield. Telegraph wires were humming with the news, but at Dundas, the key ticked in vain, the operator was at home eating lunch! At Millersburg, it was the same. A few citizens paused to gaze in wonderment as the horses galloped past them but no one raised a challenge.

The gang pushed on steadily, riding five abreast, pushing anyone else off the road. They stopped a farmer after leaving Millersburg and stole his horse. Later they stopped another farmer and stole a saddle. But toward twilight, the saddle girth snapped spilling Bob Younger onto the road. For the second time the wounded bandit, now in even more severe pain, scrambled up behind his brother. They travelled on, the weather turned cold, and their suffering was intense.

On September ninth, two days after the attack, three possemen had exchanged shots with the band as they were crossing a small ford on the Little Cannon River. The gang escaped unharmed. They continued to push on. Around Elysian Township they found themselves in a wild country filled with lakes, swamps, ravines, and gullies. It seemed ideal to hide in. They stole horses as they went along and finally between Elysian and German Lake they made camp, stretching their blankets over the dripping bushes in the form of a crude Indian tepee.

The next day, they abandoned their horses and continued their journey through the rugged country on foot. That evening they selected a high camping ground built on the lines of a small fort and here they remained until near morning. The next day they went on until they halted near the village of Marysburg.

On Tuesday afternoon they obtained food from a German farmer. They had been sleeping in a deserted farmhouse. In five days they had covered less than fifty miles. It was then that the gang divided. Charlie Pitts and the three Youngers went together. Jesse and Frank James went off together.

When Lavender, later, heard about their decision to split up, she could see the happening in her mind's eye. She could see Jesse, haggard and savage, snarling and ready to claw for his gun. Cole, big and blood-encrusted, ready to protect Bob Younger and Bob, burning with fever and clutching his shattered elbow and Frank James, solemn-faced, always ready to quote Shakespeare.

She went to sleep imagining the six bearded, red-eyed

men sitting in one of the dark rooms of the ramshackle deserted farmhouse. But until she heard definitely what had happened to the group she could only wonder and hope.

On the night of Wednesday, September the thirteenth, the Youngers and Pitts crossed the Blue Earth River bridge.

On Thursday, September the twenty-first, fourteen days after the abortive robbery, the telegraph wires began to hum with the news that some of the Younger-James gang had been trapped in the small village of Madelia, twenty-four miles southwest of Mankato, in Watonwan County, Minnesota. They had been trapped, after posing as fishermen, and buying eggs at a farmhouse. The egg seller recognized Cole Younger and became a dedicated Paul Revere spreading the word to farmhouses near and far that the Youngers were in the neighborhood.

A posse was formed and closed in on the so-called fishermen. In the ensuing battle, Charlie Pitts died with his boots on. The three Youngers were severely wounded. Cole Younger was riddled with eleven bullets. James Younger had five wounds and Bob Younger, two.

The outlaws were carted off to Madelia. The town was packed solid with the curious by the time the wagon moved down the main street. When the crowd shouted and waved hats and handkerchiefs, all three bandits, including the big, bearded Cole Younger, blood-soaked from his eleven bullet holes, waved their hats in response.

Their dream of one last big job was over. It was a day of celebration in Madelia. The captured Youngers lay on cots while great crowds filled the town and from dawn to dusk filed past the room where the prisoners were.

The Youngers talked freely. Cole had never been at a loss for words. He said simply, "We were victims of circumstances" and "We were drove to it, sir."

Lavender cried until her eyes were red and swollen. Cole was wounded and perhaps would not recover from those wounds. And if he did recover, what then? Would he be doomed to a life in prison? No! she thought over and over that must never be. Cole languishing in prison for the rest of his life when she needed him and wanted him so!

The newspapers still blazed with stories of the robbery of the Northfield Bank. She wondered, wearily, if people never tired of the story of the eight men in their long, linen dusters and their revolvers and their ammunition. The tale was told over and over again of their daring and how they waited for the clock in the belfry to strike the hour of one. And there was laughter too, at Jesse James' failure to try the door to the vault. It was unlocked and would have opened easily.

There were endless stories too of Clell Miller and Bill Chadwell, the two bandits killed in Northfield. It seemed two graves were dug in Northfield Cemetery and in the dead of night the two men were buried without mourners or rites. At least two rough pine boxes were buried there, but it was common belief that the two corpses were spirited away to a medical college to further anatomical science. Further rumor contended that before long a skeleton of one of them appeared in the office closet of a doctor in Northfield.

Lavender's first impulse was to rush to Cole's side. The newspaper articles stated that Cole had not only received the eleven wounds but that the always gallant Cole, despite those wounds, managed to stand up in the wagon and bow to the ladies.

Bob Younger was shot through the right lung and Jim Younger had a shattered upper jaw with a bullet lodged just beneath his brain. He was in terrible pain. A surgeon made an effort to remove the bullet by making an incision in the roof of his mouth and trying to pry loose the leaden pellet but his efforts were futile.

Lavender, reading the never-ending details in the newspapers, which seemed to arrive regularly from all parts of the country, felt pity and grief and heartache.

When the Youngers were recovered sufficiently, they were taken to the jail in Fairibault, Minnesota, to await trial. Four indictments were brought against them, and their attorney advised them to plead guilty, and thereby escape capital punishment for the death of the two bank tellers and the boy who had fled in terror because he did not understand English and did not stop.

The three Youngers, Cole, Bob and Jim, pleaded guilty. The judge sentenced them to life imprisonment in the state penitentiary at Stillwater.

Aunt Martha was furious and ranted continuously. Lavender, heartsick and tearful, listened fearfully to her ravings and wondered if perhaps the old woman was losing her mind.

Aunt Mary talked quietly, sincerely to Lavender. "Dear," she said gently, "a life sentence is forever. It is an eternity. You are young. You must leave here immediately. This is no place for you. People staring at the house all the time hoping to catch a glimpse of one of us. I have some money and I want you to take it and leave."

Lavender was stunned at the thought that Aunt Mary would think she would desert Cole.

"You are not deserting him, Lavender. You will only be carving a new life for yourself. If you wait for Cole, you will be an old woman before he is released. And then again, he may never be released."

A startled look came into Lavender's eyes. "I never thought of that!" she said slowly. "I never think of myself as getting old."

Aunt Mary sighed, "Dear, we all grow old. The young find it hard to realize but the time comes when one looks in the mirror and realizes that she is old. It's sad, but that is life. You, Lavender, are in the spring-time of life and I am in the late autumn and there is never any going back."

"You will never be old, Aunt Mary," Lavender cried looking at the older woman. "You are so beautiful."

"But beauty can fade overnight." Aunt Mary said. And when she spoke again, it was to speak of Cole. "I pity Cole," she said. "He was so young when his father was ruthlessly slain. It was then he vowed eternal vengeance against his father's murderers."

"I know," Lavender agreed softly, "but he always said of that vow of his that he carried it out. But in so doing, he has glutted himself with other men's blood, ruined his family honor, and damned his own soul."

"True, true."

"But it's never too late," Lavender said eagerly, her beautiful eyes aglow with hope. "We can go away. We can make a new a start when Cole gets out of prison."

"Lavender, do you really believe that?"

Lavender was silent.

"We have been through too much. I, myself, was

burned out of my home three times in Harrisonville, turned out in the snow and freezing weather. There's a piece of ice in my breast instead of a heart and Cole . . . well, you know Cole. . . ."

Did she really know Cole? Did she really know the handsome man with whom she had reached heights of ecstasy? Did she really know the handsome man who could bow gallantly and grin at the women as he was being carted off to prison?

"We love each other," she finally said.

"Of course you love Cole and I think Cole loves you as much as it is possible for him to love anyone."

Winter and the snows came. By Christmas, the snow was a foot deep and crusted over like hard white icing on a cake. Word drifted back from the West that cattle were dying by the thousands. And from the North, Cole pleaded with Lavender, by letter, not to come to Minnesota.

"I couldn't bear for you to see me behind bars, my darling," he wrote. "Do not despair. Our dream to start a new life together will come true."

Chapter 28

The glory of spring blazed over the midwest. Violets and jack-in-the pulpit and white varnished dogwood dazzled the lanes. The enchanted spring evenings presently faded into summer and the sleeping perfumes of Aunt Mary's roses made the air fragrant with scent. The great elm trees broke the moonshine into silver and black squares and patterns on the old house.

Cole wrote regularly and Lavender treasured his letters, reading them over and over again. She answered with long letters. She clipped verses and poems out of the newspaper. She told him of Aunt Mary's garden but she did not tell him that as the days went by Aunt Martha was becoming queer and hostile.

She wrote only that they were well and missed him, and of course, that she loved him dearly and would be waiting for him. Her days blended together, one as the other, monotonous in their sameness.

Aunt Martha took to her bed, groaning and moaning and quite irrational at times.

Lavender, washing, ironing and cooking, dreamed of that glorious day when Cole would come home. She could not understand why the James brothers were not in prison with Cole and Bob and Jim. She knew they had participated in the robbery. She had seen them riding away at dawn in their long linen dusters.

At first there had been much in the newspapers about the certainty of their participating in the robbery but as the weeks went by interest in them seemed to wane and now apparently, the authorities were satisfied with the imprisonment of the Youngers.

It didn't seem fair! But then remembering The Black Oath of the Quantrill Riders, she knew neither Cole nor Bob or Jim would reveal the fact that the Jameses had been with them. Besides Cole felt a real loyalty and a deep tie to Frank James and he would never do anything to hurt him.

The weary months of waiting went on and on. Cole's friends worked tirelessly to get him released. And Cole, in prison, busied himself writing letters to newspapers and friends. He told Lavender that these letters would become the last chapter of his book.

His letters were widely read and seized upon by the papers. She began to hope that Cole would write his way out of prison.

To her, he professed undying love and devotion. He wrote that Bob was slowly dying of tuberculosis. He had taken up the study of medicine and was reading text books to pass the time.

Jim had finally had the bullet removed from the roof of his mouth which pained him so through these months in prison. He had pleaded with a hospital intern, who made a careful investigation and finally dislodged the bullet by working at it at intervals for two days.

Cole always signed these letters to Lavender, "Your devoted slave. T. Cole Younger."

The months went by. There were times when

261

Lavender thought Cole might miraculously be released but those hopes were born to die. Nothing happened.

On one summer day Lavender and Aunt Mary sat under the grape arbor trellis. Strawberries picked early that morning were spilled on the table between them and beside each woman lay a fluffy heap of green hulls. Through the thick grape leaves, among which clusters of newly-formed grapes hung, an intermingled pattern of light and dark shadows made a lacy pattern.

They worked in silence for a while and when Lavender broke the silence it was to say, "The waiting gets harder all the time."

"Don't wait any longer, Lavender," the older woman said stopping her work to look earnestly at her companion. "The life you're living isn't normal. You should be married and have children."

"I love Cole," Lavender affirmed as she had affirmed a thousand times in the months since Cole went to prison.

"Oh, Lavender, dear, if I could just make you see."

"It's no use talking to me about it," Lavender said firmly, her beautiful eyes filling with tears.

"You could go away from here and change your name and make a new life. I love you as though you were my own daughter. And, I have to say this. As dear as Cole is to me, he will only break your heart if and when he gets out of prison."

There was silence then. Each woman was busy with her own thoughts. They were almost through hulling the berries, their fingers stained red, when Lavender, looking up from her work, asked, "Did you hear horses' hooves, Aunt Mary?"

"Well, it's probably some more of the curious who

come to stare," Aunt Mary said.

"No, it's a buggy and it's coming up to the porch. It's Hank Buffington driving. He must have brought someone from the station."

Wiping their stained hands on a wet cloth that had been lying handy nearby, they went forward to see who the visitor was. They saw Hank, his eyes bulging with admiration, helping a stylishly-clad woman out of the buggy. Then he dragged out two carpetbags from the buggy.

Lavender, staring at the newcomer, did not recognize her at first. She only saw that the woman's hair was dressed in the latest style with a sort of half pompadour in front and little tendrils of curls carefully pasted in front of each ear. Her dress was of dark green and a clever wisp of a hat of the same dark green had clusters of pink roses here and there and was topped off with a mist of green veiling. The woman paid the awe-stricken Hank and then smiled at Lavender.

Lavender recognized her when she smiled. It was Melon! But such a changed Melon!

"I didn't recognize you," Lavender cried as they hugged and kissed each other. Aunt Mary was introduced and the visitor must be taken inside to greet the bed-ridden and cross Aunt Martha.

They talked and talked trying to catch up on all the events that had taken place in the years since they had seen each other. But Lavender was so delighted to see her and she found that Melon was the same old Melon, her friend of the cabin days on the Marais des Cygnes, her friend through those days of winter and blizzard, when Ruby was flirting with John and Cole.

When the supper dishes had long been done and

Lavender and Melon were alone, they went out into the moon-washed night. The old white house looked mystically beautiful in the silver glow and the towering trees, the bushes and the daisies were silver-tipped and shining.

"Thanks for not questioning me in front of the others," Melon said.

"Questioning you?"

"I mean about what has happened to me since we were last together."

"Melon, you know I would never say anything. Aunt Mary and Aunt Martha know only that you visited me when John and I were married and living on the Marais des Cygnes."

"Then Cole didn't tell you where I've been?"

"No."

"I didn't really want you to know but I might as well tell you. I've been in St. Louis working for that bitchy Kate Clarke."

Lavender was stunned.

"Do you mean that Kate Clarke who was Quantrill's woman?"

"The same," Melon answered bluntly.

"How did Cole know?"

"I've been writing to him, Lavender. We read all the accounts in the papers. Kate thought it would be great if all we girls wrote to Cole and cheered him up."

"He didn't tell me."

"Did you hear about Belle?"

"No."

"Belle was like a mad woman when she heard about Cole being in prison. She vowed she would go to the Stillwater penitentiary and blast him out. I guess some of her 'jolly lads' as she calls them talked her out of that."

"How do you know this?" Lavender asked.

"I was still following the gang when I heard this," Melon answered. "Then I got this chance to go with Kate when Quantrill set her up in St. Louis. What the hell! I thought it was better to live in luxury than live like an animal with the old gang."

There seemed no answer to this. Lavender was silent but her face flamed.

Presently Lavender asked, "Does Cole know about Belle's intention to get him out of prison?"

"Sure. She's been writing letters to everybody she can think of, threatening and begging them to do something."

"Cole never told me."

"Don't blame Cole," Melon said. "He doesn't need or want Belle trying to get him out of prison. She'd do him more harm than good."

Presently Melon spoke again, "I been living in the lap of luxury in St. Louis. You never saw such red satin drapes and fittings as that Kate has. Blood-red carpets and white furniture. And she's got about ten of us working for her."

Lavender sighed.

"I know you think it's a hell of a life and it is Lavender, it is. Parading your wares around in front of a bunch of bastards with bulging eyes and eager hands isn't any fun. And going to bed with every Tom, Dick and Harry, that ain't no fun either! Some of 'em are mean in bed. They can pinch and they can bite and do worse things than that!"

"You're too fine for that kind of life, Melon."

"Guess who the star performer at Kate's is?" Melon asked.

"I wouldn't know."

"Well, you know her! None other than Ruby!"

"Ruby!"

"The same old lazy Ruby. She and Kate are both alike. They're both hellcats and they fight and hair-pull all the time. I'll say this for Kate. She does try to run a high-class joint. Everything is plush. But that cheap tramp, Ruby, does her best to ruin everything. I won't make you blush, Lavender. I know how sweet and clean you are. I couldn't tell you what Ruby offers to do to get the men to come in."

"But you left there, Melon. Why?"

"I could tell you I got tired of the whole setup, which I did but Lavender, there's another reason. Kate and Ruby have been having some real battles lately and then all of a sudden, Ruby starts actin' real smug, like a cat that swallowed a canary. I got real suspicious, especially when I heard them whispering your name now and then when they had their heads close together."

"My name?"

"It made me mad for them to even speak your name. You've always been someone special to me. Someone on a high throne. Someone I looked up to."

"Thank you."

"Well, one day Ruby steals my new white fur muff. It was in winter time and cold and damp. I had gone for a walk down to the river front to watch the River Belle come in. And there, parading as big as life, was Ruby with my white fur muff!"

Lavender laughed. "You mean you actually saw her with your muff?"

266

"Sure, she knew it would get attention. She tries to get pick-ups on the side. That's another reason Kate gets mad at her. Kate pays off plenty to run a ritzy establishment and she has her own contacts in the high-class hotels. And it don't do her place no good for Ruby to bring in some of these bums that she picks up."

"Did you ask her for your muff back there on the river front?" Lavender asked.

"No, I was waiting for her when she got back. I really lit into her. She was so mad she forgot to be cagey. She said she'd been writing to Cole regularly. She had an idea for them both to make a fortune. She said as soon as he got out of prison, they were going to make up an act and tour the country."

Lavender was stunned. "She thinks she and Cole will be together?"

"Yes. She wants to be billed as Quantrill's woman and he would, of course, be billed as Cole Younger, the famous outlaw."

Lavender looked up at the star-shaped leaves of the towering maple nearby and she could not have spoken if her life depended on it.

"I know this is a shock to you," Melon went on gently. "Somehow Ruby had heard that you and Cole were planning on getting married when he got out of prison. She laughed about that."

"She wouldn't have known about Cole and me if he hadn't told her," Lavender said woodenly, her heart dead within her.

"Oh, yes, Lavender, there are other ways. Whatever Cole says or does or thinks is news. And people can just make up things that they think he'll do."

"I suppose you're right."

"Cole Younger will always be front page news."

"But Melon, Ruby never was Quantrill's woman."

"So? Neither Kate or Ruby mind telling a lie if it suits their purpose. Well, after Ruby blurted this out when she was mad about me snatching my muff away from her, I put two and two together and knew that's what she and Kate had been planning and whispering about together."

"I can't believe my Cole would even think about being in an act with Ruby."

Melon went on, "The more I thought about Ruby and Kate trying to get Cole to agree to something like that, the madder I got. I decided to come here and see you."

"I'm glad you came, Melon, but I can't believe that Cole would be in any kind of an act with Ruby. He didn't even like her that winter when you and she were at my place."

"I know. I remember how she used to try to get him to go to the woods with her."

"I remember," Lavender said softly. "I remember it all."

Melon grinned. "Don't be jealous, Lavender, of me. I didn't matter one bit to Cole. I saw him look at you that winter. I knew he had you in a class all by yourself. You were someone special to him."

Lavender smiled, remembering.

"I decided I'd had enough of Kate and Ruby. Besides, I ain't gettin' any younger. That business of sellin' your body can age a woman mighty fast. I decided to get out while I could."

"Oh, Melon, I'm glad you did."

"I left St. Louis and went straight up to Stillwater Prison."

"You saw Cole?"

"Yes, I saw Cole."

"He wouldn't let me come to the prison. He wouldn't let me come to visit him."

"Of course he wouldn't. It's a horrible place. Bars and men with gray faces. No. No," she said quickly, seeing Lavender's stricken face. "No, not Cole. Cole is the same old Cole. Handsome and charming."

Charming! Lavender thought of Cole bowing and smiling to the women as he was carted off after being captured. Yes, Cole would be charming!

"I talked to him. I asked him right out what the deal was with Ruby. I said, 'Now, no use turning all that famous charm on me, Cole Younger. I want to know the truth. Ruby told me you and she was goin' to do an act together and go around the country and cash in on your fame as a gun-fighter and Quantrill's fame as a wrecker of women and a burner of Lawrenceville, Kansas.' "

"What did he say?" Lavender asked and she thought she could not bear to hear the answer.

Chapter 29

Lavender repeated her question, "What did he say?"

Melon was looking at her and Lavender saw the pity in her friend's eyes.

"Tell me," Lavender demanded.

"Cole admitted the whole plan," Melon said slowly, reluctantly.

"And he never told me a thing about it," Lavender whispered.

"He was afraid of what you would say," Melon said. "He does love you very much."

"He has a strange way of showing that love."

"Cole has always been a straight-shooter. I guess that's why I couldn't bear the thought of him getting together with that no good tramp, Ruby."

Lavender said nothing.

"He said Ruby had written to him sometime back and he hadn't paid any attention to her. But she kept writing and it began to sound pretty good to him. Cole thought he could get Frank James to go in with them. After all, the names of Younger and James would draw in the people. I asked him, what about you?"

"Me?"

"Yes, you. He said you were much too good for him. And he said, he loved you dearly."

Oh Cole, Cole, my darling, her heart sang.

"But Lavender," Melon went on and she seemed to be fumbling for words, "to men like Cole, love doesn't mean much. They've lived too fast."

"You sound like Aunt Mary," Lavender said.

"Your Aunt Mary is a very wise woman."

"She has often told me that I shouldn't wait for Cole to get out of prison."

"She's right," Melon went on. "Cole calls his show a 'Wild West Show' and his gray eyes danced when he told me about it. He's eager to do it."

"He promised me that we would go west and make a new life," Lavender said.

"You might as well face facts, Lavender," Melon went on definitely. "Cole loves you. I'm sure of that. But he also loves the thought of this exciting life he is planning. And the very thought gives him hope and something to plan for."

"He should be planning our life together."

"I know. I advised him to write to you and explain. He said sorrowfully that he didn't think you would agree to this so-called 'Wild West Show' and that he would have to choose between you and the show."

"Poor Cole."

"Poor Lavender," Melon said. "It is you who are waiting and wasting your life away."

"I love him," Lavender said firmly.

Melon sighed.

"I will be glad to wait for him forever."

"Cole seems to think it is his destiny to be an actor. He enjoys being the center of attention. He is planning the fancy boots and hat and outfit he will wear."

"He would be a very handsome actor," Lavender conceded.

"He talked of his destiny. He told me that that morning when he left you to go to Minnesota he had a strange premonition that his journey was an ill-fated one. And the night before they went into Northfield, he had had a restless night and had heard the high-pitched 'yips' of a family of coyotes. It was a sign of bad luck."

"Poor Cole. He may never get out of prison."

"That's just why you must make a new life for yourself, Lavender. You won't be young and beautiful forever."

Lavender looked at Melon and remembered Aunt Mary's words. Aunt Mary had said that one day you were young and then the next day, when you looked in the mirror, you were old. She felt a sudden fear envelop her. And suddenly she felt as she had when she and Cole were on the trail together going to Mexico to join Quantrill. She had looked at the waving grass and felt this same fear clutch her throat. She remembered now how her horse had lurched, then steadied and gone on and how the fear had enveloped her again.

She remembered how she had wanted to see the green of the honey-locusts and the red and yellow and creamy whiteness of blooms along the trail, not this waving sea of coarse prairie grass. The grass! She had wondered if it would ever stop moving. Would it ever stop waving? She remembered it had a kind of rhythm,

Blow grass blow . . .
      Blow grass blow . . .
Blow wave ripple . . .
      Blow . . .   blow . . .

She came back to the present with a start. There was

272

something about time that frightened her. The thought of time passing brought this strange fear to mind. If only time would stop for a while. Like the wind that blew the tall grass, hither and yon, the winds of time blew too. Hither and yon, and there was no stopping them.

The months went by. Melon spoke of leaving but was persuaded by Aunt Mary to stay.

"If you leave now, Lavender will spend the rest of her life waiting for an impossible dream to come true."

So Melon stayed on while Lavender waited. Cole's letters contained words of love for her. Now and then he mentioned his hope for their future life together.

Another year. Another spring. Melon was getting restless.

"Lavender," she said seriously. "The time has come for me to move on. I love you and I want you to go with me."

They were sitting on the front porch of the old farmhouse. Lilac fragrance filled the air and an owl hooted nearby.

"I couldn't leave here . . ." Lavender said and stopped. Her loving eyes were looking at the giant trees, the silver-tipped flowers.

"You're too young to bury yourself here and wait for a man who will never come," Melon said sternly. "And if he should get out of prison, there is no assurance that he won't go to St. Louis and pick up a floozy named Ruby."

Lavender said nothing.

"Listen, I have a plan, Lavender. You and I are going westward together. No," she said as she saw Lavender open her mouth to protest. "No, don't say anything. Just listen and then think about it."

Lavender sighed deeply but she was listening.

"My plan is this. I have some money. I've made plenty out of this body and saved a bit of the money. We can go West. I hear Denver is quite a town. We'll go there and open a dress shop. I'm pretty good at designing and I remember how handy you were with the needle."

Lavender's eyes were like stars. She was interested. Melon smiled and hurried on, "We'd make a great team, Lavender. You can have that new start and so can I."

"What about Cole?"

"What about him?" Melon asked. "You can't sit here and just wait for him forever. He'll have a lot more respect for you if he knows you are doing something with your life."

"Do you really think so, Melon?" Lavender asked wistfully.

"You're damn right I think so. In fact, I know so. No man wants a woman who just sits and waits."

"Let me think about it."

"Good. I want you to think long and hard about it. But Lavender, think about a pretty little dress shop with stylish dresses and hats. It would be such fun for us."

And then once again the newspapers blazed with news of the James brothers and their gang. On October 8th, 1879 in the western portion of Lafayette County, Missouri on the Chicago & Alton Railway, at Glendale, some twenty miles from Kansas City, a daring train robbery took place. No one but the Jameses or the Youngers could have so brilliantly executed the robbery. It was a perfect place for such a robbery, shadowed by high hills covered with dense forests and broken by ravines and

274

bluffs. The robbers rode to safety with thirty thousand dollars of loot.

Once again all details of the robbery of the North-field Bank were brought out and aired. Once again, readers were made aware of the dapper and handsome Cole Younger bowing to women admirers as he was carted off after being captured.

Lavender complained about this to Melon as once again the curious rode slowly past the farmhouse gawking and staring.

"You don't have to stand for this, you know," Melon said.

Lavender did not answer.

"You can go away. The Youngers and the Jameses will always be news."

But still Lavender could not be swayed. She must be faithful to Cole.

"You can be faithful to Cole out in Denver just as well. And you will be living. You can't call this living. You are hibernating like a bear. You are letting life pass you by."

And then on a sleepy late fall day shortly after the Glendale train robbery, when the leaves hung gold and red and goldenrod lined the lanes, they had a visitor. She was not an invited visitor and when Lavender and Melon heard the strident high-pitched voice they could only stare at each other in shock.

Belle Starr!

She was dressed in flame-colored velvet with not one but two white plumes waving above the brim of her matching hat. The familiar Navy Colts hung from her waist.

"What do you want?" Melon demanded.

"I came to talk to Lavender," Belle said. "You can leave Lavender and me alone."

"I'm not about to leave Lavender alone with a hellcat like you," Melon flared.

"What have you got to say to me?" Lavender asked. "Whatever it is, you can say it in front of Melon."

"I been to see Cole," Belle said flatly.

The two women looked at her.

"You know I've been doing everything I can to get him paroled," she said.

"So we've heard," Melon said darkly.

"I've had one of my 'jolly lads' goin' into the office of Cole's lawyers and drop big rolls of greenbacks 'for Cole from a friend.' Well, I'm the friend."

Lavender was silent.

"Ain't you got nothin' to say?" Belle asked Lavender.

"No."

"I told Cole you're a mealy-mouthed nothin'."

"Don't you dare say that to Lavender, you tramp," Melon cried angrily.

"I mean to say she ain't the woman for Cole. He's my man. He needs a woman like me."

"What Cole needs and wants is a woman like Lavender. A woman who is a lady."

Belle shrugged. "Well, to get back to what I was sayin'. I been up to Stillwater to see Cole. I want to be in his 'Wild West Show.' "

"What 'Wild West Show'?" Melon asked.

"You know all about it. Cole said Lavender is against it."

"He told you that?" Lavender asked.

"He told me you wanted him to go west and get married and . . ."

Lavender interrupted her. "Cole said that?" She could not believe that Cole would discuss their plans with Belle Starr.

"How else would I know about it?" Belle questioned.

"Who could believe you? You're such a liar," Melon said flatly.

"I know what Cole wants. He doesn't want to get married. He doesn't want to settle down. He wants an exciting life and I can help him live an exciting life. We've got it all planned. We'll put on a show that will make an audience sit up and take notice."

Belle began to pace the floor nervously. The plumes danced above her head. She swished the long flame-colored skirt about her.

"We could have a great act."

"Does Cole really want to put on this great act as you call it?" Lavender asked.

"Damn right he does," Belle boomed. "And you're standin' in his way."

Lavender said nothing while Melon glared at the woman.

"I got great plans for it. I'll come ridin' in on my horse, Venus. There ain't never been another horse like Venus."

Melon laughed.

"Don't you laugh. I'll have a hat all made of white plumes that wave. Maybe I'll have 'em of red, white and blue. Ain't decided that yet. I told Cole I'll even have Pearl come and be in the show. Ain't that somethin' for the audience to see? The daughter of the great outlaw and the 'Queen of the Outlaws.' I been givin' Pearl piano and dancin' lessons."

Lavender said simply, "Cole says Pearl is not his daughter."

Belle scoffed, "Of course, he says that. What man ever admits a child born of wedlock is his'n?"

There seemed no answer to this.

Belle went on, "I tell you, Cole is livin' on hopes of bein' in this great show. He's a born actor. Of course, he's the best lookin' man that was ever borned. That goldy hair and that smile melts everyone's heart."

"I can't deny that," Lavender said softly.

"Don't stand in his way," Belle begged.

"You love him, don't you, Belle?" Lavender asked. "You truly love him?"

And now both women glimpsed a side of Belle Starr that they had never seen before. Her hard face became amazingly soft, her eyes filled with tears.

"I was a little girl," she said softly, "the first time I saw Cole Younger. But I knew in that moment that I would love him forever. I remember thinking, 'You are my love, Cole Younger. You are my love.' "

Belle presently left but her words, "You are my love, Cole Younger. You are my love" rang in Lavender's ears.

It was almost twilight when she walked out to the old grape arbor and sat under its lacy shadows. The vines were almost bare, a few leaves dangled and they seemed to envelop her with a sort of security and peace.

What to do? What to do?

Belle Starr wanted Cole and so did Ruby but then, what woman could resist his charm?

She suddenly remembered Aunt Mary's words that one day you were young and then the next day when you looked in the mirror you were old. Well, she wasn't old yet! She was young and she was beautiful and she would decide now what to do with the rest of her life.

She thought now about Melon and her offer to take her in as a partner in a dress shop in Denver. It would be a new beginning. Just beyond the horizon, in a land where white and silver mountains were jutting into an aquamarine sky, she could write a new chapter in her life.

From this land that she now knew of prairies, and meadows sweet with blue-eyed grasses and buttercups and dandelions and Indian paintbrush and the memory of a dead baby with a face like a wild rose and Cole of the gray eyes and sweet crooked smile, she would escape.

Cole of the gray eyes, the winsome smile! She remembered the first time she saw him. He had grinned down at her with the face of an angel. His hair was pure gold and his eyes the gray of a dove's wing. The air about him seemed charged with a kind of vibrancy.

"Lavender," he said and the words were a caress. He took her hand in his and held it. "I've been anxious to meet John's wife."

He had slept for many weeks before her fireplace and she had watched, night after night, as the glow from the fire made a golden halo in front of the fireplace and the glow danced on the three figures. And she had watched as Ruby snuggled close to the sleeping Cole. And she had wondered with a wrench at her heart if the shameless Ruby would make love to Cole before her watching eyes?

Night after night Ruby would snuggle close but Cole would ignore her.

Even then she thought of him constantly, Cole with

the face of an angel and the golden hair and the lean body.

And that was months before the two of them had gone in search of the Christmas tree. The December day had been cold and sunless. No breath of wintry air stirred in the bare world surrounding the cabin. The trees were silent dark sentinels. The sky was low and menacing with snow as Lavender joined Cole outside the cabin.

As they walked, a hundred cowbirds rose suddenly making a lacy black and gray patchwork pattern in the sky. She remembered now how happy she was and how she had dimpled up at him as he reached over and pulled the heavy scarf closer around her shoulders.

The sharp wind whirled about them making the golden tendrils dance on her forehead. He had stopped walking and looked at her. "Lavender, Lavender," he had whispered. "You are so beautiful."

And quite simply, he had put his arms around her and kissed her tenderly on the mouth.

"Don't," she had gasped.

He had held her tightly. "I have to kiss you," he said gently and her breath was gone again.

And then the time, when Cole announced they would be leaving soon.

"It's time to move on," he had said as signs of spring began to appear and the creek overflowed with melting snow.

And she remembered how she had felt time stand still. She could not let him go. She could not stand living in this God-forsaken place without him. They had stood at twilight together, she and Cole, in the path at the end of the lane. It had been a day rich with sunshine and fragrance and birdsong.

Far off a night-bird wailed plaintively but the quiet hush of coming night lay like a benediction over the earth.

"I wish things had been different," Cole had said. "I wish we . . ."

She had interrupted him, "It's too late to think such thoughts."

"I want you, my darling," he had said very low. "I see you at night, so beautiful, so wonderful, in that bed with John and I cannot bear it."

"And I see you there in front of the fireplace with Melon and Ruby and I cannot bear it," she whispered.

"I know, my darling, I know. That's why it is time to leave. It's torture, pure torture, to see your beauty, your sweetness and not have you."

And then he had gone away.

They had only a stolen moment together. "Goodbye, my darling," he had said softly. "You've changed things. That's all right. Nothing will ever be quite the same again. And yet, I'm so glad just to have known you, to have loved you."

For the briefest moment she had been in his arms. She had felt his cheek hard against her own.

"Take care of yourself for me," she whispered. Her heart had been dead within her.

And then the best memory of all. The night he had come to her in the cabin. That rainy night! A stranger had come through the darkness as she had waited with cocked gun. The only noise had been the sloshing sound of the man's footsteps against the heavy beat of the rain. She saw the rain dripping from the stranger's wide-brimmed hat and as he came closer, she recognized him.

Cole! It was Cole Younger!

"Cole!" she cried and was in his arms. All she could think of was that Cole was here and they were together again.

She remembered how later she had gotten in bed. She had felt no shame as she waited for him. She loved him with all her heart and soul and this night belonged to them alone. The rain had continued to beat against the cabin. The branches of the giant oaks, heavy-laden from the rain, pressed on the roof and beat with a heavy ominous sound but inside the cabin it was warm and cozy.

She had pulled the sheet up to her chin and waited trembling with anticipation.

Two tallow dips were burning.

Cole had come toward the bed and seemed to fill the room with his presence. He loomed in front of her. The gleaming glow of the dips turned his hair to pure gold. He had sat on the bed and spoken softly, taking her hands in his, "Lavender, I should get on my horse and ride out of your life but I can't. Whatever the future holds, we do not know. But tonight is ours."

"Ours," she had echoed.

"When you live as I do," he went on, "you have to snatch what happiness you can. There may never be a tomorrow. There is only this moment."

She nodded. She understood.

He had drawn off his boots with the boot-jack that stood always at the fireplace. Then unbuttoning his shirt, he had stood and let his pants slide to the floor. In bed, he took her tenderly in his arms and she had relaxed against him. For a long moment he said nothing, then whispered, "Lavender, my beautiful, beautiful Lavender."

And she had lain hypnotized by his nearness, smelling the good healthy smell of him. He had pulled her gown upward from her willing body and whispered, "Let me look at your beauty."

He had drunk in her loveliness for a long moment and then breathed in awe, "Lavender, your breasts are the breasts of a goddess."

He had been tender and gentle, not at all like John. Cole had wooed her with love and she had become as clay in his hands. She had coiled her arms around his naked waist and run her fingers up and down his back feeling the strong rippling muscles, the firm skin. She had felt his response as she pressed her body to his and felt his hardness.

He was whispering sweet words to her and she felt she had never been alive before this moment. Unconsciously her hips had begun to undulate. He was whispering, "I love you, love you, love you."

Her body took up the sweet rhythm to his words as his eager hands captured her breasts and kissed them, tasting them, nibbling them. Then he had eased himself on her and taken her, loving her, penetrating her with love. She had moaned. She had moved beneath him and they had breathed together in mounting and complete ecstasy.

The memory of that ecstasy swept over her now and it was as if it had just happened.

Cole Younger belonged to her! She would never allow Belle Starr or Ruby or any other woman to have him.

He was hers alone! She jumped to her feet, her eyes blazing with determination. Tomorrow she would go to Stillwater Penitentiary and see him and tell him of her love.

She would tell him she would go wherever he wanted to go. She would do whatever he wanted to do. She loved him and would love him forever. She started hurriedly toward the house when she heard Aunt Mary calling her.

"Lavender, Lavender," she called and Lavender detected a joyous note in Aunt Mary's always lilting voice. "Come quickly. There's someone to see you."

Lavender entered the kitchen and stood transfixed. Cole Younger stood there! Cole, smiling at her with the love light in his gray eyes. Cole standing with outstretched arms!

"Cole, my dearest," she cried running to him.

And it was as if they had never been apart. Their love enveloped them with a radiance as they kissed.

Then presently, she pulled away to gasp, "You've escaped! You got away!"

"No, darling, I was released and I came as quickly as I could. I wanted to surprise you. I'm free."

"Free! What a beautiful word!" she exulted. "Dearest, I intended to come to Stillwater tomorrow to tell you that I would go with you wherever you wanted to go. That I would do whatever you wanted to do and that I loved you and would love you forever and forever."

"You are my woman, my beautiful Lavender," he whispered tenderly.

"And you are my man," she answered fervently. "Forever and forever."

PREVIEW OF LEATHER & LACE #2:
THE TREMBLING HEART

Zee smiled to herself as she recalled the joy of the previous day when she married Jesse James. She reminded herself now of the many years she had waited to become his wife. She had grown up loving Cousin Jesse, as her sister called him.

"He's kinfolk," Sister had said, "and you got no call being so taken with him. There's plenty of other fellows after you. You can have your pick!"

But for Zee, even then, there had only been Jesse. When she was fifteen, she told her best friend, Sarah, "Cross your heart and hope to die if you tell anyone this—"

"I do," Sarah had promised solemnly.

"I love Jesse," Zee confided, stammering, her throat thick and her cheeks pink.

"Don't love him!" Sarah cried, shocked. "Please don't love him. He's mean. Remember the time he shot Tom Morley's cat?"

Zee remembered. It was just because the cat scratched Jesse. It was a bad old cat anyway. Aloud, Zee said, "Jesse can be gentle."

"He's no good and he'll never be any good."

Zee put the memory from her now and dozed off, and when she awakened she felt refreshed and happy in that first delicious moment of awakening.

She stretched joyously and her quick movement jerked Jesse awake.

"I'm sorry," she said frightened and moved quickly away from him.

He shut his eyes and was instantly asleep.

Zee moved cautiously in the bed and thought again of Sarah. Sarah had been dead for seven long years. Sarah had died in childbirth at seventeen and would not know that she, Zee, was now Mrs. Jesse James.

Zee shut her eyes and willed herself to go back to sleep, but her mind skittered about like a waterbug on a brook.

In her thoughts, she was back on the Samuels' farm at Kearney, Missouri, and she and Jesse were standing together under the coffee-bean tree in the front yard.

"This is my favorite tree," he said, "and you're my favorite girl."

"Hardly a girl any longer," she answered dryly. "I've waited a long time, Jesse."

Jesse had become suddenly silent and Zee was conscious of a strange tension, of a breathlessness she had never felt before.

"Zee," he said, his voice almost a whisper.

She did not answer.

"Zee, I love you so much."

"I've always loved you," she replied, her voice as low as his.

He came close to her now and put his arms around her holding her close.

His nearness, the feeling of being softly and steadily overwhelmed, left her trembling and quivering with happiness.

Then he kissed her. It was their first really passionate kiss. He had given her little pecks on the cheek at family gatherings, little duty pecks when family parties broke up.

But this was different.

He kissed her golden hair, her eyes and the softness of

her white neck.

He kissed the palms of her hands and then took possession of her lips again.

"Oh, Zee . . . Zee!"

Her heart and her pulse beat in a sudden ecstatic rhythm.

"Jesse, I've loved you for such a long time," she said, her voice warm and caressing.

At last Jesse was declaring his love. They could now plunge into the exciting exhilarating unknown and unexplored depths of love.

She would belong to Jesse. She thought of the secret. The secret, when a man and woman became one. The very thought left her weak and trembling.

She was glad she was a virgin.

She didn't dare ask Jesse, but she supposed he had lain with many women. She had heard stories of the camp followers who followed the guerrilla band, women who cooked for the men and comforted them at night.

Yes, she had been glad that Jesse would know what to do. She hoped he would be gentle.

Jesse said, "We might have to wait to get married, but you will marry me?"

"Yes. Yes. Yes."

"I was afraid Frank was going to ask you to marry him."

She was taken aback at this. "Is that why you asked me now?"

"No, Zee. I think it's time I got married."

She did not quite believe him. She had waited too many years for him to ask her to be his wife.

He laughed and reached for her.

"Ma's watching," she cautioned.

"Let her watch," he said recklessly. "Zee, I've changed my

mind. I want us to be married right away."

She smiled. "Jesse, I will never be able to understand you. You are as changeable as the wind."

"Well, the wind just whispered to me that it was time we got married."

"Do you really believe the wind and the birds talk to you?" she asked seriously.

"I know they do. I would have been dead long ago if the wind and the birds didn't warn me and help me."

"I'm glad the wind told you for us to get married now. You know I've hoped we could get married long before now," she reminded him. "You've always been reluctant."

"It's a dangerous life for a woman. You'll get tired waiting for your man."

"I've dreamed of being always with you," she said softly, "and sharing your life."